Alan Gibbons

Alan Gibbons has twice been shortlisted for the Carnegie Medal, with *The Edge* and *Shadow of the Minotaur*, which also won the Blue Peter Book Award in the 'Book I Couldn't Put Down' category. Visit his website at www.alangibbons.co.uk

Acclaim for *Scared to Death* . . .

'Very definitely scary . . . builds tension slowly and cleverly and is ultimately a more rewarding read for it'
– Jill Murphy, the bookbag

'entertainingly gruesome stuff'   *The Daily Telegraph*

. . . and *The Demon Assassin*

'A genuinely scary time-shift novel'   *The Bookseller*

'Another gripping, action packed story full of mystery and excitement'   *Primary Times*

D1392460

Also by Alan Gibbons

Hell's underground 2

THE DEMON ASSASSIN

ALAN GIBBONS

Orion
Children's Books

First published in Great Britain in 2008
by Orion Children's Books
This paperback edition first published in Great Britain in 2009
by Orion Children's Books
a division of the Orion Publishing Group Ltd
Orion House
5 Upper St Martin's Lane
London WC2H 9EA
An Hachette UK Company

1 3 5 7 9 10 8 6 4 2

A catalogue record for this book is available from the British Library

ISBN 978 1 84255 751 8

Typeset at The Spartan Press Ltd,
Lymington, Hants

Printed and bound in the UK by
CPI Mackays, Chatham ME5 8TD

The Orion Publishing Group's policy is to use papers that
are natural, renewable and recyclable products and
made from wood grown in sustainable forests. The logging
and manufacturing processes are expected to conform to
the environmental regulations of the country of origin.

www.orionbooks.co.uk

Prologue

5 November, present day

Paul isn't there. The instant Mum sees his room is empty her heart stutters. The PC, usually left on twenty-four-seven, is switched off. There's none of Paul's usual clutter on the floor or on the table: no discarded clothes, no books lying face down on the desk, no DVDs or computer games. For once, everything is neatly filed away. He's even made the bed. The whole place has the appearance of a hotel bedroom.

'Paul,' she cries, knowing there's no point, 'Paul!'

Paul's girlfriend Netty hovers behind the distraught Mrs Rector, feeling like an intruder on a mother's grief. Mum grabs the phone and calls him. She gets a recorded message: the number you have called is unavailable.

'What in God's name is he up to this time?' Mum groans, seeking solace in Netty's face. But there isn't a trace of reassurance in Netty's expression. Like Mrs Rector, she knows that there is no innocent explanation for Paul's disappearance. Mum calls Paul's mobile again. His voice mail announces the same recorded message. While Mum's trembling fingers are returning the phone to its usual place on the hall table, Netty crosses Paul's room and picks up a sheet of lined notepaper. It was lying behind his computer monitor. Maybe the draught blew it there when Mum opened the door.

'What is it?' Mum asks, dismayed by the shadow that passes over the girl's face.

Netty passes it to her without speaking.

Mum.
I've gone back to where it all started. I think I know what I've got to do.
Love,
Paul.

'Netty,' Mum says, 'do you know anything about this?'

Netty shakes her head. 'Not really, it's just . . .'

'Go on.'

'It's the last few days. Paul's been strange, kind of broody. Didn't you notice?'

Mum shakes her head. 'After everything that's happened, I suppose I've been too tied up in my own thoughts.'

'You know Paul and I went on that river cruise on the Thames this morning?' Netty asks.

Mum nods, urging Netty to continue with a look.

'He said he saw something. He didn't really make much sense. He said he saw pictures in the water.'

By this point Mum's instincts are screaming. 'And you didn't ask what he meant?'

Netty lowers her eyes. 'No.'

Mum feels a chill slither through the marrow of her bones. Pictures, Netty said. Mum knows all about Paul's visions. She's heard him talk about the stark spectral images, of terror, of creatures from London's dark heart. For a long time her son has been a tormented soul, haunted by an unwanted destiny. She remembers his black-outs and panic attacks and looks at the note again.

'*Where it all started,*' she murmurs.

Her mind goes back to the night when horror exploded into their lives. It came in the form of a fiend from Hell. It came in the form of her other son. He found Paul one evening on a station platform and that night the killings started.

'It's got to be Whitechapel,' Mum says. 'The tube. Netty, will you come with me?'

There isn't a moment's hesitation. 'Of course.'

It's a ten-minute walk to the tube. Running, they complete the journey in five.

'What did he see?' Mum asks. 'Didn't he tell you anything at all?' She drops her voice. 'Did he mention Redman?'

Netty shakes her head. From that moment on, they stand silently, each lost in her own thoughts. Within a single square mile Redman had butchered five people. He'd murdered them – the policeman, the teacher, the gangster, the student, the boy. It was Paul who had put a stop to Redman's killing spree. So what more was there to do? Why this all-too-brief, teasing note? Neither Mum nor Netty had the answer. Two stops down the line, they arrive at Whitechapel.

Mum doesn't know what to expect, only that, after everything that has happened, she should imagine the worst, then know the real thing is going to surpass it. It was true of Redman's killing spree. It's bound to be true of this latest crisis. They run up the steps and check the other platforms. They ask around. Has anybody seen a fifteen-year-old boy wearing a black jacket? Nobody has.

'But he's got to be here,' Mum says. Fear is clawing at her throat. 'What platform would he have been on the night he met John?'

'He was going home,' Netty said, twisting round. 'It's this one.'

They both turn and retrace their steps to where they got off their train. There are only two people on the platform and no trains waiting.

'He's got to be here,' Mum says. 'Do you see him?'

Then she sees the expression on Netty's face. Mum follows the direction of her stare. Just for a moment she sees him. There's a train carriage standing at the platform. It belongs to a different age. And there's

Paul, looking straight ahead as if he no longer belongs in the twenty-first century.

'Paul!' Mum screams, hammering on the closed doors. She tries to prise the doors open, tries and fails. 'Paul!'

She slaps her palm against the window. Very slowly, Paul turns and looks at them. A sad, distant smile flits across his face. He holds it for a moment and raises his hand to wave. He mouths a single word. 'Goodbye.'

Mum pounds helplessly at the carriage window but it dissolves into thin air. With nothing to hold onto, she almost topples forward onto the line but Netty tugs her back. There's the translucent after-image of a parting tube train, then nothing. A tortured scream of loss explodes from Mum's throat and she slumps back against Netty, sobbing uncontrollably. Netty does her best to comfort her, vaguely aware of a pair of bystanders staring at them with furrowed brows. Neither of them saw the ghost carriage. Paul makes no effort to look back. He keeps his gaze fixed on the darkness that is racing towards him. His journey has begun. He's entered Hell's Underground.

The train thunders on through the roaring gloom. Paul looks out of the window. There are no over ground sections to the journey this time, nor lights to illuminate the tunnel. On and on he plummets, alone, into the abyss. The bulbs in the carriage glow brightly for a second then stutter. He hears footsteps. Somebody's coming. Paul looks up and is surprised to see a ticket inspector. He looks perfectly ordinary though the uniform, like the train, belongs to the 1940s, his destination.

'Tickets please,' the inspector says.

Without thinking, Paul holds out his ticket. The inspector takes it and frowns.

'This ticket is invalid, Sir.'

Paul looks up, bewildered. He has left his own familiar world. What are the rules? Before he can speak, the inspector pulls out a small blue notepad. There are carbon papers between the pages. He licks the end of a pencil and writes a replacement ticket.

'There you go, Sir. That'll take you where you want to go.'

The inspector hands Paul his ticket. Everything is now neatly printed.

Sunday, 29 December, 1940. Paul reads the remaining details. Bank Station. There's even a time. 6.30pm.

Paul sees the inspector turning to go.

'Wait,' he says. 'Aren't you going to help me? What's supposed to happen next?'

'Now your journey is underway,' the inspector says. 'Yours is a path of loneliness and self-discovery. The way is long and beset with many dangers. At the end of it there lies a dethroned King and a white chapel. To find your enemy you must find yourself.' He touches the peak of his cap. 'Good luck.'

With that he turns. Paul stares in horror. The back of the inspector's skull is a gory mess of shattered bone, gelatinous blood and brain matter.

'Are you a ghost?' Paul asks.

But the inspector carries on down the carriage, oblivious to the question. He steps through the far door and is gone. The train starts to slow. Paul cranes to see. There's a light up ahead.

The brakes squeal. The carriage shudders and fills with the acrid stench of smoke and burning rubber. There's something else, the sulphurous perfume of brimstone. Paul wonders what's waiting for him at his journey's end. He left his London at the beginning of the twenty-first century. Soon he will enter the same city in the early years of World War II, the time of his country's greatest crisis. There will be fire. There will be terror. There will be a reckoning. A man's life is in the balance. If he dies, history will change. Evil will rise. Paul has the destiny of a great city in his hands. He has turned his back on his own world to fight for its right to survive in another. The point of brightness becomes a sequence of light and dark. The train is pulling into the station. The battle begins.

One

London. Sunday, 29 December, 1940

The train juddered to a halt. The wheels made a noise on the track like a knife grinding. Immediately, Paul glimpsed the wartime posters on the wall.

Look Out in the Black Out.

Walk facing the traffic where you can see and be seen.

Can it really be true? he wondered. Is it that easy? Have I stepped back in time? Stirring himself, he left the train. Though he had made his journey alone, he now found himself swept along by bustling crowds. There was the staccato chorus of high heels and half a dozen young women overtook him, chatting excitedly. Next, a man in a sports jacket and wide, flapping flannel trousers pushed past.

It was impossible not to eavesdrop on the snatches

of conversation around him. A woman in a flowered dress was looking forward to a nice cup of cha. An elderly man grumbled that it was time they gave Jerry something back. Paul couldn't help but be fascinated by these echoes of a past England come to life. Falling in behind the other passengers, men and women who seemed to have materialised from nowhere, Paul headed for the exit, without any idea where he was going. He was in search of a man, not a destination. He was looking for Detective Inspector George Temple of the Special Branch, the man whose life he had to save.

Making his way through the rotunda-shaped booking hall, he gazed at his surroundings. As the crowds disgorged by the tube train thinned, Paul examined every male face. Temple's name had been contained in an old diary, the thinnest of clues but a signpost at least. So which of these anonymous faces belonged to Temple? Paul was beginning to realize the difficulty of his mission. He started climbing to street level. The station was emptying quickly. No more than a dozen people remained and most were rapidly vanishing out of view up the stairs. Soon, everyone would be gone, and with them any chance of thwarting the murder plot. Had he left it too late?

Taking a chance, he called, 'Temple.'

A man at the top of the stairs halted. His leather-soled shoes scraped as he paused. Then the man crouched low and glanced back into the station. Paul flattened his back against the wall to avoid being spotted. He saw a tall, lean man in a mackintosh. His

10

black, Brylcreemed hair was just visible under the brim of his trilby hat.

'Hello,' Temple asked, 'who's there? Did somebody call my name?'

Paul stayed where he was, heart thumping. It was too early to declare himself. What could he say? Explain why he was here? Temple would just laugh in his face. No, Paul's story was so strange, so utterly unbelievable, Temple wouldn't even give him a hearing. There was only one way to convince the policeman and that was to do something to prove himself and the story he had to tell. Paul stepped out into the late December gloom and watched Temple walk down the street. He could hear the six o'clock chimes of Big Ben ringing out across the river. He followed, grateful for his Nike trainers. He padded softly after the shadowy figure of the detective, taking care not to let the gap between them shorten too much. The last thing he wanted was to attract Temple's attention a second time.

He needn't have worried. Temple was wrapped up in his own thoughts. He kept his eyes trained on the way ahead. That's when the air-raid sirens sounded. It was a prolonged, unearthly wailing like banshees gathering over a haunted moor. Paul skidded to a halt while the rest of the crowd started to head for cover. Some hurried. Most seemed to treat it as part of an irksome routine. The streets emptied instantly. The long queues of pale, weary-looking people at the bus stops reluctantly gave up their wait for a ride home

11

and joined the general exodus. The air raid siren was quickly replaced by a second sound, the distant crackle of guns. The anti-aircraft batteries were opening up. Simultaneously, searchlights started to swing across the sky, illuminating the lines of barrage balloons. Their beams were mimicked by another set of lights at street level. Air raid wardens had appeared, their dimmed torches creeping along the pavements.

All the sights and sounds were new to Paul: vivid, startling and strange. He watched as people vanished from the street. They'd been living this nightmare for one hundred and fourteen consecutive days. A quarter of the British population was clustered here, more or less defenceless while the skies rained fire.

Soon, Paul and Temple were alone on the darkened streets. Temple wasn't looking for shelter. He was moving fast. Come hell, high water or Nazi bombardment, he was going to keep his rendezvous. The *ack ack* was continuing to growl across the rooftops. Temple didn't even look up. Instead, he quickened his pace and headed in the direction of St Paul's. Paul followed, uncomfortably aware of the rumble of planes overhead and Temple's assassin lurking somewhere in these bleak, wintry streets.

'Hey, you there,' a voice barked, 'didn't you hear the siren?'

A man in a black uniform and helmet emerged from the murk.

'I'm just going,' Paul said.

No sooner had the words left his lips than there was

a sound like a heavy rain shower or the rustling of autumn leaves.

'What's that?' Paul asked, startled.

'Where've you been hiding?' the ARP warden demanded. 'Haven't you heard the sounds of incendiaries before?'

Paul gazed skywards and saw the falling objects. 'Firebombs.'

'That's right, sonny,' the warden told him, 'IBs, Hitler's New Year presents, call them what you will. Now stop asking ruddy stupid questions and get off the street. You'll get your bleedin' head blown off, you will.'

Paul started walking but not in the direction the warden had pointed. The dull, rolling roar of aircraft drowned out the man's renewed protests, then more incendiaries fell, creating dazzling white points in the night. Already, the street was ringed by flame. The firebombs were falling in thick showers now and one or two fires were blazing out of control. Fear boiled over Paul's skin but he couldn't give up his pursuit of Temple.

Keeping the detective's silhouette in view, Paul hurried after him. The night was heavy with the bombers' drone, the increasing number of fires casting an eerie, scarlet glow. Flames leaped above the houses and offices and cinders pelted the roofs. At each new explosion, Paul flinched. After one particularly loud detonation, he cowered behind a blast wall of sandbags but Temple didn't seem to notice any of it. On he went through the night, dodging waves of howling sparks and embers. The detective had to be either very brave or very stupid. Scrambling out from behind his shelter, Paul ran to keep Temple in sight. The sky filled with planes, planes and more planes, unloading their deadly cargo over the city below. The Luftwaffe seemed to be intent on reducing London to ash.

To Paul's relief, Temple stopped and pulled out a notepad. He had a small pencil flashlight in his hand. He held the page in the torch beam, nodded and continued to the end of the street. He turned the corner, a hazy figure framed by the blazing warehouses of Paternoster Row, Ivy Lane and London House Yard. The narrow City streets were being devoured by runaway conflagrations.

As Paul followed through the flame and the dust, he cast his mind back to the twist of destiny that had brought him to this corner of Hell. There was something in his blood, a rottenness almost as old as time. The men in his family did things, terrible things. They destroyed the lives of others. In doing so, they often destroyed themselves. It was a contamination from which Paul would not be free until he had uprooted its source deep in London's sooty heart. His bloodline made him a reluctant cousin to the shadowy killer who was prowling nearby.

'Where are you?' Paul wondered out loud.

It was the right time. What happened next? All Paul understood was this: the whole world was falling apart around him. Walls and coping stones were crashing to

the ground. The streets were cratered and full of debris
and everywhere burning brands pelted down. Even the
clouds were stained crimson by the reflected glow of
the flames. And the inferno was becoming more intense, creating a haven for the killer in the dark.
Turning the next corner, Paul saw Temple picking his
way past a burned out fire appliance. What drove this
man on? Wearily, Paul kept up his pursuit. His eyes
darted left and right. Any second he expected the
assassin to spring out from the sheets of flame that
roared from every direction.

The atmosphere at the centre of the firestorm was
stifling. A high wind was adding to the hellishness of
the scene, hot gales sweeping through buildings amid a
snowstorm of golden sparks. For the first time Paul
was beginning to hear the clang of collapsing girders
and the crash of floors giving way. He passed a group
of fire fighters and half expected to be challenged but
they were too intent on the job in hand. For a moment
Paul stood transfixed by the courage of these red-eyed,
smudge-faced men. He was starting to realize just how
safe it had been, that world in which he had grown up.
He stumbled forward, wondering if he had the courage
to go on.

That's when, at last, he saw a silhouetted figure
appear to Temple's left, emerging out of a blizzard of
hot brands. A burst of *ack ack* illuminated the stranger's face. Paul had seen the telltale signs before, in
the face of Redman – John Redman, his nemesis, his
brother. Paul recognized the same translucent skin,

the same soulless eyes as the murderer who had taken the lives of five people. They were the marks of the demon. But Temple didn't see the monster in the stranger he was meeting, just the man. Oblivious to the danger, Temple turned to talk to the newcomer.

'You must be Shadow,' he said. 'You spoke to my superior, Superintendent John Ketsch,' Temple said. 'We followed up the tips you gave him. They were accurate.'

'I told you I had inside information.'

Paul saw what the demon was doing. He'd fed Temple just enough leads to bait the hook and draw him to a meeting.

Temple spoke again. 'It's obvious you are who you say you are.'

Shadow listened. His eyes remained expressionless.

'So let's get down to business, Mr—'

'Why don't we just stick to the name I gave you?' the demon suggested. 'Call me Shadow.'

'Very well,' Temple continued. 'Shadow it is. You have information about an assassination attempt on Mr Churchill.'

Now Paul understood why Temple was ready to brave the Blitz and attend the meeting. He'd come on a matter of national security, the protection of the Prime Minister. More bombs shrieked down. The ground jumped beneath their feet. Even the hitherto unflappable Temple flinched this time.

'You could have chosen a better night for a meeting,' he said ruefully as slabs of masonry peeled from a nearby building. 'Now, tell me what you've got for us and we can get out of this madness.'

A thin smile curled across the Shadow's face. The demon made a telltale movement towards Temple. Paul's heart set up a warning clamour.

'Look out!' he cried.

At last Temple recognized the danger. He blocked the sudden assault with his shoulder and threw a right jab. His knuckles found soft flesh and he succeeded in propelling his attacker backwards. Shadow grunted and staggered for a moment then renewed the attack. Beneath a blood-red sky, a life-or-death struggle began. Temple swung a punch that rocked the demon back on his heels. It was the detective's turn to smile. Paul sensed that Temple thought he'd won.

'No,' he cried, rushing forward, 'don't drop your guard.'

Temple half-turned, catching Paul's eye. 'Who the hell are you?' he demanded. Then he realized where he'd heard the voice before. 'You're the one who called to me in the tube station, aren't you?'

Paul nodded then turned his gaze on the demon, who was approaching once more. He was in no hurry. He wore an amused smile, as if he was telling the detective that his efforts to hurt him were ridiculously puny. It was Temple's turn to notice the deathly pallor of his opponent's face. Shadow snarled. The drawn-back lips revealed inhuman, needle-sharp teeth, in double rows.

'What in God's name!' Temple gasped at the sight of the man's hideous maw.

'Don't look into his eyes,' Paul warned. 'You'll be dead if you do.'

Temple tore his stare away from the demon then, realizing that he was facing a danger beyond his imagining, he drew his gun and shot his assailant through the shoulder. Blood and flesh spattered the wall and pavement behind him. Shadow stumbled back, uttering a wounded animal squeal as he did so. But the gunshot didn't stop him for long. Reaching into his wounded flesh, he dug for the bullet with bloody fingers, and plucked it out, scooping gobbets of flesh and decals of thick, dark blood with it. Paul saw Temple's eyes widen in disbelief. The demon grinned triumphantly, the curved, serrated fangs gleaming, and flicked the bullet in Temple's direction. It tinkled uselessly on the pavement. To the policeman's amazement, the movement of the attacker's ruined shoulder seemed unimpaired by the damage. Paul saw that Temple was paralysed by the sights he had witnessed. He stepped between monster and man and prepared to confront the demon himself.

'Step aside, boy!' Shadow growled. 'This is no business of yours.'

'You're wrong,' Paul retorted. 'I know what you are. I know who sent you. Do you want me to speak your master's name?'

The demon's eyes narrowed as he searched Paul's face, curious to find out if he knew as much as he claimed. Paul didn't disappoint. It was the likes of Redman and Shadow who became demon assassins but they were mere pawns. Behind them, there was a greater power at work.

'You serve King Lud,' Paul said. 'You serve the terror man.'

In response, Shadow hurled Paul to one side, winding him. The demon watched him for a moment, curiosity blazing in his dark eyes. Then he turned and slammed Temple into a wall, blasting the air from his lungs. Body ablaze with pain, Temple crumpled to the pavement and the gun spun from his hand.

Two

Germany, Sunday, 29 December, 1940

*S*even hundred and eighty miles away from the intense conflagration sweeping east and central London there is about to be a meeting that could change the course of history. It will be held near the town of Berchtesgarden, in the Bavarian Alps. On this December night, the man in charge is the leader of the RHSA, the counter-espionage unit of the feared SS. His name is Reinhard Heydrich.

One of Heydrich's lieutenants telephoned earlier. He sounded excited. He claimed to have discovered a new secret weapon in the struggle to break the resistance of the United Kingdom. Heydrich rises from his chair and walks across the room. He is growing impatient. How much longer? Heydrich slaps his black leather gloves in his palm as he waits for Gessler and his man to appear from the lift. Heydrich pauses in front of the fireplace in the south wall and waits for the doors to open. He hopes this isn't just another of Gessler's hare-brained schemes. His last suggestion was to try to poison Winston Churchill's cigars.

Finally, the lift hums and Heydrich and his bodyguards turn towards the doors.

Gessler steps out accompanied by a tall Englishman with a square-jawed face and dark, hawkish eyes. He strides into the room, head held high. Heydrich watches the Englander keenly. He's heard rumours about Gessler's protégé and he's curious to see what's so special about him. Harry doesn't disappoint. A confident figure, broad-shouldered and powerful who oozes menace, he seems to dominate the room.

'So this is your secret weapon, Gessler,' Heydrich observes, looking Harry up and down.

'This is Harry Rector,' Gessler replies. 'I discovered him among the British volunteers.'

Since the outbreak of war there has been a trickle of British traitors. One day they will form a unit of the SS. Harry smiles. In truth, Gessler didn't discover him at all. According to the wishes of his true master Harry entered Germany with the express purpose of being noticed. But he's happy to allow Gessler his moment of glory. He notes the SS guards in their black uniforms with lightning flashes on their collars. They're Waffen-SS, some of the most feared warriors on the planet. Harry also registers the trio of ferocious Alsatians straining at the leash.

21

'Step forward, Herr Rector,' Heydrich says.

Harry does as he's told. As he reaches the centre of the room, the Alsatians growl and their hackles rise. They smell something unusual in this newcomer, something feral and dangerous. Breathing in the sour scent of the man-beast before them, their instincts scream. The dogs have been trained to be predators. In Harry's presence they feel more like his prey. They don't for one second take their eyes off the new arrival. Heydrich notices their reaction.

'Do you like dogs, Herr Rector?'

'Not much,' Harry answers, 'the taste is a little earthy for my liking.'

There's a moment of stunned silence then everybody laughs.

'You have a strange sense of humour, Herr Rector,' Heydrich observes. 'So tell me, why does Gessler here think so highly of you?'

'Maybe it's because I'm very good at what I do. Believe me, I can be of use to you. I have certain abilities as you may have heard.'

'Maybe you would like to demonstrate these . . . abilities,' Heydrich suggests.

Harry had been expecting this. 'Set me a test.'

Heydrich nods to the dogs' trainer and the man sets them on Harry. Harry sees them coming, three huge beasts, their lips peeled back to expose glistening fangs. He turns unhurriedly to face them, his body nonetheless appearing coiled and ready for battle. Harry Rector is in complete control of the situation. The dogs rush forward, biting and snarling. That's when Harry snaps open his right hand. Simultaneously, his eyes blaze. Immediately, the dogs yelp as if struck by some invisible weapon. Though Harry has made no physical contact with the animals, their bodies jack-knife in the air. They land painfully, rib cages crunching, spines twisting, jaws striking the floor, and there they lie, whimpering and cowed.

'Impressive,' Heydrich comments, breaking the shocked silence that followed the performance. 'Some kind of hypnotism, I suppose.'

Harry prefers to remain silent and let the watching men wonder how he subdued the dogs, reducing them to mewling wrecks with a look.

'It's a good party trick,' Heydrich continues, 'but not, I imagine, beyond the skills of a circus entertainer, a Harry Houdini. I think we need a more meaningful test.'

Instinctively, Harry glances sideways at the two SS guards he noticed on the way in. He knows how these men think. They dream of the day they'll win the Knight's Cross with Oak Leaves, Swords and Diamonds, their country's highest honour. They're keen to impress.

'Kill the Englander,' Heydrich orders in a voice devoid of passion.

The first man attacks, drawing his dagger. Harry disarms him with a brutal, clubbing chop that renders his victim's right arm quite useless. The second SS man draws a Walther pistol and points it at Harry's chest. Harry disables him as effectively as he did the first. To the amazement of the onlookers, the gunman's face drains of blood. He gasps in pain, clutching the pistol so hard his knuckles turn white. His hand starts to tremble. Then his mouth sags open and he screams in agony. As the observers exchange puzzled glances, he falls to his knees pleading for mercy. It is only then that the reason for his strange behaviour becomes apparent. The flesh of his right hand is melting like wax from the wick of a candle, sliding from his bones in liquid, yellowish streams.

'Gott in Himmel,' Heydrich murmurs, at the same time impressed and appalled by the spectacle that has unfolded before him.

Harry grins and steps forward. He forces open the soldier's fleshless fingers. The revolver clatters to the floor. The handle is glowing like a heated poker.

'Do you still think I do, what was it, yes, party tricks?' he enquires. 'Well, do you?' He is haughty, arrogant. 'When did Houdini do something like that?'

'This is beyond impressive,' Heydrich says. 'You have a great gift, Herr Rector.'

'It's a gift you desperately need,' Harry replies.

Heydrich bristles for a moment. Few men talk so boldly in his presence. 'And why would we need a traitor Englander? Most of Europe already sits in our palm. It is merely a matter of time before Britain falls too.' His eyes narrow. 'Explain. Why do we need you?'

'You need me,' Harry replies without flinching, 'because Winston Churchill stands in your way. Some of the other British leaders are ready to sue for a negotiated peace. Not Churchill. He is Britain's hope. He symbolizes the resistance of a nation. If you let him live, he will eventually find a way to bring America into the war against you. If that happens you will surely lose.'

There's a gasp of utter amazement. Nobody speaks to a member of the Nazi leadership like that. But, to everyone's surprise, Heydrich raises his hand to put a stop to the protests. 'Go on.'

'Just get me within striking distance of England,' Harry says. 'I suggest you parachute me into neutral Ireland. I will make my own way from there. Give the word, and I will remove this obstacle to the Reich's triumph.'

This time his words aren't met with dubious stares or laughter. He has earned the respect of one of Germany's most powerful men.

'There's no hurry,' Heydrich says. 'I will consider your offer. But we may not need your services. Even as we speak, we have someone closing in on Herr Churchill.'

'He will fail,' Harry tells him.

'I think not,' Heydrich says. 'He's the best man at his trade, the finest shot at our disposal. He is a great example of Aryan manhood.'

Harry lets the words hang in the air for a moment then answers.

'Exactly,' he says, 'the best man.'

Heydrich wonders what Harry means by that.

'But there are limits to what your assassin can do by himself. Churchill has a most vigilant guardian at his side.'

'Walter Thompson?' Heydrich says. 'Yes, we know

about Churchill's bodyguard. May I remind you what our Reich Minister of Propaganda broadcast recently on this very subject. 'All the Thompsons in England won't prevent us assassinating Churchill.'

'As you wish,' Harry says. 'But if your best man fails, I shall be ready to serve you. I await your summons.'

Heydrich watches Harry stride back to the lift followed by Gessler. He admires the straight back, the proud gait. What a pity this Rector isn't German. As the lift descends, Heydrich makes up his mind. If the latest assassination attempt fails, he will give this odd Englander the job.

Three

London, Sunday, 29 December, 1940

Temple shook himself alert and felt for his gun. He saw Shadow back-hand Paul out of the way then kick the weapon aside. Shadow registered that the detective had recovered and drove a vicious kick into his shoulder, sending Temple to the floor. Temple's head snapped back and cracked sickeningly against the pavement. When he looked up through a wave of pain he met the assassin's stare. The dark eyes drew him in.

'No,' Paul cried, throwing himself at Shadow, 'if you want to live, you've got to look away.'

But Shadow had skewered Temple. The detective was already transfixed by the demon's nightmarish gaze. The monstrous eyes were scarlet slashes in a face that was little more than a translucent sheet of skin drawn taut over the skull beneath. Temple felt as if he was drowning in those blood-red pits. His senses swam. Soon his mind was filling with a kaleidoscope of horrors. Temple saw the faces of his wife and baby son cowering before some unseen threat. Fear roared in his ears.

'My Connie,' he gasped through parched lips, 'Denis. No, leave them alone!'

The desperate words were like an invitation to the demon. His gaze probed deeper, opening doors in Temple's mind, blazing through every passage and byway where his most hidden thoughts might lurk. Paul tried to break the spell but Shadow cuffed him aside a second time. Shadow searched for the detective's worst fears and found them. Temple had seen the worst mankind can do. Every time he left home, he feared for his family, facing the Blitz alone. This most basic of fears was the way to crack the detective. Shadow grinned.

Temple's throat constricted. He saw a dark outline fall over Connie. She shrank back, hugging her baby son in her arms. Menacing hands closed on the screaming infant. Temple's head started to toss from side to side, struggling to defeat the paralysis that had seized him. His breathing became laboured. Paul had seen this before. Shadow was scaring his victim to death. It was the one power shared by all demon kind, the urge to spread fear.

Without thinking, Paul grabbed the nearest object – a red-hot shard of ordnance, a jagged splinter of metal from an exploded shell – but the moment his fingers closed round it he shrieked in agony. The shrapnel fragment hissed as it burned into the tender flesh of his palm. Again, Paul howled in pain. It was so intense that, just for a moment, his vision blurred. Then some conscious part of his mind managed to hang on to a childhood memory, a red door. You can master the pain, he told himself. You have an affinity with fire.

The sharp edge of the agony dulled. Yes, somehow, fire was his element. Paul focused on the shrapnel. Shapes fluttered around it, swirling into a black tunnel. Then the pain was gone. Swinging his arm in a downward movement, he drove the point of his improvised weapon into the demon's thigh. It was Shadow's turn to scream. Pulling out the shrapnel, Paul stabbed again, this time plunging the point into his enemy's stomach. He watched as blood stained the demon's clothing. Shadow turned uncomprehending eyes on Paul, then there was a flash of recognition.

'It's true,' the demon said, 'the seed is in your blood. You're one of us.'

He made a grab for Paul but the boy sprang back.

'Why fight me?' the demon demanded, fighting to staunch the blood. 'Why, if you were born into the demon brotherhood, do you betray your own kind?' He threw a contemptuous look at Temple, who was now curled up in a foetal position. 'The mortal sort are weaklings. How can you take sides with *them*?'

Temple was surfacing from his waking nightmare. He battled back to his knees and looked in the direction of the two figures. The thunder of the air raid prevented him hearing Paul's answer. Instead, he resumed his search for his gun.

'Go,' Paul addressed the wounded demon. 'You've failed in your mission. Just leave.'

'Failed, have I?' Shadow retorted. 'Think again, boy.'

He drew his hand away from his stomach wound. Already, the bleeding had stopped. Astonished by his opponent's powers of recovery, Paul gripped the shrapnel dagger again. He went as if to stab but, to his horror, this time he saw not one demon, but three.

'Let's play a game,' Shadow chuckled. 'I call it *hunt the Shadow*. Well, which one's which?'

Paul stabbed wildly at the first figure he saw. His weapon slashed through empty air. In the same split-second a searing pain lanced through his arm and he let go. The demon grinned and shook his head.

'You're as weak as the mortals you defend,' Shadow said. 'I am about to teach you a lesson you'll never forget.'

With that, he seized Paul by the shoulders and forced him back into the burning building. It was little more than a hollow-eyed ruin, engulfed in clouds of embers and sparks. Through one shattered window Paul could see St Paul's, a spectral island in a sea of billowing smoke. The dome was stained scarlet by the garish light of the firestorm. Paul wondered whether he or the great cathedral would survive the night of fire.

At the same moment Paul vanished into the conflagration, Temple finally succeeded in recovering his gun. Shielding his face, he stepped into the building after them. The heat was intense. Where were they? Then the plumes of flame gaped open for an instant and he saw a pair of struggling, silhouetted figures. Paul was retreating under the onslaught of his bigger, stronger opponent. Temple knew it was only a matter of time before the boy succumbed. But the lad had saved his life. He had to repay the debt.

'You take the side of mortal men,' Shadow snarled. 'You, who carry the demon seed in your blood. I still want to know why.'

Paul retreated through the swarms of sparks. His lungs burned with the sour, sickening reek of the flames.

'Why?' Shadow demanded. 'You were born to serve the Master. You're like me.'

'I'm not like you!' Paul cried. 'I don't want to be this way.'

Shadow leered. 'You have no choice. It's your nature.'

With that, he propelled Paul backwards against a blazing timber. Paul writhed in agony as his clothes caught fire. Shadow continued to advance.

'Maybe you're right,' he said. 'You're too weak to belong to the demon brotherhood.'

He was toying with Paul now, inflicting pain with glee. Paul stumbled backwards, barely able to defend himself. Suddenly a bullet pinged off a blackened

31

timber. To his left, Paul saw Temple. The firearm bucked once more. This time the bullet found its mark and shattered the demon's jaw. Shadow's tongue lolled grotesquely amid blood, shattered bone and splintered teeth. By now Shadow was barely conscious but he remained dangerous. His attention drifted from Paul to Temple. He'd allowed Paul to distract him. Driving his foot into Paul's chest in a fit of rage, Shadow turned to face Temple once more.

'Playtime's over,' the demon announced, his voice distorted by the horrific destruction wrought by Temple's bullet. But the next words were unmistakeable. 'Get ready to die.'

Temple wondered what drove this madman on. He took his pistol in both hands and prepared to fire. That's when the sky split asunder, shredded by metal debris. A bomb had exploded nearby. This new shock was all it took to shatter the fragile shell of the building. What was left of the roof gave way with an ear-splitting roar. Temple flung himself backwards and landed, sprawling, on the pavement outside. But the boy and the assassin were engulfed in the ensuing avalanche of masonry, steel girders, brick and timbers.

'Dear God,' Temple murmured in horror, 'how could anyone live through that?'

But inside the building boy and demon survived, if only just. Paul rubbed dust from his eyes and spat out the sooty debris he'd swallowed. He was trembling violently, a result of the terrible burns that covered much of his body. Shadow too was badly injured, a mutilated, bloody mannequin; the flesh down one side of his body had been torn away but he was still capable of some limited movement. Paul saw the monster clawing towards him, driven on by an all-consuming hatred. In an attempt to defend himself, Paul seized the demon's scorched hand. Immediately, Shadow winced. There was fear in his eyes. What did it mean? Moments before, the creature had seemed invincible, shrugging off wounds that would have killed any normal man. Suddenly he seemed as helpless as a newborn baby.

'You're scared of me!' Paul said, numb with disbelief.

Shadow didn't reply. His whole body was wracked with convulsions. Then Paul understood. *It's not just his injuries. I'm doing this.* Paul's fingers seemed to be sinking into Shadow's body, cutting deep. Paul could feel Shadow's life force throbbing against his fingers. The demon's strength was flowing into Paul's body, the way blood flows during a transfusion.

I'm absorbing what's left of your life force.

Then he said out loud. 'You said I was weak. You were wrong.'

Shadow was fading fast. Paul gloated. 'You will die so I can live.'

He saw Shadow's eyes begging him for mercy. Paul didn't feel an ounce of pity. He felt triumph. He felt joy. He turned down the plea with a cold stare and continued to tighten his grip. The mystical transfusion

33

gathered pace. Paul was siphoning away the last of Shadow's strength and using it to cling to life himself.

'Please,' Shadow groaned.

'Who's the master now?' Paul demanded.

Then he watched Shadow perish. Desperately weak from the struggle, Paul reflected on his victory. I've absorbed the last of your power, he thought, gazing down at Shadow, but will it be enough to protect me from the inferno? The firestorm was a more dangerous opponent than Shadow. He had some kind of connection with the marching flames but they could consume him nevertheless. Paul staggered. Alert though he still was, the pain that raked his flesh was almost unbearable. The firelight flickered in Paul's fading consciousness and he heard Temple's voice once more, as if from far off.

Paul managed to croak a plea for help. 'I'm here.'

Then the world swam away.

'Hold on,' Temple yelled. 'I'm coming.' He was about to plunge back into the building when he heard somebody behind him. A fire crew had arrived and they were unloading their hoses. Temple glanced in their direction as he braced himself to re-enter the building.

'Don't be a fool,' the senior officer shouted. He made a grab for Temple's sleeve.

'I have to,' Temple said, shrugging him away. 'There's somebody alive in there.'

The detective plunged forward and started to fight his way through the conflagration. He cast a nervous glance at what was left of the walls. They could come down at any moment. Where was the boy? Temple picked his way through the rubble, occasionally retreating when another sheet of flame advanced through the darkness. Then he saw Paul. Most of his clothes were burned away and he was unconscious. But there was something Temple couldn't explain. There was a kind of aura around the boy. The flames had parted like theatre curtains, leading him to the spot where he was lying.

'Am I going mad?' Temple asked out loud as he struggled to explain the amazing spectacle.

Praying he was doing the right thing, the policeman picked Paul up and started carrying him from the scene. As he stumbled back towards the street, he saw his attacker. Shadow was now no more than a charred corpse, unrecognisable as the powerful figure who had come to take his life. By the time Temple reached the safety of the street, the fire fighters were playing streams of water on the building and an ambulance had arrived. The driver was a woman.

'Let me take a look at him,' she said.

Temple saw her wince at the sight of Paul's burns.

'It's bad, isn't it?' he asked.

The woman's colleague arrived with a stretcher. The way he reacted to Paul's injuries confirmed Temple's suspicions. 'We'll get him to hospital,' he said, 'and see what the doctors think.'

But from the tone of his voice he didn't hold out much hope.

Four

London, Wednesday, 1 January, 1941

Temple was sitting at Paul's bedside. He had visited the boy every day since the night of flame. Almost every waking moment he found himself reliving the events of the firestorm. People were calling it the second Great Fire of London. He was sure the photograph in the *Daily Mail* of St Paul's cathedral riding through a sea of billowing smoke would live forever. Somehow it symbolized London's defiance, the conviction that the nation would endure, no matter how much fire and steel the Luftwaffe rained down on London.

But other images kept flashing into Temple's mind. They were just as remarkable as Sir Christopher Wren's indomitable dome. He remembered Shadow, a man with translucent skin who had demonstrated impossible powers of endurance against fire and bullet. He relived the sea of flame that had parted like magic to guide him to the boy who'd saved his life. He hadn't told anybody what had really happened, not even Connie.

Temple looked down at the boy. He didn't even know his name. But the boy had known his. This single fact tortured Temple even more than the monstrous strength of his attacker. A father himself, Temple shook his head as he watched over the boy. The lad was still unconscious and so swathed in bandages he looked like Boris Karloff in The Mummy. Alerted to footsteps behind him, Temple glanced round. He saw a pretty young nurse enter the room. She didn't look much older than his niece, Evelyn.

'Here again?' she said brightly.

Temple nodded. 'Is there any change?'

The nurse shook her head. Something in her expression told Temple the hospital staff were only expecting one change to occur. He asked to speak to a doctor.

'Stay here,' the nurse said. 'I'll get Dr Tyler.'

When Dr Tyler appeared ten minutes later, huffing grumpily, Temple said, 'I want you to be straight with me. Is there any chance he will recover?'

Dr Tyler frowned and answered with a platitude. 'Only time will tell.'

'Don't fob me off, man!' Temple snapped. 'I want the truth.'

Dr Tyler heard the crack of authority in Temple's

voice. He hesitated then said, 'You can never say never. But I won't lie to you. He has burns over eighty per cent of his body. They're deep. Inspector Temple, there's been major tissue damage. It's the shock from the loss of fluid that causes death. A process has been set in motion that usually has only one outcome.'

Temple nodded briefly. 'Thank you for your honesty, doctor.'

Rising sadly from the bedside, he made his way down the long, blank corridors and out into the street. He felt numb. The boy had saved him and paid the ultimate price. Temple had many questions for his saviour but they would never be answered. He drove in the direction of Whitehall where he had a meeting with some of the Top Brass. Parking his car, he made his way past the bomb damage to the Clive Steps, that led from the statue of Clive of India to the front door of the War Rooms, passing a sentry. He flashed his ID and entered the Number Ten Annexe. He noticed the marigold paint of the war rooms. It reminded him of the hospital from which he had just come. Soon the labyrinth of corridors defeated him. He hesitated at a point where three corridors met.

As he fetched up at the end of one particularly gloomy passage, he looked around. He heard footsteps and a familiar figure appeared. It was his immediate superior, Superintendent John Ketsch. As usual, he was puffing away at his pipe.

'Ah, there you are, Temple,' he said, tamping down

the tobacco. 'Now that you're here we can start. Come in.'

Temple entered. There were half a dozen men in the room. Temple knew most of them. One he knew only by reputation. This was Walter Thompson, Churchill's bodyguard.

'Righty-oh, gentlemen,' Ketsch said in an artificially breezy tone. 'You must be wondering why I have called this meeting.' He ran his eyes round those present. 'The code-breakers at Bletchley Park have come up with something. A couple of days ago they intercepted a message. They ran it through their magic box of tricks and got in touch with me. We have a problem. This is the substance of the communication. There is a sniper at large in the heart of London. In the words of the intercepted message from German intelligence, Arminius is on the move.'

'Arminius?' Temple asked.

'Nobody recognized the name to begin with,' Ketsch said, 'but somebody at MI5 did Classics at Oxford. Apparently Arminius was a German tribal leader in ancient times. He led a rebellion that succeeded in smashing the Roman legions. It seems it was one of the worst defeats Rome ever suffered in the field. This Arminius is still a national hero to the Hun.'

Ketsch always called the Germans the Hun. He copied it from some of Churchill's utterances.

'So what does it mean?' one of the younger men asked.

'To the best of our knowledge,' Ketsch answered,

'we have another assassination plot. It's Mr Churchill again, of course.'

Walter Thompson shifted in his seat. Temple interpreted the gesture as an acknowledgement that he had more work to do.

'So,' Ketsch said, 'do you have any observations to make?'

Temple was the first to speak. 'On the way in here,' he said, 'I passed a single sentry. This is the hub of the war effort. Surely the War Rooms should be better protected.'

'I quite agree,' Ketsch said. 'That's the purpose of this meeting, to beef up our security measures.'

He rubbed his palms together. They made a dry, papery sound.

'Let's have some suggestions,' he said.

The meeting took just over an hour. They drew up an action plan and selected the men who would be given the responsibility to implement it. Satisfied with his morning's work, Ketsch closed the meeting. He intercepted Temple at the door.

'I say, Temple,' he murmured, 'would you mind popping back in for a moment?' He closed the door behind them.

'What is it, Sir?' Temple asked.

'I've just read your report about Sunday night,' Ketsch said, 'your meeting with this Shadow fellow. I don't suppose we've found out his real name.'

'No, Sir.'

'Ah.' Ketsch sounded disappointed.

'Is that all?' Temple asked.

'There's one more thing,' Ketsch said. 'I was wondering, is there anything you left out? It seems a tad thin on detail.'

Temple met his superior's eye. In truth, he'd left out a lot more than he'd put in and Ketsch had noticed. He wasn't stupid.

'You say that this man was a double agent,' Ketsch said. 'He lured you there with the intention of killing you.'

'That's my judgement,' Temple answered.

'That raises an obvious question,' Ketsch said. 'Why? Why go to all that trouble to kill an Inspector in the Special Branch?' He let the question hang for a moment. 'I don't wish to belittle the work you do, George, but you're rather a small fish when it comes to German intelligence. I ask again, why you?'

'I've been wondering the same myself,' Temple said.

'And this boy,' Ketsch continued. 'What part does he play? Who is he?'

'I'm sorry, Sir,' Temple said, 'I have absolutely no idea. I can only tell you that, but for his intervention, I wouldn't be standing here talking to you.' He waited a beat. 'Do you think my attacker and this Arminius are one and the same?'

'Unlikely,' Ketsch said, 'For starters, the modus operandi is different. According to Bletchley Park, Arminius is likely to be a sniper. Your man wasn't even armed with a revolver. Odd that, what kind of assassin kills with his bare hands in this day and age?

Besides, if his purpose was to murder the Prime Minister, why let himself be sidetracked? What possible reason could he have for going after a mere policeman? It would only put his mission in jeopardy.' He cleared his throat. 'Let's face it, Temple, our intelligence estimates that there are twenty thousand Nazi sympathizers active in the UK. At any one time there will be several separate plots against the Prime Minister. We have to assume that the man who died in the raid wasn't Arminius. We also have to assume there will be an attempt on the Prime Minister's life in the near future. You and Thompson will be working closely together to foil it.'

Ketsch started stuffing his briefcase with sheaves of documents.

'I'm afraid this will be disruptive to family life, Temple,' he said. 'You'd better tell Connie that your hours may be rather irregular until further notice. To be quite blunt about it, your first duty from now on is to your country, not your family.'

'Yes, Sir,' Temple said.

Five

London, Wednesday, 1 January, 1941

*R*etsch is right to remain open-minded about the identity of the man who had died in Sunday's air raid. At that very moment the man code-named Arminius is walking in St James's Park, not two hundred metres away, watching the Cabinet War Rooms. He's carrying a battered suitcase. Inside it there's the stripped down rifle he's just collected from a contact in Mile End. He isn't at all nervous about lugging the firearm across London. Arminius finds the British amusing. There's something endearingly amateur about them. They've posted just one sentry outside the War Rooms. Is this the kind of security afforded the most important men in the nation? And what kind of secret services permit their

Prime Minister to take his 'constitutional' alone in the blackout? The Gestapo would never be so careless.

Arminius strolls by at a leisurely pace. He's building up a mental map of the killing ground. Soon, he will watch Churchill plod down the Clive Steps, probably puffing on one of his fine Havana cigars. Arminius is already familiar with Churchill's portly five foot eight inch frame, his black overcoat and slouch hat. He's studied newsreels and photographs until the man is as familiar as his own father. If the British were to employ a double, Arminius would see through him in an instant. There will be no mistake.

Making his way down the gravel path, Arminius imagines Churchill trudging along, possibly lost in his thoughts, possibly chatting to his bodyguard Thompson. Arminius knows that Thompson is a skilled and loyal protector. At close quarters he would be a formidable opponent. But Arminius is going to make his kill from a distance, the way he always has. He will get Churchill in his crosshairs and blow his brains out with a single shot. He imagines the spray of blood, the heavy thud of the body on the ground. By the time Thompson works out where the shot came from, Arminius will be long gone. The perfect crime.

Arminius spends another hour gazing through the watery sunlight of a January morning, picking out the best spots from which to fire the fatal shot. Soon, he's narrowed it down to three possible locations. He will need them all. Churchill can be unpredictable. He doesn't always take the same route round the park. Satisfied with his morning's work, Arminius sets off for the rented flat in west London where he will make his final preparations. He isn't nervous. He's killed before, shooting from distance and slipping away before anybody could discover his location.

Churchill's days are numbered.

Six

London, Wednesday, 1 January, 1941

Paul Rector was hovering between life and death in the side ward of a central London hospital. Black, fluttering shapes swirled through his subconscious. These images had been haunting him for months. Now they were inviting him into a new, dangerous world. The ground shuddered at his feet. He stepped back, staring down at the deep, swirling vortex. Shrieking creatures rose like sparks caught in the up-draught of a fire. A silvery glow followed them, radiating out from a white chapel. The white chapel started to rise and Paul formed words, his lips barely moving. As he struggled to speak, a change came over him.

'A white chapel,' he murmured, 'a white church . . .'

The image of the white chapel fused with another,

instantly recognizable landmark of London's East End. His voice, still barely audible, forced out another fragment of the dream.

'. . . a white church, Spitalfields.'

In his mind's eye, the still unconscious boy saw a towering spire rising to a stiletto point in a clear, blue sky. In its shade, in the neighbouring, narrow streets the East End's most famous, and notorious son, Jack the Ripper had claimed two of his victims. Fault-lines of evil ran under the pavements.

'. . . a white church, Christ Church . . . Spitalfields.'

Pain and exhaustion were falling away. His voice grew steadily stronger until it attracted the attention of the pretty young nurse who had been on duty during Temple's visit. Nurse O'Hara stopped and stared. He was speaking. The boy they all believed to be at death's door was talking in his sleep. Nurse O'Hara rushed over to the bed and listened. She saw the rapid eye movement of her patient. He was sleeping but he was terribly agitated. She leaned in close to catch his words.

'. . . a white church, Christ Church . . . Spitalfields.'

Nurse O'Hara stood there a while, listening to him repeating the same few phrases. That's when she noticed something about the boy. The deathly pallor seemed to have gone from his face. Right there, before her very eyes, he was undergoing a kind of resurrection. Was he coming back from the dead? Pulse racing, Nurse O'Hara hurried away to get Dr Tyler. At first Dr Tyler simply frowned and dismissed her report. The

47

anonymous boy in Ward Ten? That was one patient who wasn't going to recover any time soon, he told her. He'd said as much to that short-tempered policeman. But Nurse O'Hara was so vociferous, her manner was little short of impertinent. When Dr Tyler finally followed her to Paul's bed at the far end of the ward he was amazed to see that not only was the boy capable of talking in his sleep, his eyes had actually begun to flicker open.

'Can you hear me?' Dr Tyler asked, astonished at the turn of events.

Paul blinked for a moment or two, struggling to cope with the rays of winter sunlight that were slanting across the ward.

'Would you draw the curtains please, nurse?' Dr Tyler asked.

Nurse O'Hara did as she was told. 'Is he awake?'

Dr Tyler held up his hand for quiet.

'Can you tell me your name?' he asked.

The answer came as a hoarse, exhausted whisper. 'It's . . . Paul.'

'Hello, Paul,' Dr Tyler said. 'How do you feel?'

Paul thought for a moment. 'I ache a bit.' His voice was growing stronger. 'My skin's sore and I'm so thirsty. Could I have a glass of water, please?'

Amazed that his patient could talk at all, Dr Tyler glanced at nurse O'Hara and nodded. 'Would you get one please, nurse?'

While Nurse O'Hara went to get Paul's glass of

water, Dr Tyler examined the boy. This was impossible. He was so alert.

'Do you mind if I take a look at your burns?' Dr Tyler asked.

Paul reacted with surprise and dismay. 'I'm burned!'

'You were in a fire.'

'Was I?' Paul closes his eyes for a moment. 'I don't remember.'

Dr Tyler snipped away at the bandages and the gauze beneath. To his surprise, the exposed skin was a little red. In patches it looked waxy. But where were the extensive burns he had seen when the boy was admitted? He continued snipping and peeling back the bandages. Still there was no sign of the irreparable damage he'd been expecting. Am I mad? he thought. I was here when we dressed his wounds. But, as the bandages came off, it was the same all over the rest of Paul's body.

'What exactly do you recall?'

Paul was now fully conscious.

'A fire,' he said. 'Yes, there was a fire.' His thoughts started to clear. 'I was in a burning building.'

'They found you in a warehouse not far from St Paul's,' Dr Tyler told him.

Paul stared. 'St Paul's?' He searched for an explanation and found none. 'Are you sure?'

'That's what the ambulance driver said.'

'But what was I doing *there*?' Paul's eyes batted furiously as he tried to make sense of what Dr Tyler had told him. 'I can't imagine what reason I would have to be in the centre of London at night.' One event remained vivid. Paul winced at the flashback. 'The roof caved in.'

'Now, Paul,' Dr Tyler continued, 'what's your surname?'

Paul gave another deep frown as his mind failed to penetrate the fog that shrouded his memories. 'It's . . .' He fought to drag the information up from the dark confusion of his thoughts then admitted defeat. 'I'm sorry. I don't recall.' He felt a rush of panic. 'I don't remember anything.' Tears spilled down his face. 'What happened to me?'

'That's all right,' Dr Tyler said, patting Paul's arm. 'You've been through a terrible ordeal. You must be very tired. Get some rest and we'll talk again soon. If there's anything you want, just ask Nurse O'Hara. When you're fully rested, she will remove the rest of your dressings.'

Paul lay on his back, looking up. How could he not remember his own last name? He followed the spidery cracks across the off-white ceiling. He could tell from the doctor's tone that something dramatic had happened. Then a single word lanced through his consciousness. Burns! Unable to wait for the nurse, Paul tore at his last few bandages. It brought back a vivid image. He remembered screaming in agony as tongues of flame licked his skin. He wriggled and squirmed out of his wrappings and stared. Under the bandages his skin was untouched except for a slight reddening and a few patches where it felt almost like greaseproof paper.

By what miracle had flames licked his skin without destroying it? Several minutes later nurse O'Hara returned with a carafe and a glass of water.

'Oh,' she said, 'I see you've removed the rest of your dressings.'

'I had to see for myself,' Paul said. 'Look at me. I'm as good as new. How's that possible?'

'I'll get you some pyjamas,' she said simply.

Along the corridor, Dr Tyler was in his office, consulting a list of phone numbers in a log book. There it was, the home number of the police officer who brought Paul in, Detective Inspector George Temple. He asked the operator to put him through. The phone rang for a few moments then he heard a woman's voice at the other end.

'May I speak to Detective Inspector George Temple please?' he asked.

'George isn't in at the moment,' the woman told him. 'I'm Mrs Temple. Would you like to leave your name?'

'Certainly,' Dr Tyler said. 'It's Dr John Tyler.'

'Doctor?' Connie Temple repeated. 'Is this about the boy George pulled out of the burning building?'

'That's right,' Dr Tyler said. 'So your husband's told you about it?'

'Yes,' Connie said, 'how is he?'

'That's the purpose of this phone call,' Dr Tyler said, barely able to conceal his excitement. 'The boy's awake.'

'Oh, that *is* good news!' Connie exclaimed. 'George will be so thrilled.'

'Do you think I could leave a message for your husband?' Dr Tyler asked.

'Of course,' Connie answered. 'Just give me a moment to find a pencil and a piece of paper.'

'Tell DI Temple . . .' Dr Tyler let his voice trail off for a moment. How exactly should he put it? 'Tell him that the boy's name is Paul. He's alert and apparently in rude good health.'

He heard a catch in Connie's breath.

'But surely he was badly burned,' she said, interrupting the doctor. 'George phoned to tell me he was unlikely to survive the next twenty-four hours. He was quite depressed about it. He can't have made such a rapid recovery.'

'That's why I need to talk to your husband,' Dr Tyler said. 'This is a most unusual case. You could say I've just witnessed a modern miracle.'

Soon Paul was sleeping once more, the spire of the white church still looming over his unconscious mind. The door to the side ward was closed, hiding him from view. As the boy lay recovering his strength, the light in the room dimmed and four shadowy figures emerged from the walls, silently gathering round his bed. All wore long robes and hoods. They seemed to float across the tiled floor. Had Paul woken while they surrounded him, there was one face he would have recognized – the man who had appeared to him three days earlier as the ticket inspector. But when one of the quartet spoke to the ticket inspector, he addressed him by his true name.

'He doesn't remember, Cormac.'

'Maybe it's for the best,' Cormac said. 'His ignorance of who he is will shield him from Lud's gaze.' Cormac inspected the sleeping boy. 'His memory will return soon enough. He is strong.'

'But is he the one?' the third of the hooded men asked. 'You discovered him. What do you think?'

Cormac gave only the slightest shrug of the shoulders. 'It's too early to say. He shows great promise. He destroyed Redman and he was one of the demon lord's favoured disciples.'

'That's true,' the last of the quartet agreed. 'He killed the assassin even though it was his own brother. He ignored all of Redman's pleas and completed the kill.'

'It was the same with Shadow,' Cormac said. 'Paul smiled as he took his life. There's a ruthless streak in this one. That's good.'

There was a protest. 'What if he enjoys his kills too much?'

'If he is to fulfil his destiny,' Cormac said, 'he must be able to take lives as well as save them.' He crouched over Paul. 'It's a risk we must take. Fire consumed him but already he is whole. His body has almost recovered. His mind will follow in its own time. He *is* the one. I feel it in the depths of my soul.'

Cormac sounded hopeful yet weary. He had seen too much suffering and death in the centuries he had wandered the world. Then he sensed something, a deep and gathering disturbance in the air. 'Did you feel that?'

A murmur of agreement ran round the others. Apprehension filled the room. All four of them had cause to fear the creature's approach. They had suffered at his hands.

'It's King Lud,' Cormac said. 'He's searching for the boy. I feel his eyes burning away the city around us. We must be gone before our presence leads him to the boy. In his weakened state, he might succumb to the demon lord. Imagine the consequences. If Paul Rector is the one, and Lud succeeds in winning his allegiance, all is lost. I shudder at the thought of their combined powers, the forces of the white chapel will be unstoppable.' His eyes darted round his comrades. 'Paul's destiny is written. There is nothing more we can do. He must choose it for himself. If he is truly the one we seek, he will discover himself soon enough.'

'But can he find his way alone?'

'He will have to,' Cormac said. 'The court of destiny will not permit us to guide him. He must triumph over Lud's disciple before I may speak to him again. But, if I am right and he is the demon master's true nemesis, then we will be meeting Paul Rector again before long. He may be greater than any who have gone before him.'

There were nods all round. One by one, the hooded men dissolved back into the walls. Cormac was the last to go. By the time Nurse O'Hara looked in on Paul, they had all vanished.

Seven

'You look much better,' Nurse O'Hara said. 'Dr Tyler says you can move into the general ward. You'd like some company, wouldn't you?'

Paul gazed up at her. He wasn't sure that he did. He had the strangest feeling that he hadn't been alone as he slept. It made the skin on his neck creep.

'Did I have visitors?' he asked.

'Visitors?' Nurse O'Hara said. 'We don't know who to contact. There's only the policeman who found you.'

'Was he here?'

'Not while you've been sleeping,' Nurse O'Hara answered. 'Dr Tyler's left a message for him. Do you remember anything yet?'

Paul furrowed his brow. 'Not a thing.'

He didn't raise a protest; he knew there must be

other patients in greater need of a room to themselves. Soon he dozed off once more. As he slept, Paul's mind sank deeper into sleep. Nightmares arose, blurred forms that drifted in and out of focus. Black shapes, familiar somehow, swarmed at the corner of his vision and formed a tunnel. He was aware of his feet thudding on the pavement. He was walking towards a white church. There it was, opposite Brushfield Street, the imposing edifice of Christ Church, Spitalfields. His sleeping mind told him that the building was important but it didn't explain how. He continued his silent progress down the ever-narrowing tunnel. There was the church entrance.

He saw a shadowy hand beckoning him forward. His feet carried him on.

With only the briefest hesitation, he entered. The shadows between the building's pillars pulled him in. Is this where he would learn his true identity? Was he going to find a surname to go with the first name Paul? He peered at the man in the front row of pews. His head was bowed as if he were praying. As Paul drew closer he saw that the man sitting in the far corner had a newspaper spread out on his lap. It was *The Times* dated 3 January, 1941. Written in pencil in the top right hand corner was a note: *Pam. 2.15 p.m. The Olive Tree.* Next Paul saw the man's watch. The time was set at one p.m. Paul was gazing over the man's shoulder, a disembodied spirit scrutinizing every detail of the stranger's appearance.

Finally, the shadowy finger that had guided him into

the church pointed out the man's hand. It was resting on something. Paul craned to see but he could only make out the corner of something crimson. A chill wind rushed through the church throwing open the doors. Paul felt an icy grip on his shoulders and he was dragged backwards at tremendous speed, his feet kicking uselessly at the floor, his arms flailing as he tried to grab onto something, anything. But the invisible hands ripped him out of the church and into the streets of London. Paul was travelling backwards, thumping over the pavement. Strangely, he felt no pain.

On and on he went, slaloming through the rushing traffic before soaring into the sky until he saw the Thames below him. That's when, without warning, the invisible hands relaxed their grip and he tumbled towards the cold waters below. But there was no impact.

Paul gasped and looked around. To his surprise, he was lying between crisp, white sheets in a hospital ward. He was in darkness except for a dimmed light in the nurses' station. Paul sat up. His pulse was still racing. He became aware of somebody watching from the next bed.

'It's all right, son,' the man said. 'You've had a nightmare.'

Paul nodded and the man rolled over, turning his back. But it had been no ordinary nightmare. What Paul had experienced was a curious brew of real life and macabre fantasy. It was as if somebody was manipulating him the way a puppeteer works a puppet. He fell back against the pillow and dozed again. This time one image returned from the original dream. He saw the face of a watch. It belonged to the man in the church. The time didn't change. It was frozen at one p.m.

When Paul woke again, it was the following morning. The curtains had been drawn and a breeze was stirring them. Paul watched for a moment then the face of the watch exploded into his mind. He saw Nurse O'Hara nearby making a vacant bed.

'Excuse me,' he said, 'but what time is it?'

'It's eleven thirty,' she answered. 'Do you know, I was wondering whether you would ever wake up. Still, you must need all that sleep.' She smiled. 'It's doing you good. You're on the mend.' She turned to go.

'One other thing,' Paul said. 'What day is it?'

'Today's Thursday.'

'And the date?'

'January 2nd,' Nurse O'Hara answered. 'Would you like me to tell you the year too, Paul?' She was teasing, but the question wasn't half as silly as she thought.

Paul forced a smile. 'That's OK. I know it's 1941, thanks.'

The moment nurse O'Hara went about her business the smile drained from his face. Eleven thirty, 2 January. The dream was a prophecy, an omen. It had to be. There was nothing to hang onto except this one image, plucked from a crazy dream. He had an hour and a half to get to Christ Church, Spitalfields.

Paul peered around him. Some of the patients had

gone to a day room to talk or listen to the wireless. Others were drifting in and out of sleep, just as he'd been doing. I've got to get some clothes, Paul thought. Slipping out of bed, he padded eagerly across the floor. While nobody was looking, he examined the contents of some of the lockers and pulled out a pair of trousers, a white, cotton shirt and a sleeveless jumper with a V-neck. After a little more furtive rummaging, he discovered a pair of socks and a pair of brogues that would fit. He took his finds to the toilet and dressed quickly.

Still a little unsteady on his feet, he walked slowly, glancing round all the time. The floor seemed to tilt as he walked, making him stumble from time to time. But he refused to surrender to exhaustion. He was becoming more sure of himself. The back of his neck tingled. He risked discovery at any moment. He knew that if he were to bump into Dr Tyler or Nurse O'Hara, he would have to return to bed. That would mean failing to keep his appointment with a stranger in an East End church. But finally, after taking several wrong turns, he succeeded in finding his way out onto the street. All he had to do now was discover where he was and how far it was to Spitalfields.

After a couple of minutes' walk he recognized a street junction. He was on Clerkenwell Road. It couldn't be more than two or three miles to the church. For the first time since he had recovered consciousness he felt something like optimism. The cold air washed round him. It refreshed him, stinging his cheeks. His meeting with the stranger in the church was important; every nerve in his body told him so. Walking through the city streets, he saw the bomb damage all around him. Life went on as usual. He gazed at the posters on the wall advertising Vera Lynn and Max Miller at the London Palladium. He watched the people around him, the woman whose coat had a false fur collar, the man in his double-breasted suit, the special constable in his cape. He had the strangest feeling, as if everything around him was familiar, yet new at the same time.

As he reached the East End he noticed that the bomb damage was more extensive. Here and there he had to thread his way through the rubble. He asked a passer-by the time. He had half an hour to kill. Paul was determined to arrive at precisely the appointed hour, not a moment before, not a moment after. He spent the next half hour wandering the streets. He stopped at a cinema and looked at the posters. The Gaumont was showing three films. He liked the sound of *Confessions of a Nazi Spy*. The other two, *Rebecca* and *Gone with the Wind* he wasn't so sure about. Finally, on his travels, he came across a sign: Unexploded Bomb.

'Is there really a bomb down there?' Paul asked a passer-by.

'Oh no, son,' the man said, glancing at the crater, 'it's just a ruddy big jelly baby.'

With that, he gave a loud belly laugh and walked on. Paul shook his head. Why did everybody have to be a comedian? Soon it was time to meet his stranger. He reached the church on the stroke of one o'clock and made his way inside. There, sitting at the far end of the church, was the man from his dream.

Eight

London, Thursday, 2 January, 1941

Temple phoned his wife from the War Rooms. He was permitted one personal call. There was a crackle on the line then he heard her voice.

'Connie?' he said. 'It's me. How's Denis? Good. Has that rash gone? Yes, I see. At least it's getting better. Me? Oh, I'm fine. There's a bit of a flap on here. I can't say much more. Careless talk and all that. Well, if there isn't any news, I'd better get back to work.'

'Don't hang up,' Connie said. 'There is some news. That boy of yours, Paul, he's awake.'

Temple gasped. 'Awake? But the doctor said . . .'

'I know, but it was the doctor who called me. Your boy is a living miracle.' Temple thought it was an odd word for a medical man to use. 'So Paul's going to survive?'

'I think it's better than that,' Connie told him. If I remember correctly, Dr Tyler used the words "in rude good health." '

'Right,' Temple said. 'I'll go over and see him the first chance I get.' He sounded distant, preoccupied.

'Is everything all right?' Connie asked.

'Yes,' Temple said. 'I'm just a bit surprised, that's all. I'll phone you when I can.'

He replaced the receiver and stared thoughtfully across the room. The news was as astonishing as it was welcome. But he knew what he had seen as he had helped put Paul into the ambulance. The boy he had rescued had been at death's door. Could he really have made such a sudden recovery? Temple had to see for himself but first there was the small matter of a meeting with Walter Thompson to discuss the PM's security.

The summons had come at noon, just after Paul woke up a mile or so across the capital. Temple found Thompson waiting for him at an oval, wooden table in the PM's dining room. Lunch was about to be served. There was a vacant chair with a curving, lattice back. This was where Churchill would sit.

'The PM will be here in a couple of minutes,' Thompson said. 'He doesn't like anything interrupting his lunch.'

Temple glanced at Thompson. 'We have to step up security. We have intelligence . . .'

'I've read the intelligence,' Thompson said, interrupting him. 'We both attended the same meeting.' He brushed fluff from his trouser leg. 'I have the PM's instructions. He's prepared to go along with a little heightened security on one condition. You must be discreet. He won't have his routine disrupted. Furthermore, there will be no attempt to insulate him from contact with the British people.'

'So how are we supposed to protect him?' Temple asked.

'As discretely as we can,' Thompson answered. 'I've known the PM for many years. There's no point arguing with him. Try to wrap him in cotton wool and he'll have you immediately assigned to new duties.'

'But two of us can't give him the protection he needs,' Temple protested.

'That's precisely what we've got to do,' Thompson said. 'He won't change his routine.'

Temple stood there for a moment, slightly bewildered by the brevity of the meeting. Two members of staff entered behind him, bringing in the Prime Minister's lunch. There was Dover sole, boiled potatoes and a selection of vegetables. It was finer fare than the rissoles Temple would be eating later.

'That's the PM now,' Thompson said.

Ten minutes later, Temple was parking his car outside the hospital. He marched purposefully towards Ward Ten, noticing Nurse O'Hara at her station, making some notes.

'I've come to see Paul,' Temple said. 'I hear there's been some improvement.'

'Improvement is an understatement,' Nurse O'Hara said. There's been a miracle. There isn't a mark on Paul's skin.'

'But that's impossible,' Temple said. 'We all saw the condition he was in on Sunday night. Nobody can recover that quickly.'

'Are you a religious man, Inspector Temple?' Nurse O'Hara asked.

'Not terribly,' Temple admitted.

'Then maybe you should be,' she said. 'There's no scientific explanation for what's happened here. Come and see for yourself.'

But when they reached Paul's bed, it was empty.

'Looking for the young scamp who was here, are you?' the patient in the adjoining bed asked.

'Yes,' Temple said, 'do you know where he's gone?'

'I saw him rifling through some of the lockers,' the patient said. 'He filched some clothes, got himself dressed and went out.'

Nurse O'Hara was stunned. 'He got dressed!'

'He did that.'

'When was this?' Temple demanded.

'I haven't got a watch,' the patient said. 'It must be half an hour ago, probably longer.'

'Why didn't you call me?' nurse O'Hara cried. 'We can't have patients just walking out of the hospital.'

'Not my place to interfere,' the man grumbled before rolling over.

'We've *got* to find him,' Temple said.

'I'm reporting this to matron.'

'Before you go,' Temple said, 'did he say anything? Maybe he let something drop, a detail that could help me find him.'

'I don't . . .'

'This is important,' Temple said. 'Given the circumstances in which I met him, he may be in danger. Is there anything at all?'

Nurse O'Hara thought for a moment. 'There was one thing. It seemed very odd at the time. He was talking in his sleep. He mentioned a church. It's not the kind of thing I'd expect a boy his age to be talking about.'

'A church?' Temple repeated, fastening on her words.

'It was Christ Church, Spitalfields. You know the one. It's one of the original Hawksmoor churches. It's on Commercial Street.'

'I know the place,' Temple said. 'Thank you.'

Before the words were out of his mouth, he was running down the corridor towards the exit.

Nine

Paul walked steadily towards the stranger from his dream. The man didn't look up. In fact, he didn't seem to register Paul's approach at all. Was this man friend or foe? Did he pose a danger? Paul's dream had, after all, had a strange, violent ending. A vein pulsed in Paul's temple as he recalled its bewildering conclusion. What was he doing here? Who chases a dream? The answer was simple, without memories the dream was all he had. Taking a deep breath, he made his approach.

The man noticed him coming and stiffened, suspicious. He folded his newspaper and tucked it under his chair with the rest of his belongings. Paul reached his quarry and took in the man's features. He was in his late twenties. His blond hair was cut in a short back and sides.

'I'm Paul,' he announced.

The man's brow furrowed. There was no recognition in his eyes. He spoke brusquely. 'Now what business is that of mine? Honestly, can't you find somebody else to pester? All I want is some peace and quiet to study.'

Paul was taken aback. 'I . . . you were in my dream.'

'Is this some kind of joke?' He scanned the building, searching for somebody to remove the boy.

'Yes,' Paul said, let down by the turn of events. 'I saw you just as you are now. The dream sent me.'

'Really,' the man said dismissively. 'Well, your dream must have sent you to the wrong place. Look, I don't know you from Adam. Now, if you don't mind, I'd like to get on with my work.' He reached under his seat and pulled out a notepad. Paul didn't move. 'Are you still here?' the blond man demanded irritably.

Paul remembered something. 'You've got a newspaper, haven't you?'

There was a snort of frustration. 'I have, but I don't understand what—'

'I'm going to prove that I'm not trying to waste your time,' Paul said. 'I couldn't have read it, could I? You'd already hidden all your stuff under the chair before I got to you. You probably thought I was going to steal it. That's right, isn't it?'

The man looked a little shame-faced. 'Well, yes.'

'So how do I know that you're going to meet somebody at the Olive Tree at 2.15 p.m?'

The man's eyes widened.

'Her name's Pam.'

Now he was incredulous. Without saying a word, he picked up his copy of *The Times* and unfolded it. There was the pencil note Paul had seen in his dream.

'How on earth did you do that?'

'I told you,' Paul said. 'It came to me in a dream.'

Some of the man's hostility faded. 'What's your name again?'

'Paul.'

'Very well, Paul,' he said, 'you've got my undivided attention. So tell me what you want.'

'Maybe you should tell me about yourself,' Paul said.

'Doesn't that seem rather irregular?' the man asked. 'After all, you approached me. Normally, you would be the one to introduce yourself.'

'That's just it, I can't.'

The man waited for an explanation.

'I've lost my memory,' Paul said, 'in Sunday's raid. Maybe it was the impact of the blast, I just don't know. My first name is all I've got. That's why I'm here, to find out who I am. Look, this must all seem really odd but how did I know about your meeting with Pam?'

'I really can't imagine,' the man said. 'It's got to be a trick but I can't for the life of me work out how you did it. Call me gullible, but I'm intrigued. There isn't really much to tell, to be honest. My name is Hugh Cotton. I was born in Salisbury. I was teaching History at the University of London when the war broke out.'

'But you didn't get called up by the Army?'

'No,' Cotton said, 'I didn't.' He patted his left thigh.

69

'I had a riding accident when I was ten. My femur was shattered. I still walk with a pronounced limp. I'd be very little use on the battlefield, you see. At the moment, I work on military broadcasting for the BBC.'

It was an unremarkable story. Paul wondered why the dream had brought him to Cotton. 'And you don't know who I am?' he asked.

'Not a clue, old man,' Cotton replied.

'Maybe there's some other connection,' Paul said, 'some reason for us being here.'

'Let's see,' Cotton said. 'Are there any other fascinating facts about Hugh Cotton, BA, MA? Well, in addition to my work for the BBC and my academic studies, I have an interest in, what shall we say, the seamier side of our great city.' He picked up a book. Paul recognized it as the crimson object from his dream. 'This is my latest work, published two years ago. I am presently engaged in researching a sequel. Mind you, it's going to be a devil of a job getting it published. They're rationing paper, you know.'

He was getting off the subject so Paul interrupted. 'What's your book about?'

Cotton looked pleased to be asked. 'Actually, it concerns the criminal underworld of East London in Victorian times. I've always found the subject fascinating. I once wrote a pamphlet about the Jack the Ripper case.'

Somewhere in the back of his mind, Paul felt a tug of recognition. 'So your book's about Jack the Ripper?'

'No,' Cotton answered, 'I've moved on. The events

70

in my new book occurred some fifty years before the Whitechapel murders. Have you read *Oliver Twist*?'

'Yes, I think I have. Why?'

Cotton explained. 'The story of Oliver Twist is set in London's rookeries or slums in the last century. These districts were swarming with criminals at the time. For some, crime was the only means of survival. One day I came across the story of one such rookery in Flower and Dean Street. Have you heard of it?'

'I don't think so,' Paul confessed. 'Where is it?'

'We're right on top of it,' Cotton said, warming to his theme. 'It was one of the most notorious streets in London. The events in my book occurred not a hundred yards from where we're sitting.' He paused. 'Look, I could chat to you all afternoon about the Flowery and I really am curious about this magic trick of yours, but I have to go.' He smiled and held up his newspaper with the handwritten note. 'It's my meeting with Pam. I have to get all the way across town.'

Paul frowned. 'But you can't go.'

'Why not?' Cotton asked. 'Because you saw me in your dream?'

Paul felt stupid but there was only one answer. 'Yes.'

Cotton rose to his feet. Paul noticed that he had little mobility in his left leg, the result of his childhood riding accident.

'Please stay,' Paul begged. 'There has to be something you can tell me.'

'I'm afraid not,' Cotton said. 'Sorry, old son, I'd love to help but I really do have to leave.'

Paul continued to protest but Cotton limped down the aisle and let himself out into the street. Paul slumped back in the pew, terribly disappointed in the outcome of his meeting. He stared at the ceiling, wondering what to do next, when his fingers came into contact with something. It was Cotton's book.

'Mr Cotton,' he cried, 'you've forgotten this.'

There was no answer so Paul leapt up to give chase. That's when he heard the door creak open. 'Mr Cotton?' he said hopefully.

But it was Temple. Paul looked surprised, but he tried to shove past.

'Hey, slow down,' Temple said. 'What's the big hurry?'

'Mr Cotton forgot his book,' Paul answered. 'Anyway, what are you doing here?'

'Cotton? Who's Cotton?'

Paul looked right and left along Commercial Street but there was no sign of Hugh Cotton. He sighed. 'Just somebody I was talking to.' Paul posed a question with his eyes. 'So how did you know where to find me?'

'I went to the hospital,' Temple said. 'Nurse O'Hara heard you talking in your sleep. You mentioned this church.'

Paul nodded.

'What was so important you had to abscond from your hospital bed?' Temple asked.

'You wouldn't understand,' Paul said.

Temple smiled. 'Listen Paul,' he said, 'I have to know what's going on here. First, a boy I've never met calls my name in an Underground station. Then I encounter . . . frankly, I don't know what to make of my attacker. Finally, this boy saves my life before miraculously recovering from fatal burns.' He hesitated. 'The doctor says you don't have a mark.'

Paul unbuttoned his shirt and showed the top of his chest.

'Dear God!' Temple said. 'I saw your flesh horribly blackened and blistered. But how can this be?'

Paul shrugged. 'I don't understand it myself.'

'It's rather a remarkable chain of events,' Temple said, recovering himself. 'Don't you think you owe me an explanation?'

Paul stared. 'You just said I saved your life. Is that true?'

'Yes,' Temple said. 'It's true. You don't remember?'

Paul shook his head. 'Only my name.'

Temple was sceptical of Paul's story. 'They said at the hospital that you had amnesia. It all sounded rather far-fetched. Are you sure you don't remember Sunday night? I found it pretty unforgettable myself.'

Paul shook his head slowly.

'Look me in the eye,' Temple said, 'and tell me you don't remember.'

Paul returned his gaze. 'I don't remember.'

Finally, Temple took pity on him. 'Do you have anywhere to go?'

Another no.

'No family at all?'

'Nobody I can remember.'

'I have a spare room at home,' Temple said. 'I'm sure I could clear it with the authorities for you to stay with me. Would that be OK?'

Paul nodded without lifting his head or looking at the detective.

'That's decided then,' Temple said. 'By the way, we'd better call in at the hospital on the way to return those clothes. They're not yours are they?'

'I took them from the other patients.'

'Technically, that's stealing.' Temple smiled and patted Paul on the shoulder. 'Don't worry, you're not in any trouble. I'll square it with the matron. She comes across like an old battle-axe but she's a decent old stick underneath the fierce exterior.'

Paul followed Temple out to the car. If only Temple knew the trouble he was really in.

Ten

Temple drew up in front of a neat semi-detached house in Enfield.

'Nice place,' Paul said.

'It should be,' Temple said. 'It cost us £1,300 three years ago. It was a bit steep on a copper's wage but we needed a family home, what with young Denis coming along.'

Paul got out of the Bullnose Oxford, rolling the name Denis round his mind. It was familiar. He tried to make the connection to a life that was tantalisingly out of reach. He looked at the suburban street. There were pollarded trees along the pavement. In addition to the lopped-off branches, there were a few other tell-tale signs of the conflict engulfing the nation. Bands of white paint marked the tree trunks, kerbs and lamp posts. House windows were taped. Otherwise, the war seemed a very long way away in this quiet middle-class neighbourhood. Temple stopped his car and sat drumming his fingers on the steering wheel. They'd been at the hospital for over an hour while Dr Tyler gave Paul an examination. It had eaten up time Temple didn't have. The detective was under pressure. He looked at his watch.

'I've got to be back in Whitehall in half an hour,' he said. 'I'm going to introduce you to my wife, then I'll have to be making tracks.'

'Because there's a flap on,' Paul said.

Temple stared at him askance. 'Did you eavesdrop on my phone call at the hospital?'

Paul grinned. 'I did my best.'

Temple wanted to sound stern but there was something disarming about his young charge. Temple was usually highly secretive about his phone calls. They dealt with matters of national security. But Paul had saved his life. It was the kind of thing that tended to soften hearts, even those belonging to a time-worn cop who'd seen too much of the dark side of human nature.

'You're giving me a place to stay,' Paul said. 'I'm just grateful for that.'

'OK then,' Temple said. 'Time to introduce you to Mrs T.' He opened the front door and led the way inside. Immediately, Paul saw baby Temple in his pram.

'This must be Denis,' he said, gazing down at the gurgling infant.

'Yes,' Temple said proudly as he scooped up his baby son, 'this is His Lordship.'

Temple's wife appeared at the doorway.

'Oh hello, dear,' she said. 'I thought I heard the front door. I was just going to take Denis out for some fresh air.' She looked at Paul and her eyes lit in a way that told him he was going to like her. 'This can't be our miracle boy, can it? I'm Connie, George's wife. How are you feeling?'

'I'm fine, thanks,' Paul said.

Connie Temple stared at the threadbare clothes he was wearing. 'Dear me, is that the best the hospital could come up with?'

'My own clothes were destroyed,' Paul told her, 'in the air raid.'

'Everything was burned off his back,' Temple explained. 'The nurses kitted him out from a store of cast-offs they had.' He didn't mention that Paul had stolen his first set of clothes from other patients' lockers. 'We'll get him something better later. Sit down in the parlour, Paul. I want a quick word with my wife.'

Paul could hear them talking. Temple tried to keep his voice down but Paul got the gist of it anyway. He was surprised by how much he could hear. Temple was explaining that he wanted to have Paul to stay with somebody he could trust. There were things about the boy he had to know. Temple promised that he would be around as much as he could but Connie would have to take responsibility for Paul while he was working. When Temple reappeared, Paul smiled.

'Connie's happy with the arrangement,' he told Paul. 'If there's anything you need, just ask. Mind you, there isn't much to be had, the way things are. Even eggs are a luxury. That reminds me, I'll have to get you issued with a ration book. The Superintendent should be able to pull some strings and gee things along.'

Temple turned to face Connie.

'I'm off now,' he told her, planting a kiss on her cheek. 'I'll phone when I can.' He glanced back at Paul. 'Keep an eye on him, won't you?'

'Of course I will,' Connie said. 'You go to work. There's no need to worry.'

Connie was a welcoming hostess. She showed Paul to the spare room. There was a single bed, a wardrobe and a dressing table with a mirror. There was even a washstand. Paul glanced out of the window. His room looked out onto the railway line. Connie looked on, cradling baby Denis in the crook of her arm.

'Will this do?' she asked.

'Thank you,' Paul said. 'This is great.'

'It's comfortable enough,' Connie said. 'This is where we put George's Mum when she stays.'

Just then a cat brushed against Paul's legs. He knelt down and stroked its chin.

'That's Spitfire,' Connie said. 'Keep your door locked or you'll have cat hair everywhere.' She shooed the tortoiseshell out onto the landing. 'Have a nap if you like. You need to recover your strength.'

'I'm fine,' Paul insisted, 'honestly.'

'Well, it's your decision,' Connie said. 'I'm going to

walk down to the shops. I need some vegetables to make soup . . . if they have any. Will you be all right on your own? You can come along if you like.'

'I'll be fine,' Paul said.

Connie nodded and left the room. A few minutes later the front door slammed. Paul lay down for a while but sleep didn't come so he set about exploring the house. He checked out the bathroom then padded downstairs. There was a sitting room, a kitchen, a dining room and a small front parlour. In the sitting room Paul examined the photos on the sideboard. There were several sepia-coloured prints of soldiers from the First World War. He also discovered a recent photograph of an elderly woman standing in front of an ivy-grown cottage. Paul wondered if this was Temple's mother, or Connie's. His thoughts were interrupted by the telephone.

'Hello?' he said, picking up.

'Is that George?' a woman's voice asked.

'No,' Paul said. 'My name's Paul. I'm his guest.'

'Oh, I see.' There was a moment's silence. 'This is George's twin sister Brenda. Could you remind him that he agreed to have Evelyn round tomorrow? I have to work late.'

'Yes sure,' Paul said. 'I'll tell him.' He repeated the message. 'Evelyn's staying tomorrow.'

'Thank you,' Brenda said. She waited a beat then asked a question, 'Are you something to do with George's job? You sound quite young.'

'I got hurt,' Paul said. 'I had nowhere to go. Mr

Temple offered to take me in.' He wasn't sure what to say next. 'It's quite a long story.'

'I'm sure George will tell me in his own good time,' Brenda said. 'Will you be around tomorrow?'

'Yes,' Paul said, 'I think so.'

'How old are you, Paul, if you don't mind me being nosy?'

'I'm fifteen.'

There, Paul thought, that's something else I know.

'The same age as my daughter Evelyn,' Brenda said. 'Oh, how lovely. You should have a lot in common. Don't forget to give George the message.'

'I won't,' Paul said.

He hung up and stood in the sitting room, watching the afternoon light start to fade. He thought about what Brenda had said and grimaced. Just how much would he have in common with this Evelyn? Finding nothing to do, he returned to his room. By the time Connie got back he was fast asleep.

Eleven

London, Thursday, 2 January, 1941

*A*bout an hour after Paul dozes off on the bed, Temple
is standing next to Walter Thompson on the Clive
Steps, impatiently waiting for Churchill to appear.
Thompson's in his second decade guarding the Prime
Minister. Temple is only meeting the Old Man for the
second time. But both detectives are focused on his safety.

'I do wish the PM would reconsider these evening
walks,' Temple says.

'You'd better face it,' Thompson replies, his eyes never
leaving the darkened landscape of St James's park.
'You're not going to get him to change his mind. The
Old Man is too set in his ways.'

Temple nods ruefully. He's offered his advice to the
Prime Minister and been roundly rebuked for it.

Churchill enjoys his constitutionals and nothing, not the Luftwaffe and not some Hun assassin, will make him suspend them.

'Don't you think it's rather reckless though?' Temple asks. 'Just look out there. Imagine how much cover there is for a sniper.'

'I have been at the Prime Minister's side through many a hairy situation,' Thompson says. 'Egyptian nationalists, the IRA, they've all been after him. I don't think he'd have it any other way. He's a man of action. Taking risks is part of his nature.' He smiles, thinking of past adventures. 'Maybe it's all of his nature.'

'Even so,' Temple says. 'This is different. He's leading the nation through its greatest crisis. Never have we faced such a dangerous foe. Honestly Thompson, if something were to happen how could anyone replace him?'

'Quite,' Thompson says, continuing to scan the park before them.

So many shadows. So many hiding places.

'And the assassins are becoming ever more dangerous,' Temple says. He wants to tell somebody about his life or death struggle with a supernatural enemy. His memories just won't let go. At any moment that colourless face will flash into his mind. He sees the soulless eyes, the double row of deadly fangs and he feels the same panicky rush of adrenalin he felt the first time the monster loomed out of the darkness. He's got to get it off his chest. Is Thompson the man?

'I suppose you heard what happened on Sunday night?' Temple says.

'Yes,' Thompson replies. 'You had a bit of a close shave, I hear.'

'It was no ordinary assassin,' Temple tells him. 'I shot him in the shoulder and still he came back for more. Thompson, he reached into his own flesh and pulled out the bullet. There was something . . . devilish about him.'

Thompson frowns. 'Devilish? That's an odd thing to say. Whatever do you mean?'

But that's when Churchill finally appears, ending the conversation.

Churchill and Thompson set off together. Temple sighs and follows. He dismisses thoughts of the demon and fixes his mind on the task in hand. It's a wise decision. Just a hundred yards away, Arminius is completing the assembly of his modified Kar 98k sniper rifle. He fixes the sight and picks out the bulky form of Churchill in his crosshairs. He smiles as the full moon slides out from behind the clouds, illuminating the park with is silvery light. It's a good night for a kill. He has taken up position looking across the lake. He has Birdcage Walk at his back. From his observations of Churchill's movements, he expects his target to walk anti-clockwise around the lake. Arminius is going to make the kill as his quarry passes the Queen Victoria Memorial.

Oblivious to Arminius' presence, Churchill and his bodyguards reach the lake. They're working their way along the far side, facing Marlborough Gate, when the air raid sirens start to howl.

'We'd better get back, Prime Minister,' Thompson says.

Arminius watches the odd procession. He can see from the way the bodyguards shadow Churchill that they're tense. They want to hurry the Prime Minister but Churchill isn't a man to be hurried. Arminius smiles. The stubborn old fool's playing right into my hands, he tells himself. In less than a minute I will have a perfect shot. Arminius lies full length on the bowed tree trunk he's selected for support and squints down the sight. He can hear the sounds of the raid. There's the whistle of falling bombs, the cannon fire of RAF fighters racing up to meet the attackers, the boom of anti aircraft guns. None of it distracts Arminius. Over several years he's honed the ability to block out every distraction. All he hears as he hugs the tree trunk and looks down the sight is the thud of his own heartbeat. This is his night of destiny. He's about to become the greatest hero of the German people.

Temple raises his eyes and sees a sky of flickering scarlet. The East End has copped it again. Poor beggars. He listens to the violent thud of bombs and prays that Enfield isn't a target too. Dear God, if anything were to happen to Connie and little Denis. There's the muffled thud and whoosh of a bomb somewhere nearby. It sounds as if the Luftwaffe is hitting parts of the West End too. Temple is tempted to seize the PM's arm and hurry him back to the War Rooms. He knows it would be counter-productive. The Old Man's as stubborn as he's brave. Besides, it would be the end of his career if he were to manhandle the Prime Minister.

Arminius has his finger on the trigger. Any moment

now Churchill's frame will fill the sight. Then Arminius will squeeze and blow his victim's brains out. Many snipers would go for a heart shot. The body provides a bigger target than the head. Even if the bullet misses the heart itself, it might pierce an artery or hit another of the major organs. Either way, it will probably cause enough tissue damage to result in death. But Arminius is the best man Germany can muster. He always goes for the head. He always completes the kill. It never takes more than one shot to take a target down. He is always long gone before anybody can discover his hiding place.

'Any moment now,' he murmurs.

As Temple trudges round the lake after Churchill and Thompson, he is painfully aware how vulnerable the Old Man is. The moon is bloated and swollen. The park is awash with its eerie light. They couldn't have picked a worse night to be out in the park.

'If there is a sniper out there,' Temple thinks 'then we're giving him one heck of a helping hand.' A shudder runs through his bloodstream. The crackles and thuds of the falling bombs sharpen his senses. Some inexplicable instinct tells him that they're being watched. At that moment a shadow crosses his soul. He jogs forward and falls in alongside the PM. 'I've got a bad feeling,' he confides in Thompson.

'Why, have you seen something?' Thompson asks.

'No,' Temple answers. 'It's the full moon. Tonight's the night. Think about it. The conditions are perfect. He's out there. I know it.'

Arminius curses under his breath. One of the

bodyguards obscures his view. If he fires now he will risk killing the wrong man. What good's a mere detective? He's going to deliver the British war leader himself. Arminius lowers the rifle and glances back towards Whitehall. It's time to adopt his back-up plan instead. The trio have only one route back to the War Rooms and it will take them right past him. He will have to make his shot from closer range. The kill is more certain from there. Unfortunately, his proximity to his victim means that he's more likely to be spotted by the bodyguards. And it will be much more difficult to make his escape afterwards. But he will do it for the Fatherland, even if it costs him his life.

Temple listens as a droning Heinkel bomber draws bursts of fire from the ground. London is taking a severe pounding. There's a crimson glow over the roofs of Whitehall. The air feels singed. Temple has his hands on his Weobley .38 pistol. Thompson too is making quiet preparations for a fight.

'Where is he?' Temple says grimly.

That's when a stick of incendiaries falls, illuminating the city with brilliant ribbons of fire. Temple glimpses a reflection. The tiny flash only registers for a split second but he knows what he's seen. The roots of his hair go rigid.

'There!' he says, drawing his pistol. 'A light.'

'Where?' Thompson demands.

'Look in the direction of Horse Guards Parade. You'll see some trees.'

'I've got the position,' Thompson says as he steps in front of Churchill.

'I'll rush him,' Temple says. 'You get the PM away.'

Arminius sees Temple starting to run towards him. He shifts position twice, three times, trying to get a bead on Churchill. It's no use. His guardians put themselves in the firing line. Arminius has no choice but to break cover. Shoving the rifle stock against his shoulder, he gets off a shot but he has fired in a hurry and the angle's wrong. It pings uselessly a couple of yards from Churchill, tossing up a puff of dust and gravel. Arminius curses. Temple has done just enough to distract him. Taking several steps to the right, Arminius prepares to fire again. But Temple's gun roars first, tearing a gouge out of the tree trunk just behind Arminius' head.

'Throw down the weapon!' Temple bawls. 'Drop it or I shoot to kill.'

Arminius is in two minds. Should he try to complete the kill or concentrate his efforts on escape? There's only one choice. If he can only gather his thoughts, he might still hit Churchill. What if it does cost him his life? Because of this one act of heroism, Germany will surely win the War. My name will echo through eternity, Arminius tells himself. His mind made up, he shoulders the rifle again and aims at the pair of fleeing figures.

Temple can see the blurred silhouette of the stalking assassin. His heart is slamming. For all his efforts, the PM isn't out of danger yet. He's an old man in ill-health. He can't run. Distracted for a moment by the scream of tracer bullets as they race across the sky, he flicks his *attention back to Arminius. Even at this distance he knows that the gunman is aiming at Churchill, not him. Temple plants his feet and takes his pistol in a two-handed grip. He gets off two shots and hears Arminius' body hit the ground. A glossy pool of blood spreads like a halo. It's over. The PM and Thompson join him a moment later.*

'Let's see what he looks like,' Thompson says.

Temple rolls the body over. Sightless eyes stare up at the night sky. Arminius' forehead is a torn mess of bone and blood. Churchill doesn't dwell long on the face of the assassin. Straightening the brim of his slouch hat, he sets off towards the War Rooms. He has work to do. When the PM is out of hearing, Temple glances at Thompson, then down at Arminius.

'This gunman won't be the last,' he says. 'The Nazis are intensifying their efforts. They want the Old Man dead, and sooner rather than later.'

Twelve

London, Friday, 3 January, 1941

Connie Temple woke Paul with a knock on his door.

'Rise and shine, lazybones' she called brightly from the landing. 'It's eight o'clock.'

Paul sat up and stifled a yawn. A shaft of wintry sunlight fell between the curtains and made him squint against its brightness.

'I'm awake, Mrs Temple,' he called.

'Connie,' she said, correcting him, 'call me Connie. If you're staying a while, we don't want to be too stuffy, do we?'

'Connie it is,' Paul said.

'Come down when you're ready,' Connie told him. 'It's tea and toast. Only margarine, I'm afraid, but I've saved you two rashers of bacon.'

Paul listened to Connie's footsteps on the stairs. Soon he heard the bacon sizzling in the pan. His stomach grumbled. Scrambling out from under the bedclothes, he brushed his teeth, then washed and dressed. As he stood over the basin with the cool breeze from the window on his skin he felt better than he had for days. He wondered at his own resilience. The night of fire was a distant dream. He was alone and had no idea who he was, yet he was happy with a comfortable bed and a cooked breakfast. Maybe that's all life is, the chance to survive for another day, to have something nourishing in your stomach and the morning sun on your face.

'Isn't Mr Temple back?' Paul asked, reaching the bottom of the stairs.

'No,' Connie answered from the kitchen, 'he phoned last night. There's some big emergency. He slept over at work.'

Paul wondered about the big emergency for a moment then made the toast and bacon into a sandwich. There was sugar in his tea. Something told him he didn't usually drink sweetened tea but it was hot and refreshing and he drank it to the dregs.

'That was great, thanks,' he said.

Connie's face glowed. 'You like your bacon nice and crispy then?'

'Yes, for some reason it tastes better than . . .' he stopped in mid-sentence before completing it. 'Than at home.' He had the oddest sensation. He felt a pang of longing for a place he couldn't remember.

'And where is home exactly?' Connie asked.

Paul answered without a moment's hesitation. 'Mile End.'

'There you go,' Connie said. 'You can't have total amnesia, can you?'

Paul picked absent-mindedly at a pull in his jumper. She was right. Now and then an elusive memory would dart through his mind before vanishing once more. He should have been relieved that his memory was returning. But something about the first flashback of home was disturbing. It left a feeling of hollowness in his stomach. Something bad had happened there.

'Mile End's not so far,' Connie said. 'I bet your parents will be worried about you.'

'Yes, I'm sure they are.'

But already Paul knew it wasn't a case of *they*. There was only Mum. He was still unable to dredge her face up from the depths of his consciousness, but he was sure it wouldn't be long before he had total recall.

'I'll tell George to call the local police station,' Connie said. 'They might have you on their missing persons list. You don't remember anything else, do you? A street name maybe.'

Paul let his arms drop at his sides. 'I'm sorry, I really don't.'

'There's no need to get yourself in a tizzy over it,' Connie said, realizing she might be pushing him too hard. 'Just relax and let your mind recover in its own good time. Rest as much as you wish. You'll talk when you're ready.' She gave him a reassuring smile. 'I didn't mean to pry.'

'That's all right,' Paul told her. 'Can I do the washing up for you?'

Connie looked surprised.

'I'd like to,' Paul said. 'You can get on with the baby.'

Connie smiled. 'Thank you,' she said. 'I'll take you up on it.' She picked up Denis and wrinkled her nose. 'Oh dear, who's a smelly little boy?'

Paul washed and wiped the dishes, glancing over occasionally as Connie changed Denis.

'Do be a dear and switch on the wireless,' Connie said as she pinned the nappy.

Paul started putting the breakfast things away in a cupboard when he remembered something. 'I forgot to say, there was a phone call yesterday. Brenda rang.'

'Don't tell me,' Connie said, 'she wants to know if Evelyn can stay.'

'That's right,' Paul said.

'Brenda works as a telephone operator for the London Fire Brigade,' Connie explained. 'Sometimes they call her in to cover absence. On those occasions she leaves Evelyn with us.'

'Doesn't she have a husband?' Paul asked.

'He's over in North Africa fighting in the desert,' Connie answered. 'An artillery officer, involved in the campaign around Tobruk.'

'Of course,' Paul said, 'he's in the Army. I should have known.'

'Evelyn's no problem,' Connie said. 'It's nice having her round. She's such a lovely girl, very bright. I bet you'll be glad to talk to somebody your own age, instead of an old fuddy-duddy like me.'

'You're not old,' Paul protested.

'Why, thank you, kind Sir,' Connie said with a giggle in her voice. 'Oh, I picked your book up when I was tidying. It's over there on the sideboard.'

Paul glanced across the room. He'd forgotten all about Hugh Cotton's book.

'Why don't you take it in the parlour and have a quiet read?' Connie suggested. 'You need to relax.'

'That's not a bad idea,' Paul said. He crossed the hall to the tiny, quiet parlour then settled into an armchair. He examined the front cover and its title, *The Demon Seed*. He immediately felt the same sense of familiarity mixed with stirrings of unease much as he had when he had said the words Mile End.

'The demon seed,' he murmured slowly.

When his mind failed to turn up any new clues to his identity, he turned to the frontispiece of the book. Vince Malum Bono, he read. He puzzled over the Latin inscription for a few moments then he went to find Connie.

'You don't know any Latin, do you?' he asked.

'I did it for five years,' Connie said, 'then I dropped it at Sixth Form.'

Paul showed her the book. 'I was wondering what this means.'

'*Vince Malum Bono*,' Connie read. 'Oh, that's easy. Good conquers evil.'

'Oh right,' Paul said, feeling stupid, 'thanks.'

He realised that it was obvious. 'Vince' as in invincible. Then 'malum' was like malevolent and 'bono' was like *bon* in French.

'I should have been able to work it out myself,' he said. 'I'm really stupid.'

Connie pursed her lips. 'I'm sure you're not.'

He returned to the parlour and started reading. The first two chapters told the story of a gang of cut-throat child thieves, the Rat Boys, who terrorized parts of East London in the early nineteenth century. Paul noticed that some of the street names such as Hanbury Street and Dorset Street, seemed familiar. The extensive notes explained why. Jack the Ripper had struck in both locations. But that was nearly half a century after the events Cotton was describing. Cotton was an academic and Paul found the book hard going at times. There were footnotes and long passages of social history. It was when Paul got to Chapter Three that things started to get interesting.

The boys were recruited by the master 'thief-trainer' a notorious underworld figure by the name of Samuel Rector.

Paul stopped. 'Rector' leapt out from the page as if the print had caught fire. Now he knew his surname. I'm Paul *Rector*. It came floating to the front of his mind like a corpse in the Thames. Round it was wrapped all sorts of other debris but Paul couldn't make sense of it yet.

Rector's early childhood is shrouded in mystery but he came to the attention of the authorities at a fairly tender age. First reports indicate that he was little more than a common thief and occasionally a bare-knuckle street fighter, earning a handful of coins by challenging all comers. In early manhood, his criminal activities took a more sinister turn. He was implicated in several grue- some murders but each time he got off scot-free. This was often because witnesses simply disappeared.

Paul laid the book face down on the arm of the chair. Samuel Rector's story seemed familiar somehow: the brushes with the law, the violence, the increasingly serious criminal activities. Was this the demon seed of the book's title?

'But what's it got to do with me?'

It wasn't long before another passage caught his eye.

The Rat Boys used an attic in Flower and Dean Street as a base from which to launch their raids. What set them apart from the other street gangs was their utter ruthlessness and savagery and their distinctive modus operandi. Increasingly, they used the city's sewers and underground channels to travel from crime to crime. Some contemporary commentators believed that the boys were in fact half-human and half-rat though most serious historians dismiss this as no more than a lurid invention, the kind of story you'd find in the Penny Dreadfuls of the period.

What can't be dismissed is the fact that there were several gruesome and unexplained murders during the Rat Boys' reign of terror. Several bodies were discovered with hideous injuries to the throat and face. There was a great scare with many in the community believing that hellish beasts were on the loose. Increasingly, the attacks centred on the area around Whitechapel, Aldgate and Spitalfields, the same territory haunted by the infamous Jack the Ripper forty years later. One local cleric would describe the maze of streets and alleys as the mouth of Hell.

Paul stared at the page. It was as if his own story was hidden somewhere between the lines and was struggling to claw its way out. What kind of person am I? Do I have something to do with this Samuel Rector? Is that why my dream sent me to Cotton? Paul was about to resume his reading when he became aware of two figures standing in the doorway. He turned to see Connie and a teenage girl.

Paul was quite bowled over by the new arrival. She had the most stunning, dark eyes. He scrambled to his feet, knocking his book to the floor in his haste. 'You must be Evelyn.' His throat was dry.

'That's right,' Evelyn replied, 'and you're the mysterious Paul. Mum's been very curious about you ever since that phone call. She wants me to take back a full report.'

'Well, introductions over,' Connie said, 'I think I'll make us all a sandwich.'

'Would you like me to help, Aunty Connie?' Evelyn asked.

'No need,' Connie said. 'Denis is having a nap. Why don't I leave you two to get to know each other?'

Without another word, she departed in the direction of the kitchen leaving Paul and Evelyn looking awkwardly at each other. It was Evelyn who broke the silence.

'Aunt Connie says you've got amnesia,' she said.

'That's right,' Paul said. 'I was in a fire.'

'Whatever were you doing out in the Blitz?' Evelyn asked.

Paul laughed. 'That's what I don't remember.'

'Oh, of course,' Evelyn said. 'Silly of me. Do you know, I've never met anyone who's lost their memory before.'

'Well, here I am,' Paul said.

'What's it like?' Evelyn asked. 'Don't you remember anything at all? It can't be total memory loss. You wouldn't even know how to walk, would you?'

'I remember my name,' Paul said. He smiled. 'I also remember how to walk. One foot in front of the other, very complex.'

Yes, he knew his first name, last name too, though he wasn't going to tell her that, not until he knew more about the Rectors.

'And that's it?'

'Not quite,' Paul said. 'The memories are there, only they're like shadows, dark shapes trying to surface. Though I don't remember much, I have a feel for the person I was . . . am.'

'So your memory isn't gone for good? It's going to come back?'

'Yes, I think so. The doctor thinks so too.'

Paul remembered the sense of unease he'd felt when he read the title of Cotton's book. Maybe he didn't want to remember.

'You know what?' Evelyn said. 'I'm going to jog your memory. Let's try a quiz.'

'I'm not sure . . .'

'Oh, don't be a spoil sport,' Evelyn said. 'What's your favourite colour?'

'Red.' For some reason, he remembered a red door. There was a name too, Redman.

'There you are,' Evelyn said. 'You've started remembering already.'

But Paul felt as if he were gazing into a dark pit. There was fire deep inside and something else, something evil. Evelyn noticed the look on his face. 'Are you OK?'

'Yes, why wouldn't I be?'

'You're sure?' Evelyn asked. 'We can stop if you like.'

'No,' Paul said, 'ask me some more.' Curiosity outweighed apprehension. 'I think it's helping.'

'What's your favourite sport?'

'That's easy, football.'

'Favourite team?'

'West Ham.'

'See, you're doing really well.'

'That's enough about me,' Paul said. 'What's *your* favourite sport?'

'Tennis, I suppose,' Evelyn replied. 'I used to play lawn tennis every Sunday before the War but my friends were evacuated to the country. You should try it, Paul. It strengthens your wrist and arms.' She stuck out her hand. 'Here. Feel.'

Paul liked touching her. She felt warm and soft. But it made him a bit self-conscious.

'Do you feel the muscles?' Evelyn said. 'They're quite well-developed.'

Paul released her arm. 'Yes, I'm sure they are.'

There was an uncomfortable moment, then she bent forward and picked up his book.

'What are you reading?' she asked. 'Crikey, *The Demon Seed*. What's this about?'

'I've only just started it,' Paul said.

'What's it about *so far*?'

'A gang of kids terrorize Victorian London.'

'So it's a novel?'

'No,' Paul told her, 'it's history. It's meant to be a true story.'

Evelyn read the book at the page where it had fallen open. 'History? It reads just like a gothic page-turner. Oh honestly, have you read Chapter Twenty?'

Paul shook his head. 'I'm nowhere near that far on. Why, what's it say?'

Evelyn handed him the book so he could read for himself.

Samuel Rector was condemned to be publicly hanged at Newgate Prison.

That name, Rector. His name.

In the final days before the execution, he wrote this testament:
'I serve a greater cause than mortal men can imagine. I have stolen. I have killed. I have devoured human flesh.

Paul stopped. 'Devoured human flesh!'
Evelyn rolled her eyes. 'I know. How gruesome.'
Paul read on.

As the great lord, my master, is my witness, I regret nothing I have done. This world we live in is a stale and mediocre place. We go about our lives with our heads bowed. We do not dare to live our lives to the full, lest some priest or judge tells us that what we are doing is wrong. Our rulers insist on law and order. But it is their law, their order. One day a new Kingdom will arise devoted to the joy of mischief, the pursuit of pure pleasure. We will be free to satisfy our appetites just as the wild beasts in the field are free. What we want we shall take, regardless of rules and restrictions.

'This I swear: the grave will not imprison me, nor will it imprison my master. Our enemies have their triumph now, but they will pay for what they have done. Their reward will be eternal agony. Ours will be eternal mischief.'

'Now tell me that isn't odd,' Evelyn said. 'It sounds like downright Satanism if you ask me. Wherever did you get it?'

'The author gave it to me,' Paul said, 'a man by the name of Hugh Cotton.'

'You've met the man who wrote it?' Evelyn asked, trying her best to sound scandalized. She affected a low, sinister voice. 'Do you know devil-worshippers?' She sounded quite excited.

'No, of course not,' Paul said. 'I only met him once. I wanted to ask him about the things in the book but he was in a hurry.'

'I don't quite understand,' Evelyn said. 'How did you get to know him?'

But before Paul could answer Connie called from the kitchen. 'Your sandwiches are ready.'

Paul rose from the armchair.

'What's that?' Evelyn asked, looking past him. She pointed to where Paul had been sitting. An envelope was poking out from the cushion. I think it fell out of the book.'

It was a letter addressed to Hugh Cotton.

'He must have been using it as a book mark,' Paul said.

Evelyn examined it. 'Now you can ask him all the questions you like,' she said. 'You've got his address.' She nudged him. 'Imagine, you can visit a devil-worshipper's lair.'

Paul found himself smiling at the description of Hugh Cotton. He pictured the thin, awkward, bookish man in his late twenties. Anyone less like a Satanist he couldn't imagine. No, Paul thought, tucking the letter in his pocket. I don't know any devil-worshippers. But I have a terrible feeling I might know the devils.

Thirteen

Germany, Friday, 3 January, 1941

One of the devils is woken at six a.m. by fists hammering on his door. On a clear, crisp winter's morning Harry Rector is picked up from his Munich flat and driven to an airfield in southern Bavaria. Nobody tells him where he's going but he immediately knows the purpose of the trip. The moment the Mercedes pulls in beside several other vehicles, Harry recognizes the figure of Heinrich Gessler. Though he's been expecting the call for some time, he still feels a tingle of anticipation. The fun is about to start.

'Your man failed, didn't he?' Harry says.

He's tempted to gloat. They wanted to keep it in the family. A Nazi plot for a Nazi Europe, the triumph of

Hitler's blue-eyed Aryan heroes. But they can't do it without him.

'Arminius is dead,' Heydrich tells him evenly, resenting Harry's gloating tone, 'just as you predicted.' For a moment, he wonders whether Harry might be a double agent. But the Englander has been under constant supervision for months. There's no way he could have been in touch with the British authorities. 'How could you be so sure the British would foil the attempt?' he asks, burning with curiosity about his protégé.

'Let's just say I have an instinct for these things,' Harry says. 'What happened exactly?'

'Churchill's bodyguards did their job,' Heydrich said. 'Thompson protected the Prime Minister just as he has been protecting him for nearly twenty years. We may have underestimated him. But it was a second man who proved vital. He shot Arminius dead.'

'Temple,' Harry says, 'the detective's name is George Temple.'

Harry knows that one day soon he and this Temple will have a tryst with destiny. They will meet. One of them will lose. It won't be me, Harry tells himself.

'Temple, you say?' Gessler mutters.

Full of curiosity, he reaches into his car and pulls out a clipboard. He runs his eyes over the report he's just been given and chuckles. There's the name Harry gave him, George Temple.

'You're astonishing, Harry,' Gessler says. 'Temple's the name I have in my notes. How could you possibly know?'

Harry shrugs. If he told Gessler the truth, the German

would never believe him. 'It would take too long to explain,' Harry says. 'So what am I doing here?'

It's a mischievous question. Harry knows exactly why he's here. But he likes the Nazi High Command chasing after him. He wants them to say pretty please.

'Come this way,' Gessler says. 'Bitte.'

There's the magic word. Bitte. Please. It isn't the kind of word usually associated with the Nazis. Gessler leads Harry into the nearest hangar. There's a Dornier 17 and two Ju 88 night fighters. Harry sees Heydrich waiting for him. Harry goes through the formality of the Nazi salute though he finds all this Sieg Heiling thoroughly tiresome.

'Good morning, Herr Rector,' Heydrich says. 'Are you enjoying our hospitality?'

'I'm quite happy, thank you,' Harry says. 'I assume you have decided to call on my services. You need me.'

'You will have the honour of serving the Reich,' Heydrich says coldly.

He hands Harry a newspaper, the Berliner Illustrierte Zeitung. Harry reads the headline: 'Die City von London brennt.' Harry knows enough German to understand what it says. The City of London is burning.

'You see, Herr Rector,' Heydrich says. 'The Luftwaffe are systematically breaking the spirit of the citizens of London. Night after night, we are pounding them into submission. Unfortunately, one obstacle remains. Herr Churchill continues to stiffen their resistance. He's the lynch-pin who holds them together. For that reason, we must destroy him. We're growing weary of these repeated *failures. It would seem an appropriate time to use your considerable gifts.'*

'And I am happy to oblige,' Harry says.

'We agree to your plan,' Heydrich continues. 'You will parachute into neutral Ireland and make your way from there. Why Ireland?'

'Landing in mainland Britain is too great a risk,' Harry says.

'Even for you?' Heydrich sniffs sarcastically.

'Even for me,' Harry says. 'I've got many talents but I am not bullet-proof. Even the Home Guard could pick off a man floating to the ground on a parachute. When do I leave?'

'It will be a matter of days,' Heydrich replies. 'First, however, you must pass one final test. We must be quite sure you have the ability to get to Churchill. It's not the same as fighting a couple of Waffen-SS soldiers . . . or my poor dogs. They are still quite traumatized, you know.'

'I'm ready for any test,' Harry says.

Heydrich snaps his fingers. One of his staff hurries away to make the arrangements.

'Have you had breakfast?' Heydrich asks.

'No,' Harry says, glancing at Gessler, 'your men dragged me out of bed at the crack of dawn.'

'Then you must have something,' Heydrich says. 'Once you have eaten, you have a short flight then a night's rest. Tomorrow morning we will see what you're made of. By the way, if you succeed, what do you want in return for your service to the Reich?'

'I'll tell you later,' Harry answers, 'when I've completed my test.'

Fourteen

London, Friday, 3 January, 1941

Temple arrived home in time for the evening meal. Connie had made a large saucepan of vegetable soup and there were thick slices of white bread to go with it. A pot of tea was brewing. Already, Paul felt comfortable in the Temple household. Connie had seated Evelyn directly opposite Paul. He was trying not to stare but Evelyn was the kind of girl who seemed to look better every time you looked at her. She was bubbly and full of fun and she seemed to be enjoying all the attention Paul was giving her.

'So how are you settling in, Paul?' Temple asked.

'Fine,' Paul answered, still darting the odd glance in Evelyn's direction. Another girl's face flickered through his mind but only for the briefest of moments, then a name, Netty.

'You spent the rest of the morning reading, didn't you Paul?' Connie said. She'd already appointed herself his mentor. 'There's another bookworm in the house. I think he'll fit in just fine.'

'I'm delighted to hear you're fitting in,' Temple said. 'So what are you reading?'

It was Evelyn's turn to speak for Paul. 'It's not for the faint-hearted, I can tell you. You should read it, Uncle George. It's just your sort of thing, all those nefarious villains and murderers.'

'I'll have you know,' Temple replied, 'that I see quite enough of the dark side of life at work. I prefer something lighter when I come home.'

'No, you don't!' Connie laughed.

'Yes, I do.'

'Tell me then,' Connie asked, 'what are you reading at the moment?'

Temple looked uncomfortable, like a child caught raiding the biscuit tin. '*Brighton Rock* by Graham Greene.'

'And what's that about?'

'A young gangster.'

'There,' Connie exclaimed. 'Point proven.'

'Anyway,' Temple said, his nose out of joint, 'I thought we were discussing *Paul's* book.'

Paul said nothing. After what happened on Sunday night, he wasn't sure what Temple would make of *The Demon Seed*. Temple didn't press the matter. He looked tired and he wanted to enjoy the first meal he had shared with his family in a couple of days. 'I've brought you some clothes,' he said, pointing to a brown paper parcel.

Paul finished his soup and went over to have a look. There were two pairs of flannel trousers, some shirts, a sleeveless jumper and a couple of sweaters. There was also a pair of shoes in a white cardboard box.

'It's all second-hand, I'm afraid,' Temple said, 'but they're in better condition than the things they gave you at the hospital.' He thought for a moment then added: 'The shoes are new of course. I wouldn't ask you to wear somebody else's shoes. So what do you think?'

Paul nodded. 'They're great, thank you.'

The conversation meandered, then Temple exchanged a meaningful glance with Connie. She took the hint and started clearing away the plates.

'Would you like to help me with the washing up?' she asked Evelyn. 'I think we need to leave the boys to talk.'

Evelyn smiled and helped Connie clear the table. When they were gone, Temple led the way into the parlour and closed the door. 'How's the memory, Paul? Evelyn seems to think it's starting to come back.'

Paul was reluctant to tell Temple everything. 'Just the fire. What are you getting at?'

'A man tried to kill me.'

Paul listened without interrupting. He didn't remember the incident clearly but it didn't come as a surprise either. Somewhere in the back alleys of his mind a door was threatening to creak open, but there was an obstacle on the other side. Paul had neither the will nor the inclination to force it open.

'That's not all,' Temple said. 'You tried to warn me. You knew my name. But we've never met, I'm sure of that. How did you know I was in danger?' He waited for an answer that didn't come. 'Don't you have any idea?'

'None.'

'I see,' Temple said, not sounding entirely convinced. His eyes lighted on *The Demon Seed*. Paul had brought it to the table with him. 'Can I have a look?'

Paul passed it to him and Temple started to flick through the pages. He was about to put it down when something caught his eye.

'Something wrong?' Paul asked.

Temple took a few moments to reply. 'No . . . it's just a coincidence, I suppose. It's the name Rector.'

Paul's heart lurched. He knew now that the door in his mind was almost ready to burst open.'What about it?' he asked apprehensively.

'It's part of East End folklore,' Temple replied. 'Everybody's heard of Samuel Rector. He made a name for himself as a prize-fighter, but that's not why he's remembered. It's his criminal activities. The Rat Boy case was one of the most notorious in the early days of the Metropolitan Police, after it replaced the Bow Street Runners.'

Paul was wondering why Temple was so interested

in a hundred-year old case when the detective continued.

'The thing is,' Temple said, 'it's another of the clan I'm really interested in, a surviving member of the Rector family.'

He had Paul's attention.

'His name's Harry. Believe me, we're very interested in *his* whereabouts.'

Harry Rector. The name exploded on Paul's consciousness.

'Paul,' Temple said, rising from his seat, 'you don't look well. Are you having a relapse?'

When Paul didn't answer, Temple made for the hall. 'Don't move. I'm going to phone Dr Tyler.'

'No,' Paul said, 'I'm not ill. That isn't it at all.'

Temple frowned. 'What then?'

'It's the name Rector,' Paul said. 'It's all coming back.'

Temple was utterly perplexed. 'What is?'

'It's my name too. I'm Paul Rector.'

Fifteen

10 November, present day

Detective Sergeant Hussein is standing by DI Ditchburn's grave in Walthamstow churchyard. She will never fully understand what happened. She still has nightmares about John Redman. With his one stare he had unleashed the full horror of death on her mind: blood, splintered bone, trickling brain matter, maggots squirming through stinking gangrenous flesh. *Her* death and Paul Rector saved her from it.

She's relived that night many times. So many impossible things have happened. She's seen a man kill with a stare. She's looked on helplessly as Paul fought his final struggle with Redman, how they stepped over into, what, another dimension, the lair of the Ripper? She has always believed in Hell as an idea. Now she experiences it night after night as a real place that beckons her. She knows now that devils walked the Earth.

Hussein leaves her flowers on Ditchburn's grave and walks to her car. It only takes her half an hour to reach the Lychgate estate. She gazes up at the dark orange walkways, the crumbling rust-stained concrete and the graffiti and wonders about so many things. Was Redman really what Paul said, his brother risen from the dead? Are such things possible, and where is Paul now? She knocks on the Rector family's door and Mrs Rector answers. This is her third visit since Paul's disappearance.

'Come in,' Mrs Rector says.

Hussein follows her inside. 'We've had a sighting of a boy who answers Paul's description,' she says.

Mrs Rector doesn't even make eye contact. 'Where?'

'Luton.'

Mrs Rector shakes her head. 'It isn't him.'

'How can you be so sure?' Hussein asks.

'He hasn't left London,' Mrs Rector answers.

'But how can you be so certain?'

'He's my son. I feel his presence. He'll never leave the city.'

Hussein's gaze floats round the room. She's notices one change. Mrs Rector has moved her sons' photographs. Now they're on open display in the living room. One photo shows them together, side by side at the London Dungeon. They look about seven years old. Paul is immediately recognizable. Hussein examines John next. Her blood freezes. It's him all right, Redman. Everything Paul said about his family was true. There is a demon seed. Hussein shudders.

'Is there anything else?' Mrs Rector asks.

'No,' Hussein says, 'not really, I just wanted to keep you abreast of developments.'

That isn't the real reason. Her superiors just want her to be seen to be doing something. It's all about keeping the TV and newspapers happy.

'Very well,' Mrs Rector says, 'you've done what you had to. Now I'd like you to leave.'

Hussein lets herself out of the flat. She's relieved to be out in the afternoon air again. At the top of the stairs she glances back.

Where are you, Paul Rector?

Sixteen

London, Friday, 3 January, 1941

'Is this some kind of joke?' Temple demanded.

Paul averted his eyes. 'No.'

'Quite a coincidence, isn't it?' Temple asked, scepticism evident in his voice. 'I read the name Rector in this book and you tell me it's your name too. Do you really think I'm that wet behind the ears, Paul? I know you've been through a lot, but don't go spinning yarns.'

'I'm not making it up,' Paul insisted. 'My name *is* Rector. I knew the moment I started reading the first chapter about Samuel's days as a boxer.'

Temple leaned forward, resting his arms on his knees. 'Don't stop there. What exactly do you remember?'

'Just the name so far,' Paul said. 'But there's this feeling too.'

'So how did you feel when you read the name Rector in the book?' Temple asked.

'It gave me a sense of foreboding,' Paul answered, 'and guilt. I know I've done something really bad.'

'But you're not sure what?'

'No.' Paul sighed. 'Not yet. I know you must find this hard to understand but I'm not trying to be awkward. I've only had one or two flashbacks so far. The rest is just the shadows of memories.'

'But your memory's definitely returning?' Temple asked. He watched Paul's face. 'You're starting to remember but you don't really want to, that's it, isn't it? You're scared of what you might have done?'

Paul swallowed hard. In his mind's eye the door was swinging wider. There were shapes in the darkness. 'Yes.'

'But it can't all be bad,' Temple said. 'Do you remember what I told you in the car yesterday? You saved my life.'

'Can you go through the events of Sunday night again?' Paul asked. 'It might jog my memory.'

Temple told his story, starting at the moment Paul called his name at Bank Station and ending with the arrival of the ambulance crew. Paul listened intently. Shadow's death bled into his mind like a slow motion film.

'Are you really trying to tell me something was protecting me from the flames?' he demanded.

'That's exactly what I'm saying,' Temple said. 'It's as if there was an invisible wall around you, preventing the worst of the burns. Does it help?'

'A bit,' Paul said. 'I'm afraid I still don't remember much in detail.'

They were interrupted by Connie. She popped her head round the door. 'Evelyn and I are going to listen to the wireless in the parlour,' she said. 'Come and join us when you're finished.'

Temple smiled. 'We'll do that.'

As soon as Connie was gone he patted Paul's forearm. 'We might as well leave matters where they are,' he said. 'Things will come back to you when you least expect them. Are you joining us?'

'No,' Paul answered. 'I'm feeling tired. I'm going to get an early night.'

'Fair enough, old son,' Temple said.

With that, he crossed the hall. It was some time before Paul moved. He had good reason to sit deep in thought. He hadn't told Temple the whole truth. The door was almost open wide. In his mind's eye he pictured Mum and his girlfriend Netty. He was consumed by a yearning to see their faces and hear their voices. But other, more menacing, shapes were forming in the darkness. He was waiting for the devils.

Seventeen

Germany, Friday, 3 January, 1941

Chief among the devils is Harry Rector. Preparations
are being made to give him a warm reception.
*Sturmbannfuhrer Heinrich Bruckner has been called to
the telephone. Dropping the receiver into the cradle, he
marches down a long, windowless corridor. The walls
around him are so thick they muffle every noise from the
outside world. They belong to Schloss Drachenhohle, the
Dragon's Lair Castle, a seemingly impenetrable fortress
that stands atop thickly-wooded mountain slopes. The
only sound is the thud of Bruckner's jack boots on the
stone floor. When he opens the door to the common room
he has been sharing with his unit, the men snap to
attention. They are Waffen-SS, crack soldiers who
have been at the cutting edge of Germany's remorseless*

advance across the continent. He sweeps the faces of his men with a gaze that demonstrates his pride in them. 'Our mission is about to begin,' he announces.

The faces in front of him glow.

'What do we have to do?' Heinz Schleicher demands. 'You said it was highly confidential.'

'It's a Secret Service operation,' Bruckner informs his men.

'What is our role in this operation?' Ernst Fischer demands. He's Bruckner's deputy, a tough-minded Saxon with an appetite for battle and a fierce loathing of failure.

'There will be an attempt to storm the castle,' Bruckner says. 'It is our job to prevent Schloss Drachenhohle from falling to the invader.'

'What invader?' radio operator Markus Schmidt demands. 'All our enemies are in headlong retreat. Who would be foolish enough to storm a castle in the heart of the Fatherland?'

'As I tried to explain,' Bruckner says, 'this is an internal operation, a test.'

'So these are just war games?'

'Not exactly,' Bruckner says. 'The intruder must be tested to the limit.'

'You said intruder,' Schmidt says. 'You can't mean there is only one man.'

A newcomer answers the question. A tall, lean, blond-haired man has entered the room. Bruckner's unit recognize him immediately. Karl Jager is already a legend, even this early in the War.

'That's right,' Jager says. 'There will be one man.'

At that, the entire company dissolve into helpless laughter.

'One,' Jager says finally. 'But he will be a formidable opponent.'

'Does it matter if we hand him over dead or alive?' Schmidt asks, brimming with self-confidence.

'The High Command need this man's services,' Jager says. 'He is to be taken alive. If he succeeds in penetrating the castle, he will have succeeded.' He glances at Bruckner. 'We must begin preparations.'

Bruckner nods and wonders why his superiors consider it necessary to reinforce an already formidable Waffen-SS unit with one of the toughest men in the Army, and all this to take on a single individual. What was going on?

Eighteen

London, Saturday, 4 January, 1941

'Good morning, Mr Rector,' Evelyn said, putting heavy emphasis on Paul's newly-discovered surname.

'Temple told you that, did he?' Paul said, taking a seat at the breakfast table.

'Oh dear,' Evelyn said, hearing the note of complaint in his voice, 'who got out of the wrong side of bed this morning?'

Paul made no attempt to deny it. He'd found it hard to sleep. For hours he'd been turning things over in his mind. He'd continued to think about Mum and Netty. There were times he'd been able to smell Netty's rain-damp hair. But she was a whole lifetime away, sixty years in the future. He'd also been thinking about

Samuel Rector, of course. Then there was Harry. He remembered what Temple had said: a surviving member of the Rector family. Paul wondered why Temple was so interested in him. But the thing that had really kept him awake was the stuff he'd started to read in Hugh Cotton's book. What is the demon seed, he wondered, and why does it keep gnawing away at the back of my mind this way? Those shapes in the dark, did they represent the demon seed somehow?

'I think it's all very mysterious and exciting,' Evelyn said. 'I've never met an amnesiac before. Have you remembered anything else?' When Paul didn't answer she pressed him. 'Well, have you?'

'Not really,' Paul answered, lying. 'Where's Temple?'

'He's standing at the front door,' Evelyn told him. 'A motorcycle courier arrived about five minutes ago.' She pressed her forefinger to her lips. 'Government business. Very hush-hush.'

'I thought I heard something,' Paul said. 'A motorcycle courier. I wonder what he wants.'

'He's delivering classified material, of course,' Evelyn said. 'I was spying on them until Aunt Connie chased me in here.'

'Did you see what it was?' Paul asked.

'An envelope,' Evelyn said. She tapped her nose. 'I can't tell you any more.'

'In other words,' Paul said, 'you don't know anything.'

Evelyn laughed. 'Well, there is that.'

Paul laughed too. 'At least you're honest.'

Temple walked in on them at that very moment. He was carrying a fat foolscap envelope.

'Something interesting, Uncle George?' Evelyn asked.

Temple took his seat. 'Now haven't we discussed this, Evelyn? What did I tell you?'

Evelyn rolled her eyes and repeated Temple's advice in a sulky monotone. 'It's top secret. Don't be nosy. Careless talk costs life.'

'Quite right,' Temple said. 'So don't forget it.' He put the envelope on the table unopened.

'Aren't you going to at least take a little look inside?' Evelyn asked.

Temple shook his head. 'I'll do it later. Honestly, Evelyn, what have we just been discussing?'

Evelyn did a little girl pout. 'Sorry.'

Temple's eyes wrinkled. He gave her an affectionate smile. It was evident he adored his niece.

'No sign of breakfast yet?' he asked.

Evelyn started to get up. 'I'll see if Aunt Connie needs a hand.'

'No, you chat to Paul,' Temple said. 'I'll help her.' He saw Evelyn's eyes light on the envelope. 'And don't even think about interfering with my package, young lady. It's sealed.' He chuckled. 'Why do you think I didn't open it myself? So I'd know if anyone interfered with it. Hands off.'

'That's telling you,' Paul said, as soon as Temple had gone.

Evelyn wrinkled her nose. 'You don't really think I'd open his letters, do you? I was only teasing. Uncle George does vital war work.'

Temple and Connie returned with toast, jam, tea and a few slices of cooked meat.

'This is great,' Paul said. He looked around the company. 'I mean, this is really great.'

He didn't mean the food. Connie, Temple and Evelyn almost filled the void created by the absence of Mum and Netty. Almost.

'Let's do something tomorrow,' Paul said impulsively when Temple's twin sister Brenda called for Evelyn an hour later.

'Not tomorrow,' Evelyn said. 'I've got piano practice. Mum insists.'

They agreed on Monday. Paul was sad to see Evelyn go. As he headed for the parlour to continue reading *The Demon Seed*, Temple called him into the living room 'You were right about Harry Rector,' he said. 'You're related to him all right.'

'How do you know?' Paul asked. Dread mounted within.

'I should have seen the resemblance earlier,' Temple said. 'How are you related to him?'

Paul wasn't sure how to answer. 'He's a distant relative.' There was an element of truth in that. 'We've never met. I've heard stories, that's all.'

Temple pulled a photograph out of the envelope the courier had delivered. 'Would you like to see him?'

'Of course.'

Temple handed Paul the photo. Harry was older – a man in his thirties, but in every other respect the similarity was striking. This was no flat image. The dark eyes seemed alive. Paul's flesh prickled. He felt a rush of heat.

'Why are you so interested in Harry?' he asked.

He was starting to tug at his shirt collar. His skin was on fire.

'Are you feeling all right?' Temple asked.

'Yes, I'm fine,' Paul answered.

Temple hesitated before making his decision. 'Harry Rector's a career criminal. He came to my notice before the war. That's not why I'm interested in him now though. Our Harry's stepped up a division. He's playing with the big boys.'

Paul had to concentrate to hear what Temple was saying. His field of vision was narrowing to form a dark circle. The circle tightened around Harry's face.

'Paul, I don't know how to tell you this, but your relative's a traitor.'

Paul's head was pounding. Harry Rector. Traitor. He was feeling dizzy.

'Paul,' Temple said, 'are you really all right?'

'Harry Rector,' Paul gasped, feeling feverish, 'hanged for treason, 1942.' He stared at Temple. His eyes were wide with panic. 'Temple, it's coming back.' The door in his mind swung wide open. Memories started rushed through unhindered. 'I know why I'm here.' The final swarm of recollections invaded his mind like a thunderclap. 'Oh God, I remember everything. Harry's going to kill Churchill. That's why I came to warn you.'

'Slow down a bit, old chap,' Temple said. 'I think you need to start from the very beginning. You know about the conspiracy to assassinate the PM. What else?'

Paul eased himself into the nearest armchair, hugging his stomach. He was gulping in mouthfuls of air in an attempt to steady his nerves. The heat and the dizziness were starting to relax their hold.

'Some of the things I'm going to tell you will be hard to believe,' Paul said, still not making eye contact. 'Do you promise to listen without interrupting?'

Temple nodded.

Paul took a final deep breath and started his tale. 'I discovered a few weeks ago that my family was different from other people's. Every few generations one of the Rector men starts to show signs of a genetic disorder. It starts with the onset of adolescence, with seizures and dizziness. Then the dark thoughts begin.' He hesitated. 'Somewhere between thirteen and fifteen years old, they start to exhibit supernatural powers. But it isn't a blessing, it's a curse. They become violent. Usually, they become so hard to control that they lose contact with their family and slip into crime. Finally, they sell themselves to the forces of evil. They become assassins. The family call it the demon seed. I know the names of three sufferers: Samuel Rector, Harry Rector and my brother John.'

'Your brother's part of this?' Temple said, then

remembered his promise. 'Sorry, I didn't mean to interrupt.'

'That's all right,' Paul said. 'It's painful for me.' For Temple's sake, he skipped over the more incredible parts of the story, of journeys through time and Hellish spirits. 'John grew up to kill. He murdered six people.'

Temple read Paul's features with a practised policeman's eye. He believed him. There was no disguising the horror in the boy's eyes. 'There's one thing I don't understand,' he said. 'I don't know of any such case.'

Paul knew he had to gloss over this part of the story. 'I thought you were going to let me finish,' he said.

Temple drew back. 'Continue.'

'The Rector men aren't evil to begin with,' Paul explained. 'Sometimes they struggle to control the demon in their head but the outcome is always the same. By the time they reach early manhood, there's nothing left of their original personality.'

'A kind of Jekyll and Hyde?' Temple suggested.

'I suppose so,' Paul replied. 'But once you change, you can't go back to what you were.' He hesitated. 'You won't believe the next part.'

'Try me.'

'There's an evil presence in this city. He's as old as time. His name is King Lud.'

'Isn't he meant to be the city's founder?' Temple asked. 'There's a pub in the city called the King Lud. It's in Ludgate.'

'The King Lud I've encountered is an imprisoned demon,' Paul said. 'From afar, he controls people's lives and destroys them too. He takes his disciples' souls.' Temple continued to look slightly uncomfortable listening to the tale, but Paul pressed on. 'It isn't just my family. There are others out there. Shadow had to come from somewhere.' He frowned. 'Look, I don't understand it any more than you do but at the root of the whole thing there's a white chapel, only it isn't like a church. It's a different kind of temple, a place of horror. I see it in my dreams.'

'And that's where this King Lud is?' Temple asked, unsure what to make of Paul's story.

'Yes,' Paul said, 'I think he's imprisoned inside it somewhere beneath London. He has to live through the minds of others. He uses them to do his bidding. That's pretty much all I know.'

'It's quite a tale,' Temple commented. Only a week earlier he would have dismissed it with his policeman's scepticism. But he'd *seen* Shadow. He still shuddered at the double row of needle-like teeth and the hypnotic eyes. He'd also seen a boy rise from the dead.

'You don't believe me,' Paul said.

'I didn't say that,' Temple said. 'My mind's been in turmoil for days. That creature. The way he tore a bullet from his own flesh.' He relived the moment. 'My God, those *eyes*. It was pure terror.' He gave Paul a sidelong glance. 'If you hadn't come to my rescue I swear, I would have gone insane.'

'Anyone who possesses the demon seed has that power,' Paul told him. 'We can scare people to death.'

Temple stiffened. 'You said *we*,' he said. 'Are you telling me you can do it?'

Paul nodded. 'Do you want me to show you?'

'No, thank you,' Temple answered, holding up his hands. 'I couldn't go through that again.'

'There's something else I can do,' Paul said. He had a knot in his stomach. But he *had* to make Temple believe. 'Would you get that old newspaper behind you?'

Temple reached out to take the copy of the *Daily Mail* from a small mahogany table. 'Yes, you can do what you want with it.'

Paul placed it on the coffee table and took several steps back. Then he focused. He concentrated all his efforts on a story about a school that had been hit by a hundred-pound bomb. Black shapes started to flutter at the edges of his vision. Moments later the paper caught fire. Temple took it from Paul and doused the flames.

'OK,' he said, 'I'd call that a successful demonstration. It's telekinesis, isn't it, the power to affect objects with your mind?'

Paul shrugged. 'Beats me.'

'Can you move things too?'

'No,' Paul said, 'that is, I don't know. I wouldn't know where to begin.'

'And this gift runs in your family?'

Was 'gift' the right word? 'It isn't every member of the family, just a few of the men.'

'But you're not like the others,' Temple asked. 'You can't be. Everybody likes you. Our instincts – mine,

Connie's, Evelyn's – couldn't all be wrong. I think I know you, Paul. There's nothing malevolent or wicked in you. You're not like Samuel and Harry, are you? Or this John. You don't use your powers for evil purposes.'

'No,' Paul said, 'that's what I've been trying to explain. I think I have some of the same powers, but Lud doesn't have total control. For some reason, I'm able to act independently of his will.'

'But what brought you to me?' Temple said.

This was the hard part. Temple had believed him so far, even the part about King Lud. But how can I tell you I come from the future? Paul wondered.

'I have visions,' Paul replied, deciding to side-step the whole truth. 'When they come I start to feel sick.'

'Like just now?'

Paul nodded. Temple had swallowed his partial explanation.

'I've seen the future,' Paul said. 'There's going to be an assassination attempt on Winston Churchill.'

'There's already been one,' Temple said. 'That's why I haven't been home.'

'That had nothing to do with Lud,' Paul told him. 'This one's more serious. Harry's the assassin. If he succeeds, Hitler will invade.'

'But what's the connection between the demon world and our Nazi friends?' Temple asked.

'I don't know yet,' Paul said. 'But I do know *you* matter, Temple. You're the one who can stop Harry. That's why Shadow was sent to kill you. Lud was trying to change history. You have a destiny, just as I do. Lud sent one of his minions to destroy you and thwart that destiny. Some day soon you will save Churchill's life. Shadow was meant to prevent that happening. I got in the demon's way. You've seen what one demon is capable of. Harry will be stronger still.'

Temple had his eyes lowered, staring at the pattern on the carpet. Paul watched him for a while then something struck him.

'You should be more surprised,' Paul said, voicing his own thoughts, 'more disbelieving.'

By way of explanation, Temple handed Paul the envelope he had received at breakfast. 'We've already got wind of what Harry's up to.'

Paul pulled out the envelope's contents. There was a series of photographs. Temple explained. 'The first few show Harry talking to a Nazi agent here in London. They were taken last May. We'd had the pair of them under surveillance for several weeks. Then Harry vanished. Take a look at the next set.'

They showed Harry disembarking from a cargo ship.

'This is Kiel, on the north coast of Germany last June. A member of the underground resistance took it for us.' Temple explained the next few photos. 'The man Harry is meeting here is called Gessler. He is a member of the RHSA, the counter-espionage unit of the SS. That set alarm bells ringing all over Whitehall. Put a ruthless thug like Harry together with one of

Hitler's crack battalions and you've got trouble. That's why I was so keen to meet Shadow that night.'

Paul examined the photographs. 'Who's this?'

'The man in the glasses?' Temple asked.

'Yes.'

'It took us a while to discover his identity,' Temple said. 'He is Heinrich Voss, a key member of an organisation called Das Ahnenerbe. They're an SS unit that specialises in historical heritage, mythology, all kinds of hokum.'

'Like the kind of stuff I've just told you?' Paul asked pointedly.

Temple winced. 'Sorry.' He stared at the image of the bespectacled Voss. 'We're still rather confused by the role of Voss in all this. There's a London connection, by the way. Voss studied archaeology at London University.' He fumbled in his briefcase. 'I've got some stuff here.'

Paul studied the typewritten pages. One paragraph leapt out at him:

In 1936, Voss was involved in a dig in the Aldgate area.

'You've had the link between the demon world and Nazi Germany in your hands all the time,' Paul said. 'You just didn't recognize it. I'll bet you a pound to a penny that this Voss knows all about King Lud.'

'It may well be,' Temple said. 'There's a strong tradition of Paganism among some of the Nazi leaders.'

'Where's Harry now?' Paul asked. 'Do you know?'

Temple shook his head. 'MI5 have had no word from their contact in Germany for a couple of months. They think the Gestapo have got him. He's probably dead.'

'So Harry could be here already,' Paul said, nerves jangling.

'We don't think he's in the country yet,' Temple said.

He seemed to think very carefully before handing Paul a letter marked Top Secret. 'Read this. It's a communication from the code-breaking centre at Bletchey Park.'

Arminius has failed.
He's dead.
The Blutwolf is coming.

'Blutwolf?' Paul murmured.

'German for blood wolf,' Temple explained. 'It's a code-name for the next assassin. It's got to be Harry.'

Nineteen

Germany, Saturday, 4 January, 1941

The Blutwolf is sitting in the back seat of an SS staff car, eyes closed, feeling the whip of the wind on his face. He's on the last leg of his journey. Gessler's in the front seat next to the driver. The Mercedes saloon is climbing a steep, winding mountain road. Harry doesn't ask where he's going. He has seen the peaks and valleys of Hell. Compared to that, what can mortal man conjure? Whatever the Nazi High Command has in store for him, he knows he will prevail. They might make things difficult but it isn't in their interests to destroy him. He represents their best chance to assassinate Churchill.

Harry stares at the back of Gessler's head and smiles. Gessler thinks he's a confirmed Nazi. He's promised Harry the Knight's Cross if he succeeds in his mission.

What would I want with your pathetic trinkets, Harry wonders. I couldn't care less who wins this war. Demon kind have no country, no allegiance but to King Lud. My master offers me endless joy, Harry thinks, imagining a future in which chaos is unleashed on the world. The greatest riches, they will be mine. The most beautiful women, I will take my pick. The cruellest tortures, I will inflict them. When the world falls into my master's hands I will devour its treasures one by one. I will roam unhindered through time and space. The whole world will be my playground, yesterday, today and tomorrow. These wretched little men with their stupid wars, what do they know about life? How can they imagine its possibilities?

'Here we are, Harry,' Gessler announces. 'This is Schloss Drachenhohle.'

Harry opens his eyes. They sweep round a hairpin bend. For a moment he blinks as the dawn light explodes into his face. Then, there before him, Harry sees a castle atop a huge crag. The Dragon's Lair Castle. The car's starting to slow down.

'Don't you want to know what you've got to do?' Gessler asks, irritated by Harry's air of quiet confidence. 'Aren't you curious at all?'

'You'll tell me in your own good time,' Harry says. 'I'm in no hurry.'

Gessler laughs. 'You're an original, Harry, you really are. You have what the French call sang froid. You have cold blood in your veins.'

Yes, Harry thought, cold blood and a demon seed.

They park at the bottom of a steep path. The driver opens Harry's door and gestures for him to get out. Harry obeys.

'I will leave you here, Harry,' Gessler says. 'I'm going to continue my journey by car. You however will approach Schloss Drachenhohle by foot.'

'What's my objective?' Harry asks.

'See that tower?' Gessler says, pointing with a leather-gloved hand. 'The tallest of the four. It is called the North Tower. That's your destination. Do you remember the Knight's Cross I promised you? It's being worn by the most formidable Stormtrooper, a man called Karl Jager. He would rather die than surrender it. That's the mettle of the man. You must make your way to the tower. The castle is heavily guarded by Waffen SS. They have been told to defend the North.'

'How many are there?' Harry asks.

Gessler chuckles. 'Now that would be telling. Harry, I don't want to spoil the surprise. Your objective is to reach the tower and take the Knight's Cross from Jager. It should be a good contest. If you succeed, we will then keep it for you until you return victorious from England. This is no easy challenge, Harry. The castle walls are three metres thick. The doors are made of solid oak and bound with iron. The defenders are among the finest soldiers in the entire Reich. Just penetrating the castle will be seen as a success. What do you think?'

'Penetrating the castle without taking the tower would be a failure,' Harry said. 'I intend to earn my Knight's Cross.'

Gessler claps his gloved hands. 'Bravo, Harry, I do like a man with confidence in his abilities. Good luck.' He pauses. 'Oh, by the way, these are some of our best men. They are needed for the war effort. Please don't kill anyone.'

Harry grins. 'I'll do my best.'

Gessler frowns for a moment, then tells the driver to accelerate away. Harry is left alone to come up with a strategy. He ignores the path Gessler pointed out; it's bound to be heavily defended. He prefers to approach the castle by scaling the thickly-wooded slopes to the west. He moves quickly, weaving through the trees, always on the look out for snipers. He discovers the first man perched in the uppermost branches of a pine tree.

As he races up the slope, Harry undergoes a macabre transformation. Thick gobbets of blood ooze from every pore of his skin, coating him with a scarlet sheen. Simultaneously, a forest of bristles erupts all over his flesh. His eyes became lupine, a predator's eyes floating in their orbits. Where Harry Rector stood moments before there is now the blood wolf. The first Heinz Schleicher knows of the monster scaling the pine towards him is a slight vibration running up the tree trunk from below. He shifts position slightly, resting his rifle on his left arm

'What in God's name is happening?' he murmurs.

It's the last question that will ever cross Heinz Schleicher's lips. A split-second later Harry falls upon him, gripping his upper arms. He remembers Gessler's plea not to kill but his blood rage is upon him. His fangs sink deep and tear. When Schleicher's face clenches in pain, Harry's heart pounds with pleasure. He hears the Nazi's right arm tear from its socket and scraps of flesh hang from his shoulder, quivering like wings. Schleicher screams then tumbles to the earth seventy feet below.

Harry turns to his next opponent. Ernst Fischer is guarding a grille in the water-gate tunnel beneath the castle battlements. Harry starts to lope forward, sniffing the air. But Fischer has slipped into the water, ready to engage the enemy. The icy water disguises his scent. Where are you, Harry wonders. His eyes dart back and forth in the gloom of the tunnel then he sees the flash of metal to his left. Fischer goes to squeeze the trigger but Harry is too quick, punching the barrel up into the air. Bullets spit against the brickwork above their heads. There's a wet, ripping sound and Ernst Fischer is dead.

Harry, or at least the thing Harry has become, makes light work of the metal grille that protects the water tunnel. Splashing forward, he emerges into the castle's central keep. Soon, a third man races across the flagged floor. It's Markus Schmidt. He has just found Fischer's body. Harry sees a sudden shadow, a flash of silver, then a lance of pain tears his mouth wide open. Schmidt's dagger has pierced his skin.

'You killed him,' Schmidt cries. 'You killed Fischer. You broke the rules. Now I'm going to kill you.'

But before he can press the dagger home, Harry slashes open his stomach. Schmidt's entrails spill over his knees. His dying scream echoes through the castle. Harry gives a wolfish grin. Schloss Drachenhohle's defenders come

138

streaming from all directions, determined to repulse the attack. Bruckner is yelling to his men to keep their discipline. By the time Bruckner's unit discovers Schmidt's dismembered corpse, Harry is already racing up the stone steps to the chamber at the summit of the North Tower. When he reaches the door, he mimics Bruckner's voice.

'Open the door, Jager,' he barks, tugging at the door handle. 'You must let us in.'

'Why?' Jager demands. 'It's against my orders.'

'Forget your damned orders,' Harry says in fluent German. 'He's coming. You're a sitting duck in there. We have to get you out.'

'You're sure?'

'Listen to me, Jager,' Harry roars. 'If you want to live you must open the door. Now!'

Jager fumbles for the key. The moment he opens the door he realizes his mistake. But he's too late. The blood wolf flings him across the room, taking the key from him. Then the gluey scarlet sheen sinks back into his pores. Harry assumes the appearance of a mortal man once more and locks the door behind him.

'Time for some fun,' he says.

Jager catches Harry's eye and a vision bleeds into his mind. It's the nightmare he has lived with since childhood. When his father wanted to punish him, he would beat the young Jager with his belt and abandon him in the cellar with the rats. The room in which he is now standing vanishes, replaced by the windowless cellar of his childhood. He relives every moment of torture he ever

139

suffered at his father's hands. Suddenly he's back in the dark, listening to the dry scutter of their scampering paws. He imagines eyes like black beads, yellow teeth tugging at moist flesh.

'No!' Jager screams.

Harry's eyes hold him, plunging him deeper into his worst fears.

'Do you want it to end?' Harry asks.

'Yes, dear God, yes,' Jager cries, sensing the rodent hordes closing in. 'Get them away from me.'

'Then hand me the Knight's Cross,' Harry says.

Jager fights for a moment with his sense of duty, then obeys. His fingers are trembling as he thrusts the medal in Harry's direction.

'Good boy,' Harry says, talking to the wretched, snivelling child Jager has become.

Bruckner has arrived outside the door. Harry listens. 'Shoot the lock,' Bruckner says. He is interrupted by a familiar voice.

'What are you doing?' Gessler demands, climbing the steps behind them.

Gessler is accompanied by a grey-skinned man in glasses.

'The intruder's in there,' Bruckner explains. 'He's got Jager.'

'There's no need for shooting,' Gessler says. 'I have a key.'

When Bruckner's men burst in, Harry enjoys the look on their faces. Jager, a true hero of the Reich, renowned for his nerves of steel and utter ruthlessness, is kneeling on the floor, crying like a baby. He has turned his own gun on himself and at that very moment he is inserting the barrel of the pistol into his mouth. His eyes are wide with terror. It's Harry's party piece. He is forcing Jager to take his own life, but there's nothing the man can do to stay his own hand.

'Stop, Harry,' Gessler cries. 'Gruss Gott, I've already lost three good men. Let him go.'

Harry is disappointed that he won't see the proud Jager suffer the final humiliation of self-slaughter. Nevertheless, he breaks eye contact and Jager falls to his knees, sobbing uncontrollably. For the first time he registers Voss's presence and something passes between them.

'What did you do to him?' Gessler asks, gazing down at the broken man.

'Nothing much,' Harry says. 'I got him to talk about his childhood, that's all.'

'And why did you kill the others? We had an agreement.'

Voss speaks for the first time. 'Stop whining, Gessler. Harry has proved his worth and that's all that matters. I knew he would.'

Gessler nods and dismisses the troopers huddled round the doorway.

'You may go,' he says. 'There's no dishonour in failing to stop Harry. You will never come across another opponent quite like him.'

Bruckner still has his pistol drawn. He's reluctant to leave. 'He broke the rules of engagement.'

'Holster your weapon,' Gessler says. 'That's an order.'

'I want to hear it from a higher authority than you, little man,' Bruckner snarls. He jabs a finger at Harry. 'That butcher slaughtered my men.'

Voss pulls out a leather wallet containing a letter and hands it to Bruckner. 'Is this a high enough authority for you?'

Bruckner sees the signature on the letter and reluctantly holsters his pistol. It is from the Fuhrer himself.

'I still want to know what happened here,' he says.

'There will be no explanations,' Voss tells him. 'You have done your duty. That is all. Transport is waiting to take you back to Berlin.' He watches Bruckner lead his men down the stairs, taking Jager with them.

'Well Harry,' Gessler says, 'I promised you a reward. What's it to be?'

'The East End.'

'I beg your pardon.'

'You heard him,' Voss says. 'He wants the East End of London.'

'That's impossible,' Gessler protests.

But Voss slaps a second leather wallet in his hand. 'Nothing's impossible.'

Gessler hesitates for a moment then nods.

'I'm sure that can be arranged,' he says.' The Fuhrer will make you Gauleiter.' He gazes at Harry. 'But what on earth do you want it for?'

Harry winks. 'I'm thinking of opening a jellied eel stall.'

Voss and Harry laugh out loud. Gessler is mystified by the answer. This Englander really does have the oddest sense of humour.

Twenty

London, Monday, 6 January, 1941

Paul consulted the map Connie had drawn for him. He was only a couple of minutes' walk from Evelyn's house. He quickened his pace. It was a crisp winter's morning and he had the sun on his face. He felt good but there was a fly in the ointment. He'd told Temple he felt guilty. He meant about John, the demon brother he'd killed to save the ones he loved. This Monday morning he had another reason to feel guilty.

As Paul walked along the street, picking his way through the odd pile of rubble where a German bomb had fallen, he wondered if he ever would return to his own world, to St George's school and his friends. He missed them all terribly. But the hole left by them, though painful, wasn't half as gaping as he might have imagined. There had been a time, just a few days before, when he would have thought he couldn't live without his East End: the cramped flat on the Lychgate estate, Mum, his friends Moose and Tyrone, his PC and mobile, and Netty most of all. The hole was real enough but the Temples had come along to fill it. It was as if a space had been made for him here in 1941, ready for him to slot in and be part of this time. Wherever he was, whatever his destiny, he had to make do. He had to carry on living. Right now, that meant Evelyn. He walked up the garden path to her front door and knocked. He heard unoiled hinges creak somewhere in the house.

'Is Evelyn in?' he asked Brenda when the front door opened.

She couldn't have forgotten. 'She's upstairs getting ready,' Brenda said.

Evelyn wasn't there for long. Soon, she came pounding down the staircase, beaming a broad smile at him.

'Bye Mum,' she breezed, sweeping past Brenda. She grabbed Paul by the hand and they set off down the road at a cracking pace.

'You're in a hurry,' Paul said.

'You should be flattered,' Evelyn told him.

He saw her breath-taking eyes and smiled. 'I am.'

'So where are we going?'

'Do you want to meet a devil-worshipper?' Paul asked.

'The man who wrote your book?' Evelyn asked. 'Are you serious?'

'Absolutely,' Paul replied. 'I phoned Hugh Cotton this morning.'

Evelyn's eyes sparkled. 'How exciting. Where are we meeting him, in his garret?' She lowered her voice in mock horror. 'His crypt?'

'Not exactly,' Paul said. 'He works for the BBC but he's got a few hours off. He's going to wait for us at the Lyons Corner House at the junction of Tottenham Court Road and Hanway Street. Do you know it?'

Evelyn nodded. 'Let's go.'

On the way, she asked him if he'd got his memory back yet. Paul told her it was coming but he didn't give much away. He threw her one scrap, telling her his surname. It seemed to keep her happy for the time being. They found their man sitting at a table over by the window.

'Hello, Mr Cotton.'

'Hello again, Paul,' he said, looking up. 'Call me Hugh. So who's this young lady?'

'I'm Evelyn,' Evelyn said, offering her hand. 'You must be the devil-worshipper.'

Cotton burst out laughing and looked to Paul for an explanation.

'It's a private joke,' Paul said. 'Evelyn's read some excerpts from your book.'

'Mmn,' Cotton said, 'it is quite . . . demonic. I'm intrigued though. The moment I put the phone down, I wondered how you'd tracked me down. Another of your dreams?'

'Oh that,' Paul said. 'No, just amateur detective

work. You used a letter as a bookmark. It had your address and phone number on it.'

'Pity,' Cotton said, 'I thought it was black magic. Anyway, this is my treat.'

It was a shilling and sixpence for bacon and fried bread, dry toast, marmalade and a pot of tea.

'I thought there was rationing,' Paul said, marvelling at the spread.

'It doesn't mean you can't still find a decent meal in the city,' Cotton said.

The waitress arrived with their tea, toast and marmalade on a tray. Like the rest of the female staff, she was wearing a smart black and white uniform.

'This seems very posh,' Paul whispered as she walked away.

'You must have been in a Lyons before,' Evelyn said.

'Actually,' Paul said, 'I haven't.' He didn't offer an explanation and neither Evelyn nor Cotton pursued it.

'So, Paul,' Cotton said, 'what do you want from me?'

'Let me ask you a question,' Paul said. 'Hugh, do you believe I have certain . . . abilities?'

Evelyn leaned forward. He had her interest at least.

'I can't deny it,' Cotton said. 'That trick of yours in the church. Very impressive.'

'Well, you might be interested in my name too. I'm Paul Rector.'

Cotton put his teacup down suddenly. The contents slopped into the saucer. 'Is this some kind of joke?'

'I wouldn't joke about something like that,' Paul said. 'You don't exactly boast about belonging to one of the most notorious families in the city.' He could feel Evelyn's stare but he was determined to plough on with his story. 'I'm curious about Samuel Rector. My Nana had documents about him in an old suitcase in her house.'

'Does she still have them?' Cotton asked excitedly.

'Sorry,' Paul said, 'they got burned. You can probably understand why.'

Cotton nodded. 'Sheep don't get much blacker, I suppose. Is that why you didn't mention it in the church?'

'No,' Paul said, 'I had amnesia. I told you.'

'That's right, you did. So you've recovered?'

'Things are coming back,' Paul told him, careful not to contradict what he'd told Evelyn.

'So how can I help?'

'In your book you hint that Rector was more than an ordinary criminal,' Paul said. 'There's the stuff about cannibalism and the Dark Arts. Do you believe the stories?'

'My book is a work of scholarship,' Cotton said, 'not some lurid pot-boiler.'

Paul knew he was being evasive. 'That isn't an answer. Do you believe them?'

Cotton hesitated. 'If you ever repeat what I'm going to tell you, I'll deny it flatly.'

'So you do?' Evelyn cried, interrupting.

'Too many reliable people at the time were inclined to repeat them,' Cotton said. 'There are accounts by policemen, clergy, magistrates, all people in authority.

They thought there was something genuinely satanic about Samuel Rector.'

'They were right,' Paul said. He reached for the milk jug. 'Watch.'

He concentrated on the jug, allowing the black shapes to enter his vision. Immediately, the milk started to bubble.

'Dear God!' Cotton gasped.

Evelyn was equally astonished. 'You can do black magic!'

'Not so loud,' Paul said. 'I don't want people staring.'

Cotton's face was a tapestry of emotions. There was fascination and excitement. There was also a hint of fear. 'What are you trying to tell me?'

Paul wasn't sure how Temple would react to him letting Evelyn in on his secret. Just then, he didn't care. 'Some of the men in my family are drawn towards the demonic. It seems to happen every few generations. The demon seed's inside me too. I want to find out what it means. You're an expert on Samuel Rector. There have got to be things you haven't put in your book.' He saw the way Cotton was looking at him. 'Don't worry, I'm not going to grow horns. I'm different to the others. Will you help me?'

'I don't know,' Cotton said.

Paul was wondering how to convince him when a coincidence struck him. 'You taught at London University, didn't you?'

'That's right.'

'Did you ever come across somebody called Heinrich Voss?'

'Professor Voss?' Cotton said, his eyes as wide as they had been when Paul had done his trick with the newspaper. 'I studied under him about six years ago. How do you know about Professor Voss?'

'Another time,' Paul said. 'Will you help me?'

Cotton nodded. 'What do you want to know?'

Paul laid it out for him. 'I want everything you've got about Samuel, to begin with. There's something else too. All the way through the book, you refer to the ancient gates of London. I think they're important too.'

'Oddly enough,' Cotton said, 'that was Voss's area of expertise.'

Paul nodded. 'I'm not surprised. Oh, make a note of any mentions of demons or monsters, ancient Kings, that kind of stuff.'

'That's a lot of material,' Cotton said. 'It could take some time.'

Paul grinned. 'I know you'll come up trumps. Go on, you'll enjoy it.'

Cotton gave it some thought then returned the smile. 'Very well. I'll prepare some material for you. Give me your telephone number.'

Paul scribbled the number on a serviette and handed it to Cotton.

'I've got to get to work,' Cotton said. 'I'll give you a call when I've assembled the archive.'

'Thank you,' Paul said.

He watched Cotton limp towards the exit and turned to Evelyn. When he met her gaze he imagined Netty sitting opposite him and remembered the extreme danger he had once put her in. 'I shouldn't have involved you in this.'

'But you did. Why?'

'I'm alone, I suppose,' Paul explained, discovering the words without giving them a moment's thought. 'I needed someone.'

'Me?'

Netty's face invaded his mind and he looked away.

'Paul,' Evelyn said. 'What are you saying?' She reached across and touched the back of his hand.

What am I doing? Paul thought. But adore Netty as he did, she wasn't here. It was possible he would never see her again. He looked across at Evelyn.

'Do you mean me?' she asked.

Paul took a few moments to answer. 'Yes.'

Evelyn smiled and squeezed his hand. 'Does Uncle George know you have these powers?'

Paul nodded, still wondering what Netty would say if she could see them together. 'He's seen what I can do. He'll probably kill me for dragging you into it.'

'Then I won't tell him I know,' Evelyn said. She was still holding Paul's hand. 'This is so thrilling.' She glanced at the milk jug. 'Can you do anything else?'

Paul nodded. 'I can, but you don't want to know.'

'Oh, do tell.'

'All in good time,' Paul said. 'For now, let's try to act

150

as if we're two ordinary people taking in the sights of London. Is it a deal?'

'Deal,' Evelyn said. 'Where do you want to go?'

Paul thought for a moment. 'What about St Paul's?'

It wasn't long before they were within sight of Wren's great dome. Evelyn continued towards it then realised Paul wasn't following.

'Paul?' she said.

'This way,' he told her.

They reached a row of bomb-shattered warehouses. Evelyn gave him a questioning look.

'This is where I got hurt,' he explained.

'But what were you doing here?'

'I had to meet Temple,' he said finally. 'He's part of my destiny.'

'Uncle George?' Evelyn asked. 'Does it have something to do with the package he got on Saturday morning?'

Paul grinned. 'You're really sharp, you know that?' He gave the ruined building where he'd fought Shadow a last glance. 'I should get you home.'

Evelyn linked her arm through his as they walked. 'There's no hurry, you know.'

Paul's heart swelled. He really liked this girl. They walked as far as Trafalgar Square and waded through the pigeons. Just for those few moments, they didn't have a care in the world. They were about to head for the tube when they were stopped by a man in a gabardine mac and a trilby. He was holding a camera with a flash.

'Press,' he said. 'I thought you'd make a great snap for tomorrow's paper. You know the sort of thing, young sweethearts defy the Blitz. How's about it?'

'Which paper?' Evelyn asked.

'*Daily Mirror.*'

'Are you sure it will be in?' Paul asked.

'I can't say for certain,' the photographer said. 'That's up to my editor. But there's a good chance. You make a lovely couple.'

Evelyn flashed a delighted smile. 'You're on!'

Three times the photographer made them stride towards him, arm in arm, while the pigeons fluttered around them. On the third take, he was happy.

'It probably won't happen,' Paul said. But it did.

Twenty-one

Germany, Monday, 6 January, 1941

*I*t is the early hours of the morning. Harry Rector stirs in his Munich apartment. What was that? He hears a church bell chime. It's two am. Within moments, he is fully awake. His master is coming. Harry leaps out of bed and pulls on a dressing gown. His heart is pounding.

Soon he sees the telltale signs of Lud's approach. A hot draught lifts the curtains. Loose sheets of paper flutter into the air. Wherever dust has settled it starts to whip around like a cloud of swarming insects. Next, the floor seems to become molten. The polished floor starts to sink until it becomes a swirling vortex. Finally, from the heart of the dark, spinning whirlpool, a shadowy figure rises. He does not take on solid form. For now, that is beyond his powers.

Harry bows his head. 'Master.'

'When do you depart, Harry?' Lud asks.

'This evening,' Harry answers. 'They will fly me to the French coast. From there, they will transport me onwards to Ireland under cover of darkness. I will be there tomorrow night.'

Lud is satisfied. 'Good. Very good. I trust you Harry.'

'I will not fail you Master. Churchill's as good as dead.'

'However we have a problem, Harry.'

The hairs on the nape of Harry's neck bristle. There's something in Lud's voice, a tension he has never noticed before. 'Problem?'

'It's the renegade,' Lud says.

Harry's face grows tense. 'My descendant.'

'Your descendant indeed,' Lud says. 'The legend is true. A boy has lived who should have died at birth. He is both demon and man. Fate has yet to decide which part of his nature will win out. He is reaching the point of self-awareness, Harry. If his human side prevails, he will prove a most troubling obstacle to our progress.'

'He is a mere boy,' Harry says.

'A boy with great powers,' Lud says. 'His abilities still lie dormant and untapped. We must win him over to our side.'

'And if he refuses.'

'Then we will destroy him.'

'Does that mean my mission has changed?' Harry asks.

'No,' Lud tells him. 'Not yet. The boy is still weak and

untrained. I have other disciples. They will find him and put my proposal to him. Then, as you say, if he refuses he will die. Your mission is of vital importance if I am to break my bonds and walk the Earth once more. You will continue on your original path.'

'Yet you sound concerned, Master.'

'The renegade has been shrouded from my gaze,' Lud says. 'He has allies.'

'The priests of Beltane,' Harry says.

'My thoughts entirely,' Lud concurs. 'The fire lords rise again. Their generations-long exile is at an end. They think they've found their champion.'

'Then the endgame is in sight,' Harry says.

'It is,' Lud agrees. 'It will conclude with my liberation and triumph . . . or my destruction.'

Harry nods. 'We will slay Churchill and destroy the renegade. Victory is certain.'

'Nothing is certain,' Lud says, reprimanding his disciple. 'If we are to conquer, we must be strong. There will be no distractions, Harry. Prove yourself worthy of my trust.'

'And the renegade?'

'I sense him already. I am about to unleash the dogs of war.'

Twenty-two

The Irish Sea, Tuesday, 7 January, 1941

T wenty-four hours later, Harry is approaching the coast. His controllers have chosen an ageing, unmarked Junkers Ju-52 transport to get him to Ireland. By nightfall on this bitterly cold evening, he is sick of its droning and rattling. He zips his flying jacket to his throat as protection against the icy blasts of air that are stabbing through the fuselage.

'How long now?' he demands.

His companion in the belly of the Junker holds up the fingers of two hands. Ten minutes. Harry checks his parachute.

'I thought you were some kind of superman,' the RHSA agent shouts. 'You should be able to fly.'

Harry knows the man only by his first name, Otto.

'The stories about me are wildly exaggerated,' Harry tells him. 'Drop me out of a plane from ten thousand feet without a functioning parachute and I will die, just like any other man.'

He peels off the flying jacket and replaces it with the trench coat he's going to wear when he lands in Ireland. He straps on a small rucksack. It contains a change of clothes and some other items. 'What's more, I feel the cold just like you do.'

Otto nods. 'I've been intrigued by all the stories about you. I just wondered what the truth was.'

Keep wondering, Harry thinks. You won't get anything out of me. For the next few minutes they sit side by side, listening to the steady growl of the Junker's engines then, finally, Otto opens the door and points down. Cold air rushes in and stings their eyes.

'Ireland,' Otto says simply.

Harry holds onto both sides of the door. 'Tell me when to jump.'

He watches the greyish green land rushing beneath him. The seconds tick by then Otto slaps him on the back.

'Go,' he shouts, 'and good luck.'

Harry grins. 'I don't need luck.'

Then he's gone. His parachute blossoms in the sky like a white flower. High above, a patch of cold starlight shows between the clouds. The ground is soon rushing up at him. Harry bends his legs and executes a textbook landing. Unhurriedly, he gathers his parachute. In minutes he has used the small shovel from his rucksack to bury it. That done, he glances around him. He should be *in County Monaghan, near to Clones. From here it's a short journey across the border into Northern Ireland. Tomorrow night, Harry thinks, I'll be on the ferry from Belfast to Liverpool. That's when the excitement really begins.*

Twenty-three

London, Tuesday, 7 January, 1941

Hugh Cotton was on his way home from the BBC. 'Professor Voss,' he murmured. 'Well, well.' He stumbled over some chunks of masonry that were overlapping the pavement. When he tripped over the rubble, he almost dropped the armful of books he was carrying.

He hugged his precious tomes. He had his evening mapped out already. The fat volumes he was carrying would fill in the gaps in Paul's knowledge of his family's past. The boy had come along at just the right time. Only yesterday, Cotton had discovered a link between Samuel Rector and his Rat Boys and another part of London's past. He also had another name to follow up in this labyrinthine tale, a civil engineer by the name of Arthur Strachan.

Cotton was keen to collate what he had. But they would have to wait. His attention had been drawn to a scene of utter devastation. His route home had taken him past a row of houses that had been hit in last night's raid. The whole street looked like a mouth with half the teeth knocked out. Everywhere was coated grey with plaster dust and smoke was still rising from the scorched beams. The nearest house was nothing but a latticework of blackened roof timbers, twisted girders and sagging tiles. Cotton stopped and gazed at the torn frame of the exposed staircase. A family's belongings were still strewn about. There were the remains of a candlewick bedspread, a toy pram and the twisted wreckage of an Ascot gas heater. Cotton became aware of a middle-aged man standing next to him.

'Mate, it was Hell on earth here last night,' he said. 'Blimey, you should have seen the fires!'

'How many were hurt?' Cotton asked.

'Hurt?' the man said. 'There were three dead in this street alone, one of them a little girl.'

Cotton instinctively looked at the toy pram. 'How awful.'

'Bleedin' criminal,' his neighbour said. 'Come over here.' He pointed to a crater. 'Look at that. What diameter do you think it is?'

'I don't know,' Cotton said, 'a few feet.'

'That's a hundred-pound bomb,' the man said. 'Now

old Adolf's thumping us with thousand pounders. He wants to knock the living daylights out of us, he does.'

Cotton nodded. 'Yes, I'd say that's about the size of it.'

The man fired off his parting comment. 'A right liberty, that's what I call it.'

Cotton watched him go. He had half a dozen conversations like that every day. London was full of bomb bores, instant experts who had nothing better to do than try to lecture you about the ins and outs of aerial bombardment. With a sigh, he turned towards home. Cotton's street had thankfully been spared the worst. There were few signs of bomb damage. He reached his building and opened the door. Once inside, he checked his mail then climbed to the second floor where he had a large bachelor flat. He had been engaged to Pam Hitchin for two years but he was increasingly reluctant to give up his independence. He liked the single man's existence. He wondered whether they would ever tie the knot.

Setting down his books on the landing table, Cotton fumbled for his keys in his jacket pocket. He couldn't quite put his finger on why, but he hesitated before inserting the key in the lock. Finally, he turned the key and entered. It was as if there had been an intruder, somebody who sat in his armchair and ran his fingers over his bookcase. Everything was in the right place but the rooms had undergone a subtle transformation. It was all a question of atmosphere.

There it was again, a faint smell, a kind of animal

musk. The first time he smelled it, the day he met that strange boy in the church, he wondered about rats. He'd even put out poison and a couple of traps. But there was no sign of vermin. Nonetheless, he didn't feel at home here any longer. He had lost his peace of mind. Every time he entered the hallway, Evil whispered to him. It slid round corners and cackled behind his ear.

Cotton put his books on the desk. As he let go, his fingers were unsteady. He scanned the room. There, he told himself, everything is as it should be. But he couldn't escape the thought that he was sharing the flat with somebody. Yes, not something but some*body*.

It was only with the greatest difficulty that he forced himself to go and make a cup of tea. He stood in the kitchen, waiting for the kettle to boil and listened. There were the barely audible sounds that he had been hearing ever since he was forced to flee the church. He poured out the tea with a trembling hand and carried the cup into the living room. The moment he stepped through the door he gasped and dropped the drink. The cup smashed, spraying hot, brown liquid across the mat.

The moving shadows that had been slinking around the walls for days had finally combined, forming a dark spiral in the middle of the floor. Cotton stared, watching the black vortex emerge, accelerate. It was utterly hypnotic. Then he saw the first shapes, a dark figure, a kind of building, very bright, but far away. In spite of the intense sense of foreboding that was creeping over him, Cotton forced himself to look.

'The white chapel,' he murmured, remembering his research.

White spires. White walls. There was Christ Church, Spitalfields of course, where he had first met Paul. But the chapel Cotton saw now was different. Evil dwelt within it. Then the screeching began, a chorus of tortured howls and wails that seemed to emanate from the wall of that strange, white church. The spirit of Hell had awoken.

'Who are you?' Cotton croaked, seeing the dark figure emerging from the vortex. 'Why don't you speak?'

A tongue of dark flame licked from the spinning whirlpool and crackled through the air.

'Bring me the boy,' a voice demanded. 'You must bring me the boy.'

'No,' Cotton cried, 'go away. Leave me alone.' He could sense the wreaths of black flame licking around him, folding him in its hot embrace.

'You must bring me the boy!' the voice growled.

'I can't. I don't know where he is.'

'You met him,' the voice boomed in contradiction. 'I saw the boy. He had a girl with him.'

Cotton's scalp froze.

'You know!' Lud snarled.

The black flame licked towards Cotton, splitting into two smaller tongues. They floated mere inches from his eyes.

'When are you going to see him again?' Lud demanded.

Cotton was determined not to betray his young friend. 'I'm not.'

The flame probed his face, the points of black fire hesitating less than a quarter of an inch now from Cotton's eyes. Then they blazed forward, searing his eyeballs and slashing deep into his consciousness. Cotton screamed.

'Don't lie to me!' the voice howled, almost splitting Cotton's mind in two. 'I'll roast you on the fires of Hell. Can you imagine the agony I can inflict?'

The black fire scorched through Cotton's veins. He screamed again, this time in helpless agony.

'Can you?'

'Yes,' Cotton answered, barely conscious. 'Please, no more. I'll do anything, just stop torturing me. I can't bear it.'

'You will arrange a meeting with the renegade Paul Rector,' the voice answered. 'Don't think about warning him of my presence. I am always looking over your shoulder, Hugh Cotton. You can't escape my stare. You know that, don't you?'

Cotton felt as if a swarm of insects had alighted on his skin. 'Yes.'

'When you need me,' the dark, shimmering figure told him, 'just say my name. I am Lud.'

Cotton could barely stand. He steadied himself by resting a hand on his writing desk.

'I am Lud and I will have this boy. Serve me, Cotton.

Serve me or suffer the consequences. I know how to prolong a man's death throes for months, years before I give him peace. You understand that, don't you?'

'Yes.'

'So you will serve me? You are my slave?'

'Yes.'

The black flame retreated. Hugh Cotton stood, his eyes closed, not daring to look into the face of Lud. When he finally reopened them the vortex was gone. He went over to the sash window and opened it. He drew a shuddering breath into his lungs. Fog was rolling over the city and the light was fading. It would be dark soon. But, with Lud's voice floating through his brain, Cotton wasn't looking forward to going to bed. He wouldn't sleep a wink that night.

Twenty-four

Irish Sea, Tuesday, 7 January, 1941

Harry's on the Belfast to Liverpool ferry, leaning against the railings. It's a fine night, if choppy. He's in high spirits. After months kicking his heels in Germany here he is, speeding, or rather chugging towards his destiny. He watches the perfect black waves and the cresting bubbles. He feels the sharp kiss of the sea spray on his skin and looks forward to England. Most days Harry would prefer his creature comforts to a windlashed deck but it's refreshing to take the night air. He listens to the sounds of the packed bar. Raucous laughter eddies out into the night. Soon he hears an unsteady tread on the deck. A drunk is reeling towards the railings. He's going to be sick. Suddenly the boat pitches and he staggers into Harry.

'Watch where you're going,' the drunk slurs.

Harry turns slowly and shakes his head. He looks the man up and down. 'Don't go blaming me because you can't take your drink.' He knows he's being provocative, but he can't help it. He hasn't had any fun since the assault on Schloss Drachenhohle. His words draw the inevitable reaction.

'You give me an apology right now,' the drunk says, 'or I'll teach you some manners. I was Ulster under-eighteen amateur champion. Middleweight. You've probably heard of me. I'm Billy Gray.'

'Run along back to your pals, son,' Harry drawls, making a show of indifference. 'Goodnight, Billy.'

Billy's eyes flash and he makes a grab for Harry.

Harry evades it easily. 'This is your last chance to walk away,' he warns the Ulsterman. 'If you don't you'll have to face the consequences.' He grins. He knows Billy's going to do no such thing.

'Are you trying to wind me up?' Billy demands.

Harry laughs. 'I didn't see any key in your back.'

'Don't try to be funny with me,' Billy cries. 'I'll rip your throat out, so I will.'

He swings at Harry and punches thin air. Immediately, Harry darts out a hand. He seizes Billy by the neck. His fingers are like bands of steel in Billy's flesh.

The Ulsterman struggles for air. 'Let me go, you madman. I can't breathe.'

Harry smirks. 'Say sorry and I'll let you walk away.'

Billy responds with a string of swear words.

Harry shakes his head. 'You haven't got much

common sense, have you son? You're what I call a silly Billy.' He considers what to do. 'I thought you were going to rip my throat out. Maybe I should show you how it's done.'

Billy Gray's eyes widen in horror as Harry undergoes a macabre transformation. He sees the merciless eyes of the blood wolf.

'No!'

'Too late,' the blood wolf snarls. 'You had your chance. Now it's my turn.'

Fangs tear into soft flesh. Billy's feet drum for a moment on the deck then his eyes roll back and he is still. The only sound that competes with the boom of the wind is the wet crackle of chewing, followed by a loud splash as a body falls into the sea.

Twenty-five

London, Wednesday, 8 January, 1941

Paul dreamed he returned to Christ Church Spitalfields. In the way of dreams, the church doors
opened by themselves. Dust and street litter danced
ahead of him. He saw his man sitting on a chair at the
far end of the building just as he had seen Hugh Cotton
that first time. He walked along the aisle, his footsteps
echoing loudly. Strangely, each footfall started to
pound more loudly than the last until there was
thunder crashing inside Paul's head. He wanted to cry
out, so intense was the clashing sound, but suddenly
the hammer blows ceased and a sepulchral silence
descended upon the building. Paul drew level with the
seated man.

'I'm Paul,' he said. But when the man turned it

wasn't Hugh Cotton's face Paul saw. The features belonged instead to Harry Rector. 'You!'

Paul took a step back. There was a gleam of teeth. Harry was smiling. But it was a chilling, hideously menacing grin. Then Paul knew why Harry's smile disturbed him so. There was blood on his teeth. Paul shrank back in horror.

'Something wrong, Paul?' Harry asked.

'Your mouth,' Paul stammered. 'There's blood.'

Harry wiped his mouth and looked at the scarlet smear on the back of his hand. Then he winked and licked it off.

'There's always blood, Paul,' he said. 'That's just the way things are.' He pinched Paul's cheek. 'You should know. You're part of the demon brotherhood and boys will be boys.'

Instantly, the doors of the church blew open and a cold wind howled.

'I know this,' Paul said, his voice mixing with the dreamlike music of the wind. 'I've seen it before.'

'Have you, Paul?' Harry asked. 'Have you really?'

Then he raised his hands and rose into the air. With a final smirk, he rode the wind out across the London skyline.

'No,' Paul cried. 'Come back.'

Even before the words left his lips, invisible arms seized him and swept him out into the night sky. Paul tilted his head and saw Harry silhouetted against the moonlight. London raced by below. Paul saw the Thames just as he had seen it before. This time he didn't fall. His journey went on and on, northwards over hills and valleys, mountains and glistening lakes, darkened cities and roads. A grey sea came next, ribbed by white-crested waves.

'Where are you taking me?' Paul cried to the formless spirits that were bearing him forward through the night.

At last Paul saw the ferry. Harry was waiting. Paul watched helplessly as the demon assassin fed on his dying victim. Then, as casually as if he was tossing a rubbish sack overboard, Harry consigned Billy Gray to the waves.

The moment Paul was fully awake, he kicked off the clothes and leaped out of bed. Throwing open the door, he pounded along the landing.

'Temple,' he screamed, 'you've got to wake up.'

He beat his fists against the door.

'Wake up,' he yelled again. 'It's Harry. I know where he is.'

Temple opened the door to his room. 'What in God's name are you doing, Paul?' he asked. 'It's half past five in the morning.'

'I saw Harry,' Paul told him, ignoring the questions. 'He killed a man.'

Connie was staring over her husband's shoulder. Behind her, Denis started crying.

'You've woken the baby,' Temple said. 'Have you taken leave of your senses?'

Paul forced himself to speak slowly, with

deliberation. 'You've got to listen,' he panted. 'Harry's coming.'

He saw Temple blink. He had the detective's attention. 'What?'

'I saw Harry. He was on a boat. Temple, it's begun.'

Temple saw Connie's startled expression and grabbed Paul by the arm. 'Let's talk downstairs.' He sat Paul down in the parlour. 'Now, tell me what you saw. I want every detail.'

The story came gushing out. 'Harry was on the deck of a boat. He was struggling with a younger man. Not struggling really, he was devouring him.'

'Devouring him?'

'Yes, he ripped his throat wide open.'

Temple remembered Shadow's needle teeth.

'He was a kind of wild beast,' Paul said, 'but I knew him anyway. He had blood on his teeth and his clothing. He took his shirt off and wiped away the blood. Then he threw it into the sea. He was so calm. He'd killed a man but he just discarded his shirt, opened his rucksack and put on a new one. He didn't look angry. He wasn't even breathing heavily. He didn't show any feelings at all.'

Temple interrogated Paul. What kind of boat was it? Was there any background noise? Had he seen any signs or notices, anything that might give them a clue to Harry's whereabouts? Temple knew what he was doing. Soon he had extracted enough information to place Harry on the Belfast-Liverpool ferry. Temple left the room.

'Where are you going?' Paul called after him.

'To phone Ketsch,' Temple hissed. 'Now keep your voice down. Connie's trying to get Denis back to sleep.'

Paul waited impatiently at the breakfast table. He could hear Connie pacing the floor upstairs. Finally, Temple re-entered the kitchen.

'Did you call Ketsch?' Paul demanded. 'Did you tell them what I saw?'

'I've just got off the phone.' He tugged at his ear lobe. 'I told him I'd got an anonymous tip-off. He wanted more information but I could hardly tell him how I knew Harry's whereabouts, could I?'

'But he's going to act on it?' Paul asked.

Temple nodded. 'It wasn't easy but Ketsch agreed to get in touch with Liverpool. As it happens we've got a Special Branch officer up there on another matter.'

Paul stiffened. 'One man?'

'Yes, one man.'

'You're joking, right?'

Temple raised an eyebrow. 'Ketsch was reluctant to even agree to that.'

'Surely you can't be that stupid, Temple,' Paul snapped. 'You've seen one of the demons. Tell me this man's got back-up.'

'I'm afraid not.'

'You've sent one man?' Paul cried. 'One man against Harry. Don't you understand? You've sent him to his death.'

'There's no need to get so het up,' Temple said, giving Paul an indulgent smile. 'I know Tom

173

Wainwright. Believe me, he's no novice. He knows how to handle himself.'

Paul wasn't about to be fobbed off. He stared the detective down.

'Have you forgotten Shadow?' he shot back angrily. 'Just think about it for a moment, will you? You wouldn't have survived without my help. Your friend's walking into this with his eyes closed. He doesn't even understand what he's dealing with.'

The smile left Temple's face. 'You think Harry will spot Tom?'

Paul crashed his fist down on the table.

'Of course he will,' he said. 'Harry's close to Lud, as close as you can get. He's a prince among assassins. He'll be able to spot surveillance a mile away.'

'You're serious, aren't you?' Temple said. 'You think he'll kill Tom?'

Paul nodded. 'There's nothing more certain.'

Twenty-six

Liverpool, Wednesday, 8 January, 1941

Tom Wainwright doesn't know the danger he's in. Harry spots the Special Branch detective the moment he disembarks from the ferry. He sets off in the direction of the Pier Head. Detective Sergeant Tom Wainwright follows at a discrete distance.

So this is the famous Harry Rector, Wainwright thinks. He's read Harry's file. It's a catalogue of robberies and acts of violence. Where's Harry been hiding himself all this time? Wainwright decides to tail Harry as far as he can then phone Ketsch. He's been given a watching brief only. Wainwright has a hunch where Harry's going, of course. At the Pier Head, he expects Harry to turn left and cut across the city centre to Lime Street station. Harry's planning to catch a train to London.

But things don't go according to plan. Harry wrong-foots Wainwright by entering a café. While Wainwright kicks his heels across the road, Harry orders tea and hot-buttered toast. From his window seat Harry sips his tea and watches the detective.

'So how did you get on to me so quickly?' he murmurs. Harry notices the waitress looking at him.

'Don't mind me,' she says with a winning smile. 'I talk to myself too. At least you know you're having an intelligent conversation.'

Harry grins. She's a pretty girl and she looks interested in him. But he keeps his thoughts to himself after that. He orders another pot of tea and a scone. He picks up a magazine from the next table and leafs through it like he has all the time in the world. There's an article about Madeleine Carroll, star of The Thirty-nine Steps *and* The Prisoner of Zenda. *He likes the idea of keeping the detective waiting.*

'I'll pay you now,' Harry tells the waitress. 'How much?'

'That's a shilling to you, handsome,' she says. Definitely interested.

Harry adds a shiny sixpence to the shilling.

'That's for lighting up my morning,' he says. 'It's a pity I've got to catch a train or I'd ask you to go to the pictures with me. They're showing Seven Sinners.'

'Oh, John Wayne and Marlene Dietrich. I've been meaning to go for a while. I'd have said yes.'

'Then it would have been nine sinners,' Harry observes.

The waitress blushes. 'You're a bit forward, aren't you?'

'Yes,' Harry says, 'forward enough to ask your name. I'll probably be back up this way in a week or so.'

'I'm Marie,' the waitress says.

Harry watches her all the way to the counter, admiring the sway of her hips, then he turns his gaze back to the detective. There's only one way the authorities are on to him so soon. This is the renegade Rector's doing. Maybe he will prove to be more of a challenge than Harry thought. Harry's heard the legend of the renegade demon but he's never given it much credence. What can one turncoat do against the small army Lud has at his disposal?

'Hey Marie,' Harry calls. 'There isn't a back way out of here, is there?'

'Oh, don't tell me the bobbies are after you,' Marie groans. 'Why are all the good-looking men trouble?'

'It's nothing serious,' Harry said. 'It's just a bit of black market. Now what's wrong with flogging a few silk stockings to the lovely ladies, answer me that?'

Marie smiles. 'You don't have any on you, do you?'

'Sorry,' Harry says. 'Maybe when I return. Now what about that back way?'

Marie shows him. There's a door in the far corner of the kitchen.

Harry gives her a peck on the cheek. 'You're a little smasher,' he says. 'I'm going to show you a good time on my way home.'

Marie blushes. 'Get away with you,' she says. 'I bet you never come this way again.'

'I will, you know,' Harry says. 'Did anybody tell you you've got a look of Madeleine Carroll?'

'And you're my Robert Donat, I suppose?'

'That's right,' Harry says with a wink, 'devilishly handsome and full of thrills.'

Then he's gone. Thirty seconds later, Wainwright bursts through that door.

'Where's he gone?' he demands. 'The tall man, athletic-looking.'

Marie's gaze flicks instinctively towards the back of the café. Wainwright throws the door open and steps into a cobbled alley. Seeing it deserted, he curses.

'Lost him,' he says. He jogs to the end of the alley and looked right and left. 'Damn!'

Some tracker I am, Wainwright thinks. But the hunter has just become the hunted. Harry has been hiding in the yard of a neighbouring shop. He's now standing right behind Wainwright.

'Looking for somebody?' Harry says.

Wainwright spins round. Seeing Harry there, his jaw drops.

'Oh, don't look so surprised,' Harry says. 'I spotted you the moment I walked down the gangplank. Did you bring me a welcome home present?'

Recovering himself, Wainwright decides to make the best of a botched operation. 'Harry Rector,' he says. 'My name is DS Thomas Wainwright. I would like to ask you a few questions.'

'I bet you would,' Harry says. 'Trouble is, I don't want to answer them.'

Wainwright is left tongue-tied for a moment.

'Now,' Harry says, 'look into my eyes.'

Wainwright fails to avert his gaze in time and plunges into Harry's nightmare world.

Harry shows him his father and brother on their death beds, dying horribly from cancer.

'That's your future, Tommy boy. Recognize them. That's Daddy on the right. The other one's your older brother, Clive. Cancer runs in the family. You've lain awake nights worrying if you're next. You've tried to tell yourself you're different, the exception to the rule, the one who can laugh in the face of death. Well, you're wrong. You're going to die in agony the way they did.'

Tom Wainwright sees an image of himself, wasted and yellow on a hospital bed.

'That's you in another ten years.'

But Wainwright doesn't just see the horror. He feels it. He drowns in it. The sickness claws at his flesh. The tumours gnaw deep into the very heart of him. When Marie uses the back door as a shortcut home an hour later, she finds Wainwright spread-eagled on the cobbles.

Twenty-seven

London, Thursday, 9 January, 1941

Paul discovered Temple at the breakfast table.

'I was right, wasn't I?' Paul asked. 'He killed your friend.'

Temple didn't answer directly. 'I should have listened to you.' To Paul's surprise, Temple's face brightened. 'But Tom isn't dead. A waitress found him in an alley yesterday morning. He's recovering in hospital.'

'Thank God,' Paul said. 'Your friend will never know how lucky he is. Harry could have killed him if he'd wished.'

'There's no doubt about that,' Temple said. 'You say you've got the same power. You're like Harry. You can kill people with a stare. But how can you know, unless . . . ?' His voice trailed off. 'You've used it, haven't you? You killed someone. Paul, I've got to know, who was the victim?'

Paul looked away.

'You have to tell me,' Temple said. 'How can I trust you if you don't? You're living under the same roof as my wife and child. Speak to me.'

Paul relented. 'I told you about Redman, didn't I?'

Temple nodded.

'He was my brother, John Redman,' Paul said. 'I killed my own brother.'

Temple stared. Horror swept over his flesh. Paul explained what had happened. He was halting at first, then his voice strengthened and he told the rest of the tale in a matter-of-fact way.

'King Lud had John for eight years. He sent him back to us full of evil, just like Harry. He killed his victims with relish. It was all a game to him. If I hadn't stopped him, John would have carried on killing. So I found the thing that he feared. It was fire.' The final words came out in a whisper. 'I burned him . . . alive.'

Temple felt a cold current eddy through his veins.

'I held him tight and watched him struggle,' Paul said. His manner was cold, deliberate. 'When he screamed I kept on holding. When he begged for mercy, I gave none. It wasn't easy, but I did it. I replaced his face with the faces of his victims. Do you still think you know me, Temple?'

Temple still felt the icy shudder up and down his spine. There were hidden depths to this boy he had invited into his home. 'Dear God!'

'It was the only way,' Paul said. He wanted forgiveness, absolution. 'He wasn't my brother any more. He was a demon. Lud turned him into a killer. It had to end.'

And end it did, with pleading, and pain, and horror. The savagery of what he'd had to do would never leave him.

'Even so,' Temple said. 'Your own brother . . .'

'It's something I have to live with,' Paul said. 'Maybe if you want to fight monsters you have to become one yourself.'

That was his worst fear, that the demon seed would one day claim him and make him like the others. He remembered the moment John's skin began to burn. He hadn't just felt revulsion. He'd felt *power*, the thrill of being in total command of another human being. It had been the same with Shadow. It scared him that he had been exhilarated by an act of murder. In those moments, he had grown to hate the person the demon seed had made him.

'Turn into a monster?' Temple said. 'You don't believe that.'

Paul shrugged. Temple couldn't see into the depths of Paul's soul. He didn't see the shadows that gathered there. Paul had been living with what he'd done for weeks. He'd tried to persuade himself that he'd acted in self-defence, but looking himself in the mirror wasn't getting any easier.

'You came here to save Mr Churchill,' Temple said.

'Isn't that an act of courage and self-sacrifice? Don't tell me you don't know what you're fighting for.'

The front door went and Paul heard Evelyn's voice. Temple kept an eye on the door, just in case she appeared. He didn't want his inquisitive niece eavesdropping. He patted Paul's shoulder. 'Don't worry, I'll stop Harry.'

'Where are you going?' Paul asked.

'Euston,' Temple told him. 'I'm meeting the first Liverpool train.'

'You're not going alone?' Paul asked.

'No, I've learned my lesson. Let's just hope Harry's on it.'

'And if he's not?'

It was Temple's turn to shrug.

'You should let me come,' Paul said.

Temple shook his head. 'Sorry, old son. Ketsch would never countenance it. He lives by the rule book.'

'But I can help.'

'You're going to stay here, Paul. That's an order.' Without another word, Temple picked up his battered leather briefcase and his hat and left.

'Uncle George is in a bit of a hurry,' Evelyn said, breezing into the parlour.

Paul stared out of the window. He watched the Bullnose Oxford pull away.

'Paul,' Evelyn said, 'is something wrong?'

'It's the devils,' Paul replied. 'They're coming.' He made his decision. 'Temple isn't going to leave me out of this.'

Evelyn was excited. 'Then I'm coming too.'

'You can't,' Paul said. 'Temple will be angry enough about me turning up.'

'If you try to leave me out of this,' Evelyn retorted. 'I'll have a word with Aunt Connie. Then neither of us will go.'

Paul met her gaze. He didn't doubt that she was telling the truth.

'That's agreed then,' Evelyn crowed. 'I'll cook up a story that will keep Aunt Connie happy.'

'You've done this before, haven't you?' Paul asked.

Evelyn winked. 'Once or twice.'

They travelled into central London by train.

'Did you see our photo in the *Mirror*?' Evelyn asked.

'Sorry,' Paul said, his mind still on Harry, 'what did you say?'

'The picture of us in Trafalgar Square,' Evelyn said. 'It was in yesterday's paper.'

For a moment, Harry slipped from Paul's thoughts. 'You're joking!'

'No,' Evelyn said, 'I left a message with Uncle George. Didn't he pass it on? Honestly, he's so scatter-brained.'

Paul looked at the picture on page two. It was exactly as the photographer had described it: *Young sweethearts defy Blitz*. It showed them hurrying arm in arm through a cloud of fluttering pigeons. Paul gazed at the picture and wondered what Netty would have made of it. Their eyes were bright and their faces flushed, as if there wasn't a cloud in the sky. But there were several, and the most ominous was called Harry Rector. Paul filled in some of the details.

'And you're related to him?' Evelyn asked.

'Yes,' Paul said, 'I'm afraid so.'

From time to time, he looked out of the window. The journey took them past houses that had been reduced to shattered ruins. Here and there people were queuing for water at a standpipe. They passed a shop. Its front had been blown out but there was a sign: 'more open than usual.'

At Euston, they walked through the ticket hall and peered into the main concourse.

'We'd better stop here,' Paul said.

Temple was standing at the ticket barrier. Superintendent John Ketsch and a body of uniformed and plain clothes officers were also in attendance. Evelyn tried to speak but Paul shushed her.

'I'm trying to listen,' he said.

Ketsch was speaking. 'The train gets in at ten o'clock.'

Temple nodded.

'I'd like to know more about this tip-off of yours,' Ketsch said. 'Have a report on my desk on Monday morning.'

'Can you hear them?' Evelyn asked.

'Yes,' Paul replied. 'Why, can't you?'

'Of course I can't. They're all the way over there.'

Paul estimated the distance. Evelyn was right. In normal circumstances, he would never have overheard them.

'So you *do* have other powers,' she said.

'Yes,' Paul said, 'I must do.' He watched the huge steam engines. Clouds of white smoke drifted across the platforms when one pulled in or out.

'Harry won't be on the train,' Paul said.

'How do you know?' Evelyn asked.

'Think about it,' Paul said. 'He spotted Wainwright. He knows we're onto him. He'll find another route to London.'

'But there must be so many ways he could make his way to London,' Evelyn said. 'I don't see how the police can intercept him. Uncle George says the armed forces have taken most of the Met's best officers.'

Five minutes later the Liverpool train pulled into the platform. Ketsch supervised and Temple joined the search of the carriages. Harry wasn't on board.

'What happens next?' Evelyn wondered out loud.

'I've no idea,' Paul said. 'Harry could be anywhere.'

Twenty-eight

15 November, present day

Netty Carney is doing some homework at the Idea Store in Whitechapel. She's with her best friend Charlotte. They've just joined the queue for something to eat in the café on the fourth floor.

'There's still no news about Paul?' Charlotte asks.

'Nothing,' Netty said.

'You don't think . . .'

Instinctively, they both glanced out of the window in the direction of the old Board School in Durward Street. That's where their teacher, Mrs Petersen, was murdered.

Netty shook her head. 'The killer's dead. It was Redman. You know that. No, Paul's alive somewhere. I feel it.'

Charlotte sounded sympathetic. 'You must miss him.'

'Of course I do,' Netty replied, 'desperately.' She wanted to unburden herself to Charlotte and tell her the true story of Paul's disappearance, but that just wasn't possible. They reached the front of the queue and ordered soft drinks and toasted sandwiches, then went to a table overlooking Whitechapel.

'Do you still see Paul's mum?' Charlotte asked.

'I've been round a couple of times,' Netty answered. 'It's pretty uncomfortable, really. I don't know what to say. She looks awful.'

'No wonder,' Charlotte said, 'she's lost two sons. I can't imagine how that must make you feel.'

They finished their sandwiches and drinks and walked to the lift. Suddenly, Netty stopped dead. Just round the corner from the café, the Idea Store had mounted a display of photos. The small exhibition was called 'Wartime London'.

'What are you looking at?' Charlotte asked. She followed Netty's stare. 'No way!' She took a couple of steps forward and examined the photograph, published Wednesday, 8 January, 1941 in the *Daily Mirror*. 'It can't be.' She laughed. 'No wonder you look shocked, Netty. This lad's the spitting image of Paul.'

But Netty knew it *was* Paul. She continued to stare at the couple: a pretty, dark-haired girl and her Paul. He was wearing a flannel shirt and worsted trousers. His tweed sports jacket flapped open. But it wasn't his appearance that drew Netty's gaze, it was the expression on his face. He was clinging to the girl's arm, his cheek pressed against hers, and he was beaming into the camera. She couldn't remember the last time she'd seen him looking so happy.

'Mrs Rector,' Netty said later that afternoon, 'it's me, Netty.' She knocked again. 'It's about Paul.'

Paul's mum finally appeared. There was no welcoming smile. Just a flat question. 'What do you want?'

'I've got something to show you.' Netty had persuaded the Idea Store staff to take the Trafalgar Square photo down for a moment and photocopy it for her. She handed over the reproduction and watched as Paul's mum's hand flew to her face.

'Paul!' Her expression changed. Her eyes filled with tears, joy and misery in equal parts. 'Netty, it's my boy, he's alive and well.'

Netty realised the woman needed somebody to hold and took her in her arms. 'It's good news, Mrs Rector.'

Netty let her sob into her shoulder for several moments, then they sat down in the living room.

'Where did you find it?' Mum demanded.

Netty explained.

'*He did it*,' Mum said. 'Netty, he crossed over. He went back seventy years.' She fingered the picture. 'He looks so happy.'

Netty felt a pang of jealousy. It was true. He was happy, and without her.

'I wonder who this is?' Mum wondered.

Netty shook her head. 'There was no information

about the photo. The librarian had a reproduction of the newspaper but it was a one-line caption. It didn't mention their names.

'May I keep this?' Mum asked.

'Of course,' Netty told her, 'this one's yours. I got two copies.' She caught the other woman's eye. 'Have the police been back?'

Mum nodded. 'Yes, DS Hussein has called three times in all. It feels very strange. Both of us know we won't find him in London, at least not this London. We just go through the motions.'

They talked for a while then Netty glanced at the clock. 'I'd better get going. Mum will worry if I stay out too late.'

Paul's Mum walked her to the door. 'Of course. You will come again, won't you? You're the only one I can talk to.'

On the way to the tube, Netty pulled out the photo and looked at it. Who are you, she wondered, looking at the girl by Paul's side. Then, in a fit of pique, she dropped it in a litter bin. A few metres up the road she stopped. She glanced back, turning things over in her mind. Finally, she retraced her steps and retrieved the picture. Without looking at it, she folded it once and slipped it into her jacket pocket before carrying on to Mile End tube.

Twenty-nine

Manchester, Thursday, 9 January, 1941

Harry has just walked into the yard of a haulage company half a mile from Victoria Station. A man in a worn sports jacket and corduroy trousers is standing at the door of the office. It's little more than a shed.

'Alfie Baxter?' Harry asks.

'That's right,' Baxter says. 'What can I do for you?'

'Let's talk in there,' Harry says.

Baxter blinks. Is this man trying to order him around in his own yard?

'Look here . . .' he starts.

'You've been expecting a call from my company, Whitechapel Parts,' Harry says, giving Baxter the agreed password. 'I decided to come in person.'

Baxter understands immediately. 'Follow me.'

Once inside the office, Baxter holds out his right hand.
'It's a pleasure to meet you,' I'm honoured to be of service.
To think, an agent of the Reich in my yard.'

Harry cuts him off with a glance. He leaves Baxter's
hand hanging in the air

'You're going to drive me to Leeds,' he says.

Baxter hears the snap of authority in his voice.

'Whatever you say.'

Baxter's ready to go in ten minutes. As they turn left
out of the yard towards the Pennines, Baxter turns to
talk to Harry. He's keen to ingratiate himself.

'I was in the movement for five years,' he says, fawning
over Harry. 'I met the Leader several times.'

Harry scowls. These stupid, little men with their
stupid, little politics. Baxter's Leader is the English
aristocrat Sir Oswald Mosley, founder of an organisa-
tion called the British Union of Fascists. He fancied
himself as the English Hitler. Now he's rotting in jail, a
traitor to his country.

'What's your mission?' Baxter asks excitedly. 'Is the
invasion coming?'

Harry's head snaps round. 'Spies are supposed to be
discreet,' he warned. 'I think you should try it.'

They complete the rest of the journey in silence. When
Baxter stops the lorry, Harry fixes him with a stare.
Baxter sees the nightmare world beyond his dark eyes.

'Let me give you a word of advice,' Harry says. 'Don't
breathe a word about this trip to anybody.'

'You can rely on me,' Baxter says, 'I . . .'

'That's enough,' Harry says. 'Just keep your mouth shut.'

Without another word, he climbs out of the cab and walks off in the direction of the railway station. Later that day he's presenting his forged identity papers to Brian Sullivan, the manager of a large, rambling house on the outer edge of the East End. The wall is pockmarked by flying shrapnel and there are craters in the open ground to the rear. The house has been converted into an emergency hostel for single men who've been made homeless by the bombing. It provides a hot breakfast, an evening dinner and a take-away lunch, all for the price of a pound a week. It's exactly the kind of anonymous refuge Harry needs.

'You'll need a shilling to operate the gas meter,' Sullivan says. 'Heating isn't included in the weekly charge.'

'That's fair enough,' Harry says. 'I might be homeless. I don't expect charity.'

He looks around the poky room. The carpet and furnishings have got a tired, worn appearance. There are dusty wax flowers in a chipped vase on the window sill and the thin, faded curtains hang limply from a cracked pelmet. The light bulbs have paper caps. Cardboard has replaced two of the window panes. It isn't exactly the Ritz but it will do. Harry knows he won't be staying long. He glances at the ceiling. In places the plaster is missing.

'That was done in a raid ten days ago,' Sullivan explains, seeing the way Harry's examining the damage.

'I wish I was young enough to enlist in the Forces. Why, for two pins I'd . . .'

'This will do me just fine,' Harry says, interrupting him and ushering him towards the door. 'It's such a relief to have a roof over my head again. You can go now.'

'I was only . . .'

'I said,' Harry repeated, 'you can go. If I wanted your life history, I'd ask for it.'

'Look,' Sullivan says, 'I was only trying to make you feel at home. Most of my guests are glad of a chinwag, after what old Adolf's put them through.'

'Well I don't,' Harry retorts. 'I like my privacy, thank you very much. To be quite honest, I'm sick of hearing about the War. You've shown me the room. I'm sure you've got things to do.'

Sullivan opens the door to go. The next time he speaks, his tone of voice is frosty.

'If you need anything, just knock on the door that says Private,' he says.

'I'll remember,' Harry tells him.

As Sullivan's tread fades along the landing, muttering under his breath that you can't help some people, Harry peers through one of the remaining window panes and gazes out across the rooftops. After an interval of a couple of years, he's back in his East End. In the distance he can make out a ghost road of shattered stone and tarmac. A London bus with its shuttered headlamps is weaving its way between the bomb craters. Harry smiles to himself. Churchill is close. He can almost smell his victim's blood.

Thirty

London, Thursday, 9 January, 1941

By the time they got back to Enfield, Paul and
Evelyn were in a better mood. It had started to
rain and they were sheltering under Evelyn's umbrella. Paul could smell her hair and his cheek was
pressed against hers. As they crossed the road three
streets from the Temple's house, Paul gave way to
impulse and kissed Evelyn on the cheek, at the same
time slipping his arm round her waist and squeezing.
To his surprise, when they stepped on the pavement,
she drew him close and kissed him on the lips. Her
chest pushed against his. They stood there for a moment, looking at one another and listening to the thud
of the raindrops on the umbrella.

Paul couldn't prevent Netty's face floating into his

mind. Guilt flooded through him. He managed to stammer a few words. 'I didn't expect this to happen.'

Oblivious to his thoughts of home, Evelyn winked. 'I did. You probably think I'm a real Jezebel.'

'I might,' Paul said, 'if I knew what one was.'

'It means a wicked lady,' Evelyn said.

'I'm sure you're not one bit wicked,' Paul told her.

'No,' Evelyn replied, 'I'm not, but I do like you, Paul. I like you very much indeed.'

At that, Paul pulled away slightly. 'That might not be such a good idea.'

'Why?'

'I'll have to go home sometime,' he reminded her.

'Mile End isn't far,' Evelyn said. 'I could come and see you.'

Paul thought of Mum, Netty and his friends and seventy years of history. 'It's further than you'd think.'

Evelyn nudged him in the ribs. 'You're just teasing.'

Paul wondered how he was going to explain. He was still trying to find the words when he saw Hugh Cotton hurrying towards them. The rain had plastered Hugh's blond hair to his skull. His eyes looked wild and afraid. It was obvious something was wrong.

'Hugh,' Paul said, 'what are you doing here?'

'I was trying to find your address,' Cotton said, 'then I saw you crossing the road.' He grabbed Paul's sleeve. 'I've seen him, Paul. I've seen the creature. All those stories, you were right, they're not street mythology. They're true.'

'You've seen Lud!'

Cotton nodded. 'He appeared to me. He came into my home. Is there somewhere we can talk?'

Evelyn was looking from Paul to Hugh and back again. Her eyes were wide with curiosity.

'Not here in the street,' Paul said.

'Not at Aunt Connie's, either,' Evelyn said. 'I don't think Uncle George has told her much. He tries to protect her.'

'Where then?'

'Mum's at work,' Evelyn said. 'We can go to my house. It will only take ten minutes.'

When they reached the suburban terrace, Evelyn shook the rain from her umbrella and slipped it into the stand. Water pooled on the hall floor. 'This way,' she said.

'Tell me what's happened, Hugh,' Paul said. 'Don't leave anything out.'

Cotton explained. 'It's the flat. There's a terrible atmosphere.'

'Atmosphere?'

'Yes, it's oppressive. The heat is stifling, but it's the middle of winter. I can barely breathe when I'm there and I have the distinct impression that I'm not alone. Somebody's watching my every move. Then there's this smell.'

'What kind of smell?'

'Like an animal. But there's something else. It reminds me of sulphur.'

'Brimstone,' Paul said. 'Lud appeared from a dark vortex, didn't he? Did you see the white chapel?'

Cotton nodded. He darted a look at Evelyn, who was riveted, then continued. 'He spoke to me. His thoughts probed into my soul. Paul, I'm scared. I don't want to go back there.'

'Is there anywhere you can stay?'

'I can try,' Cotton answered. 'Pam might consent to it, though she is rather prim and proper.'

'What did Lud say?'

'He told me to deliver you to him.' Cotton's eyes were glassy with fright. 'He threatened me if I didn't get you to come to my flat.' He gnawed at the knuckles of his right hand. 'I had to warn you. I hope I did the right thing.'

'Thanks, Hugh,' Paul said, squeezing Cotton's forearm, 'it would have been so easy to betray me.'

Cotton nodded miserably. 'Don't think I didn't consider it, Paul. I agonized over my decision to come and talk to you. I'm not a brave man. I can't sleep. What am I going to do? I'm in danger, aren't I?'

Paul met Cotton's anxious look. 'Yes, I'm afraid you are.'

Cotton dropped back against the headrest. 'He hurt me, Paul. It felt as if I was being roasted from inside.'

'It wasn't real,' Paul said. 'Demon kind can use your thoughts against you.'

Cotton wasn't reassured. 'The pain was real enough. Lud said he would always be looking over my shoulder. Is that right, Paul? Does he know I'm here?'

'I don't think so,' Paul said.

'He found my flat.'

'You've been researching sites of demon infestations,' Paul said, 'Christ Church Spitalfield, the Ten Bells pub, the location of Samuel Rector's rookery. Maybe that's what put him onto you. He's dangerous but he's not all-powerful. No, it's probably just a threat. But I wouldn't drop my guard. You mustn't return to the flat until I tell you. Do you understand?'

Cotton nodded. 'But what do we do?'

Paul thought for a moment. 'I'm going to talk to Temple. If Lud is planning an ambush for me, we might be able to turn the tables on him.'

Cotton didn't like the sound of that. 'What do you mean?'

'We'll fit in with Lud's plans,' Paul explained. 'But I'm not going alone. You never know, Lud might send Harry. It could actually work to our advantage.'

'You'll need me, won't you?' Cotton asked.

'Yes,' Paul said, 'if we're going to convince Lud. Are you ready for that?'

Cotton ran his palm over his face. 'I'll have to be.'

Paul looked at Evelyn for the first time. 'Do you have a number for Temple at work?'

Evelyn shook her head. 'I don't think so. Mum's never mentioned it.'

Paul stood up. 'Stay here with Hugh. I'm going back to the house to phone Temple. Is that all right?'

Evelyn nodded. 'We'll be fine, won't we Hugh?'

Cotton gave her a thin smile. 'Yes.'

Paul walked to the front door. Unlike Cotton, he wasn't scared by the turn of events; he was excited.

Thirty-one

That evening Hugh Cotton arrived at Pam's flat with an overnight bag and rang the bell. Pam appeared and darted a furtive look down the stairwell.

'Next time, don't ring,' Pam whispered, 'just give a light tap on the door. I think you've got away with it this time, but old Mrs Law's got extraordinary hearing.' She hesitated in the doorway. 'Your phone call gave me a bit of a start.'

Pam hadn't rejected the idea of him staying out of hand. Cotton had an idea why. Pam had heard of so many whirlwind romances, young people marrying suddenly in the shadow of war, that she had started to raise the idea ever more frequently. Cotton had spent the last few weeks putting the dampener on the idea. Suddenly it was in his interests to make her think an early marriage was back on the cards.

'You don't look well,' she said.

He had bags under his eyes and there was a haunted look about him. 'I haven't been sleeping,' he said.

Cotton looked past Pam into the flat. She'd turned the sofa into a makeshift bed.

'I hope this is OK, Hugh,' she said, 'After all, we're not married.'

She heard her landlady's door creak open. Mrs Law had firm rules about gentlemen visitors. 'Come inside,' Pam said, 'we can't talk here in the doorway.'

Cotton followed her and closed the door behind him.

'What's the matter with your flat, anyway?' Pam asked. 'You were rather vague on the phone.'

Realising there was no way he could tell her about the figure that had emerged from a dark portal in the floor, Cotton stumbled through a hasty explanation.

'We've had a bit of bomb damage,' he said.

'Oh, Hugh!'

'Nothing major,' Cotton said, hating having to lie to her, 'a few windows. It's quite superficial. I wasn't in any danger. The landlord says I can move back in when the work's done.'

'And how long will it take?'

'A few days. Is that OK?'

Pam pulled a face. 'That depends on Mrs Law. She's a real stickler, you know.'

'Then Mrs Law mustn't know,' Cotton said.

'Do you think we can keep it a secret?' Pam said, giggling. 'She's got ears like a bat.'

Cotton slipped his arms round Pam's waist, suddenly feeling much closer to her than he had for weeks.

'We'll do our very best,' he whispered, pressing his lips to her cheek. 'It could be quite an adventure.'

Pam wriggled out of his grasp. 'I'm going to make some Ovaltine,' she said. 'It sends me off to sleep. Would you like some?'

'That would be nice,' Cotton replied, smiling.

Pam entered the small kitchen. The moment she was gone, the smile drained from Cotton's face. He couldn't get the monstrous silhouette of King Lud out of his mind.

Thirty-two

London, Friday, 10 January, 1941

Cotton received the phone call at seven p.m. He'd passed Pam's number to Paul.

'Temple says we're going ahead,' Paul told him.

Cotton had been dreading this moment. 'But I thought Ketsch had turned down the operation,' he said.

'You're right,' Paul said, 'he did. He wanted to know where Temple had got his information. What could he say?'

'Then I don't understand,' Cotton said. 'How can we go ahead?'

'Temple knows I'm telling the truth,' Paul explained. 'He's willing to put his career on the line and act without the support of his superiors. He's convinced two of his colleagues to work with us. Temple's called in every favour anybody owes him.'

Cotton was worried. 'But four of us against . . . *that*.'

'It's unofficial,' Paul said. 'Temple was lucky to get Wallace and Sharples. It all depends on you, Hugh. Are you ready for this?'

'What do I have to do?'

'Lud thinks he's got you petrified out of your wits,' Paul began.

Cotton interrupted. 'He's not far wrong.'

'You've got to summon him,' Paul said. 'You're the only one who can do it.'

Cotton didn't argue. As soon as he'd hung up, he threaded his way through the rubble on the approaches to his street and climbed the stairs a frightened man. He went into the bathroom and splashed water over his face then examined his reflection in the mirror – no wonder Pam had been shocked by his appearance. There was the same atmosphere in the flat as when he'd left it. He wished it were rats or some other vermin. Even the bomb blast he'd described to Pam would have been preferable to the dark figure who'd demanded to know the boy's whereabouts. Finally, he plucked up the courage to say the demon master's name.

'Lud,' he said, 'I've talked to the boy. He's agreed to come tomorrow night.'

Cotton walked into the living room and dropped heavily into an armchair. He turned on the wireless and listened to Alvar Liddel. It was a few minutes before he realised that he hadn't taken in a single word of the broadcast. All he could think about was Lud. Surely the creature would see through his lies. Wasn't he bound to sense the trap that was being laid for him? Sighing, Cotton switched the wireless off and sat in silence. Every moment he sat there he was sick with dread, wondering when Lud would appear. He remembered the satanic tongue of black flame and shuddered. Burying his head in his hands, Cotton succumbed to despair.

'God help me,' he said, to himself and the empty, brooding flat.

Still Lud didn't appear. Cotton decided to make himself a cup of tea. Hearing the kettle whistling on the hob, he went over and poured the boiling water into the pot. He was stirring the leaves when there was a blast of heat and the vortex formed – the same spectral light as before, the same dark, translucent figure dominating the room.

'You have some news for me?' Lud asked.

Cotton trembled, even though he knew the creature was unable to take on solid form. Cotton gave Lud the details.

'You've done well.'

Lud was gone as quickly as he had arrived. There was nothing left but a vague animal musk and the powerful aroma of brimstone. Cotton drank his tea to kill a few minutes. He had an idea Lud might still be watching. When he was finally convinced that he was completely alone in those four walls and there were no prying eyes watching his movements, he let himself out onto the street and returned to Pam's apartment. He slipped past the redoubtable Mrs Law without her hearing. He waited until Pam went to have a bath, then phoned Paul to tell him it was done.

'Did he believe you?' Paul asked.

'I think so,' Cotton said, keeping his voice down in case Pam heard.

'Good. Temple and his men are ready. They will protect you and capture the attacker. With any luck, Lud will send Harry and this whole thing will be over.'

But Cotton's voice was flat. 'What if it goes wrong?'

'What's going to go wrong?' Paul asked. 'Lud thinks you're too scared to double-cross him. Whoever he sends, they're going to walk into a trap. Trust me.'

Cotton tried to sound optimistic. 'I do.'

But Cotton was right to be cautious. Contrary to Paul's optimistic predictions Lud, in his subterranean crypt, had heard something in Cotton's voice. The demon master knew a lie when he heard one.

Less than half an hour later, two men were lugging a family's belongings from a recently-bombed house in a ruined Shadwell street. There was nothing charitable about their actions. From the age of thirteen, Mickey Brooks and Peter Savage had been involved in the city's criminal underworld. Their CVs included theft, extortion, even murder. Now they were members of the small army of petty criminals who scoured the bomb sites for something to steal. There was something else about the two men. The demon seed ran in their blood.

'Hey you,' somebody yelled across the rubble-strewn street as Brooks and Savage staggered over the rubble, loading anything they could carry into a thirty hundredweight Austin van. 'Where are you going with that lot?'

Savage turned to see a portly middle-aged woman waddling towards them, face red with anger.

'What's it to you?'

'That's Mrs Harris's house, that is. I'm her neighbour. What's your game?'

'Removals.'

'That isn't your stuff to take.'

'Look here, Grandma,' Savage said. 'Do yourself a favour and clear off.'

'What'll you do if I don't?' the woman, Mrs Liston, demanded.

'I'll remove *you*,' Savage warned, folding his arms across his chest.

Brooks came round the back of the van and Mrs Liston hesitated. She was feeling suddenly vulnerable. 'Don't think you can take any liberties with me,' she said, not quite as confident as she was trying to sound. 'I'll get the bobbies, I will.'

'No, you won't,' Brooks said, moving closer.

By now, Mrs Liston was wondering if she'd done the right thing tackling the two men on her own. She backed away, still mouthing half-hearted threats.

'Just you be gone by the time I get back,' she said, voice shaking, 'and don't take anything else.'

Savage watched her go. 'I've a mind to go after the old cow,' he said.

'Forget it,' Brooks said. 'She's all talk.'

He was climbing into the driver's seat when a blast of hot, dry air struck him in the face. Specks of dust stung his eyes like a thousand angry hornets. He recognized the signs and stepped down. Savage came round the corner of the van. He felt it too. 'It's the master.'

The pair watched a dark shadow come crawling up through the heaps of ash, shattered brick, splintered glass and plaster. Soon it formed into a swirling whirlpool. Then they were in the presence of their Lord. They bowed.

'What do you want of us, Master?' Savage asked.

Lud's voice growled. 'Do you know the legend of the renegade demon?'

'We do,' Brooks answered. 'A boy will be born. Death will try to claim him but he will shake off the black shroud. He will survive to become the demon brotherhood's greatest opponent.'

'It's no legend,' Lud said. 'The boy dwells within this city. He has come to this time. You will face him.'

'And kill him?'

Lud smiled as he heard the hunger in Brooks' voice. 'If necessary,' he answered. 'That depends on the choice he makes. You will bring the renegade over to my side if you can and destroy him if he refuses.' He announced the time and place of Paul's meeting with Cotton.

'The boy will not be alone,' Lud told the pair. 'Go to the Salmon and Ball in an hour. Further reinforcements will be waiting for you there.'

Brooks and Savage knew the Bethnal Green pub. It was one of their favourite watering holes.

'Go to it,' he said. 'Don't disappoint me, gentlemen. You would not like to suffer the consequences.'

Thirty-three

London, Saturday, 11 January, 1941

Paul was killing time while he waited for Temple to arrive with Cotton. Temple had insisted on picking Cotton up himself. It was a matter of security, he said. He was excited at the prospect of arresting Harry Rector and foiling the plot against Churchill. The detective's only worry was that he was acting without official approval. Paul assured him that nothing could go wrong.

Connie was busy most of the time with baby Denis so time dragged, punctuated only by a ham sandwich for lunch. Evelyn had had to go home. No amount of protests could sway Brenda. She had, she kept saying, hardly seen her daughter since Paul came to stay.

Evelyn could hardly tell her mother the real reason she didn't want to go home.

Having finished *The Demon Seed*, Paul found himself reading the strangest stuff: *Meccano Magazine*, *Radio Times*, even a boys' comic called *The Champion* that had been left by one of Connie's nephews. By mid-afternoon, having exhausted something called *Laughs on the Home Front* and having decided wartime Londoners didn't survive because of their sense of humour, Paul was glancing repeatedly at the clock. Temple should have arrived with Cotton. Had something gone wrong?

'What's keeping you?' Paul murmured.

But he needn't have worried. The Bullnose Oxford pulled up a couple of minutes later, disgorging Temple, Cotton and another man. Cotton didn't even say hello when he followed the detectives through the front door. Instead, he rummaged in an old briefcase, while Temple and Wallace went through to the kitchen.

'Take a look at this folder,' he said. 'You were asking me about the ancient gates to the city of London.'

'That's right,' Paul said. 'Aldgate seems to be at the heart of everything. The name just keeps cropping up.'

'Somebody else thought so too,' Cotton said.

'Who?'

'Professor Heinrich Voss,' Cotton said. 'I checked the library records back to 1936. His range of interests matches yours exactly.'

'Including the railway?' Paul asked. 'There's stuff about the old Minories station in your book.'

'The old London and Blackwall Company?' Cotton answered. 'Yes, Voss researched it. Why?'

'The railway lines seem important somehow, Whitechapel, Aldgate, now Minories.' He repeated the phrase that had been running through his mind for weeks. 'Fault-lines of evil.' He waited a beat. 'In your book, you mention Ludgate too. That's got to have something to do with King Lud.'

'It's possible,' Cotton said, spreading out a map. 'Judging by Voss's reading list, he thought so too.'

'I wonder what it's all about,' Paul said. 'Aldgate, Ludgate, they're important, I know it. The moment I saw them in your book, they just leapt out at me.'

'You're serious, aren't you?' Cotton said. 'What do you think they signify?'

'Lud is entombed beneath the city,' Paul said, 'maybe under one of these gates. I think the gates could mark out his territory. Look, I don't understand it all yet, but I need to know more.'

'They're not real gates,' Cotton said, 'at least, not any more. Voss wrote an article about them in 1937, just before he returned to Germany. Newgate was the last one to be built and the last to be demolished, in 1771.' He went on: 'There were seven gates in all: Aldersgate, Aldgate, Bishopsgate, Cripplegate, Ludgate, Moorgate and Newgate.'

'Wasn't that a prison?' Paul asked.

'That's right,' Cotton replied. 'It was a notorious place. Many were hanged within its walls, including your ancestor Samuel Rector.'

'You say 1771?' Paul mused, trying to recall what he knew of the demon infestation. 'That's when they knocked the last gate down?'

'That's right.'

'Lud's older than that,' Paul said.

Cotton nodded. 'That's incontestable. During my research into Samuel Rector, I came across many tantalizing hints, folk tales of demons and golems and ancient kings. To some, King Lud is the ancient founder of the city, though nobody seems to talk of him as a monster. The creature could be as old as the city itself.'

'So tell me about the gates.'

'They're ancient constructions, some older than others.'

'Which are the oldest?' Paul asked.

Cotton rolled out a map on the floor and trapped the curled corners with a bottle of ink, a vase and two paperweights. 'I'll show you.'

Paul leaned forward and followed as Cotton pointed them out on the map.

'There were four original gates,' Cotton explained, 'on the north, south, east and west of the city. They were Aldersgate to the north, Ludgate to the west, Aldgate to the east and the Bridge gate to the south. Their roots lie in the old Roman city. Would you like to see?'

Of course he wanted to see.

Cotton laid out a map of Roman London. 'You will see that I have marked out the seven gates in red,' he said, 'and the four original gates in black. Some of the more lurid accounts say that they represent the dark city, London's savage heart—' He hesitated.

'What's wrong?' Paul asked him.

'Just a few days ago I would have laughed at such theories,' Cotton said.

'And now?'

'Now I believe. The link to Professor Voss has me intrigued.'

They were still poring over Cotton's documents when a car drew up outside and a third detective made his way to the front door. 'That'll be Eric,' Temple said, answering the knock.

Detective Sergeant Eric Sharples looked tense. 'I hope you know what you're doing, George.'

'Are you prepared to go on trust?' Temple asked.

Sharples nodded. 'There isn't another man on the Force I'd stick my neck out for.'

Temple smiled. 'You don't know how much this means, Eric.'

Now that everybody was there, Temple went over the plan.

'Does everyone understand the part they're going to play in this operation?' he asked.

Everybody nodded, except Cotton.

'Hugh,' Temple said, 'do you know what you've got to do?'

Cotton assented.

'Are there any final questions?' Temple asked.

'Just one,' Paul said. 'What if it isn't just one

214

assassin?' He cast his eyes round the group. 'We're few in number.'

'It's the best I can do,' Temple said. 'There aren't many men who are prepared to risk their careers.'

Three-quarters of an hour later, the five of them drove over to Cotton's flat. They stopped two streets away so that they wouldn't be seen, then Cotton walked to the flat. Paul would follow a few minutes later and Temple, Wallace and Sharples would wait for Paul's attacker or attackers to arrive. They all carried Weobley pistols.

'Don't forget,' Temple told Wallace and Sharples as Paul let himself out of the car. 'Stay out of sight. The element of surprise is vital.'

But they were the ones who were in for a surprise.

Thirty-four

Cotton opened the door to Paul and spoke to him formally, keeping up the pretence that they were still little more than strangers. He led the way to the table by the window and they sat facing one another. Paul noticed that Cotton had left the curtains open as instructed. They continued their discussion of the Roman gates of London. Cotton told Paul where archaeologists had turned up some interesting finds: temples, public baths, the first century waterfront, a fort and a hypocaust. But neither of them had their mind on the research. First one, then the other would glance around, wondering when the attack would start. After a while, Paul frowned.

'Did you hear something?'

Cotton shook his head. 'No, nothing.'

'There's a smell.'

Cotton put his hand to his mouth. That's when Paul pinpointed the noise. Something was scratching behind the walls. 'What *is* that?' he asked.

He turned and stared at the plasterwork on the far wall. It was beginning to bulge. The swellings that were beginning to appear were travelling upwards and diagonally across the walls. It was at this point that Paul at last made sense of the smell. It was sulphurous. It was the smell he had inhaled many years ago, as a small boy, in Nana's cellar. It had signalled the first appearance of the monster in his life. It was brimstone. 'Lud,' Paul said.

This they had expected. The demon master's shadowy form started to materialise in a swirling maelstrom of dust and darkness. The *real* danger was coming from a different direction. A figure burst from the wall, sending broken plaster showering across the room. It was Savage, but Paul didn't see the wartime scavenger who lived by stripping derelict houses of their contents. In demon form, Savage was a monster whose flesh was as pale and cold as lard. His spine, grotesquely expanded and protruding through his back, formed a spiny hump. Each spine rose in a long curve and swayed as he moved. He was a thing made entirely of bleached white flesh and bone except for black eyes and a black tongue. The tongue was as thick as a serpent's body and, when it flickered forth, could stretch over a metre in length. The tip formed a deadly, spiked mace.

'My God!' Cotton gasped, stumbling backwards. 'We're trapped.'

'That's right,' Lud sneered, 'you are, aren't you?'

Cotton's voice raised a shrill alarm. 'Paul, warn Temple.'

'Make the offer,' Lud said.

'Serve my Master,' Savage said, 'and you will be spared.'

'Join me,' Lud said. 'You don't belong with these weaklings.' He gazed at Cotton. 'I will take this coward as a sacrifice. Rip out his heart and I will make you my crown prince. What do you say?'

By way of an answer, Paul turned to hurl his chair at the window. 'I will never serve you.'

'Then you're a fool,' Lud said. 'My power is growing. Soon I will shake off the shackles that bind me and there will be retribution for those who opposed me.' He summoned his disciples to battle. 'Destroy them.'

Savage's tongue shot out, the mace stabbing. Paul recoiled just in time to glimpse a second creature exploding from the opposite wall. Brooks' flesh was spiny in texture. Two pairs of razored hands flailed at such a speed they seemed to blur. Brooks' head, still human, was set beneath his shoulders in the middle of the demon's chest. Paul had still another reason to act. Lud was spraying menacing streams of black fire in Cotton's direction.

'Get behind me,' Paul told him. 'If you don't, he'll kill you.'

'That's right,' Lud said, 'I will devour him.'

Transfixed with fear, Cotton stood glued to the spot.

'Hugh,' Paul pleaded, 'if you want to live, get behind me.'

Cotton finally did as he was told. Paul recovered the wooden chair Savage had torn from his hands and swung it. For a moment, Cotton thought he was wielding it in self-defence. But Paul had two powers on which he was certain he could rely: fire and fear. Smashing the chair twice against the wall from which Savage had emerged, he succeeded in breaking it to bits. Taking a leg in both hands he fixed his gaze on them. The impromptu clubs instantly burst into flame. With these, Paul fought to keep his demon assailants at bay.

'Where in God's name is Temple?' Cotton cried. 'Surely he knows what's happening.'

'Oh, he knows,' Lud chuckled, 'but I'm afraid he has his hands full.'

As Paul retreated across the room, with Cotton behind him, he heard the crack of a gunshot. The three detectives were under attack too. Hissing, snarling, Savage spat out the clubbed tongue. In an attempt to outflank him, Brooks slashed with his steely claws. But Paul was becoming more assured in his control of fire, his element. The flaming chair legs were much more than firebrands. They were burning with an intense white heat. It was malleable. He was able to control it with his mind. In response to Paul's thoughts, jets of flame roared across the room, torching the air around the two demons.

For all the searing force of Paul's fiery weapons, Savage and Brookes continued to attack, trying to disarm Paul. Again and again, they struck. Again and again, as the torches belched liquid fire, they fell back screaming. But the torches that Paul was brandishing were beginning to dim already. The wood had all but turned into ash.

'There are two more chair legs,' Paul cried. 'Pass them to me.'

'Deny him,' Lud ordered.

Savage was too quick for Paul. His swollen, black tongue flicked out, sending the chair legs spinning out of reach. Paul could feel his heart banging in his chest. What now?

'The Master will reward us richly,' Brookes said.

His voice was less than human. It was as if his vocal chords were coated with some thick, gelatinous goo. His eyes bored into Paul's.

'You are an untrained boy, renegade. Your powers are great, so they say, but you can't begin to understand what they are. An apprentice needs a Master. You have none.'

Brooks had meant to weaken Paul's resolve with his mocking words. It was a mistake. Paul remembered what had happened in his struggle with Shadow. He had to strike, decisively and without mercy. Summoning what last reserves of energy there were in the firebrands he was wielding, he drove the shards of white heat into Brooks' heart. The demon squealed and writhed, then he fell still. Paul looked for Savage but his opponent was upon him before he could prepare himself for the inevitable onslaught. Savage hurled him to the floor, simultaneously flinging the hapless Cotton across the room.

'You're defenceless now,' the demon master crowed. 'Finish it, disciple!'

Savage didn't need any urging. His tongue snaked out and thumped into Paul's chest, cutting a gash across his collarbone. Paul stumbled back, falling against Cotton who was on all fours, wincing at the collision with the wall.

'You're bleeding,' Cotton gasped in horror.

Paul ignored the comment. Focusing on his hands, he succeeded in turning them into flaming brands. Half-recovered, he threw himself at Savage, pounding him with fiery blows. The demon was made to retreat but the tongue was maddeningly effective, preventing Paul from pressing his advantage. Any moment it might strike past his defence.

'Kill him, Paul!' Cotton yelled, his voice shrill.

Paul tensed, knowing he had to pierce his opponent's throat or heart, or die. It was time to kill or be killed. But his arms were like lead already

'You can do it!' Cotton urged, his heartbeat panicky and irregular.

Paul was tiring. Savage opened his black mouth. There was a loud report, utterly deafening in the confines of the flat. Paul stumbled. The demon had chosen that moment to exhibit a second awesome power. The floor seemed to jump underfoot. There was the shock of a second detonation and the windows blew in. Glass tinkled around the three figures. Barely a split-second later, a volcano of dust, brick, glass and timber erupted into the air. Half the roof was torn away and Paul was lifted off his feet, landing on Cotton. His heart turned over. He couldn't fight the demon. He was able to harness the awesome force of a thunderstorm. Then Cotton started to laugh behind him.

'What the hell are you laughing at?' Paul yelled. 'He's going to kill us.'

Cotton's eyes were wild with a kind of hysterical joy. 'He isn't the one doing this, Paul. It's an air raid.'

Paul was aware that Lud had vanished. He looked outside for confirmation that it was the Luftwaffe – not his demon opponent – that had ripped the flat asunder. It was *true*. There was a terrible glow across East London. Even as he watched, Paul saw a thousand-pounder hit. A water-main burst, drenching what few tardy souls hadn't made it to the shelters. Paul swung round. Savage wasn't the source of the explosions. He was lying face down on the floor, blood pooling round him. His head was like a crushed melon. Half the far wall had crashed down on top of him.

'Temple,' Paul said, dragging Cotton to his feet.

They ran down the stairs as yet another violent crash devastated the floor where they had been standing just a moment before. They threw themselves into the street and half ran, half crawled to the other side. Another bomb hit. It lifted Temple's bullnose Oxford from the road surface. Every window shattered. There was a thud and the vehicle sat rocking on its suspension. Paul ran towards it but there was nobody inside. He looked around frantically. There were slopes of rubble where a street had been. In the uneasy silence that followed the series of ear-splitting detonations, a loose gutter creaked on a bomb damaged roof and smoke drifted by, smelling of burning.

'Temple,' he shouted, 'where are you?'

In the far distance, the all-clear blared, but there was another sound too. It was a gunshot. Paul started to run. After a moment's hesitation, Cotton followed. Amid the webwork of twisted beams and girders up ahead, Temple and Wallace were fighting a rearguard action against three advancing demons. One was scaly, a reptile in human form. The second was insect-like, with grinding mandibles and snapping pincers. The attacking trio was made up by the most hideous creature Paul had ever seen: a being that seemed to have been constructed from body parts. But this was no Frankenstein's monster. Nobody had elected himself creator and sewn the walking cadaver together. Scraps of flesh hung here. Organs spilled there. It was a ruined corpse brought to life. As Paul ran towards the confrontation, he heard an ominous sound. Temple's gun clicked. He was out of ammunition. When Wallace tried to fire, the same dull click followed.

Paul leapt forward, still not sure what he intended. His hands continued to glow scarlet, sparks and tongues of flame flickering into the air. He saw

Temple's attackers starting to close in and roared a cry of rage. 'No!' Immediately, his hands blazed with a deep crimson glow. His palms seemed to pulsate for a moment then a hot wind whipped around him. From each hand there leapt intense bolts of flame. The nearest demons screamed as their bodies were embalmed in bubbling, crackling fire. They fell to the ground, trying to beat away the all-consuming heat but to no avail. Within seconds they had been reduced to ash. The third demon, the living cadaver, could only stare. Paul concentrated both streams of fire on him and he exploded, toasted body parts falling like hot rain. Wallace looked numb with shock. Temple was only slightly less astonished by the destruction Paul had unleashed. Terrifyingly, though the demons were destroyed, the danger had not passed. Paul was struggling to control the power he had unleashed. The streams of fire continued to writhe and twist across the street. Only with the most immense effort did Paul finally master the chaotic tendrils of flame. In the aftermath of the struggle, the city was strangely peaceful. Overhead, the stars glittered in a hard, black sky. Their light seemed to cut a hole in the glow of the many fires that were burning across London. It was Cotton who brought him back.

'How did you do that?' he asked. 'The trick with the milk jug was one thing, but this—'

'I didn't do it consciously,' Paul said, barely able to take in the scene of devastation. 'It was instinct, just instinct.'

Temple approached, followed by Wallace. Somebody was missing.

'What happened to Sharples?' Paul asked.

'Dead,' Temple told him. 'One of those things just reached through the window and dragged him out onto the street. Then the three of them tore him limb from limb as we watched. I don't know how I'm going to break it to his widow.' He sounded weary. 'Paul, he went out on a limb for me. I rewarded him by leading him to his death.'

'It's not your fault,' Paul said. 'It's mine. I thought we were laying a trap for Harry. I didn't think we were going to face five demons. I underestimated Lud's power.'

'We both did,' Temple said, his voice flat. 'Are you two all right?'

'I'm fine,' Paul said. 'I've got this cut. It stings like hell but I don't think it's serious. What about you, Hugh?'

Cotton seemed surprised to see that he was in one piece. 'I'll survive.'

'That's more than can be said of your flat,' Paul observed.

Cotton gave a grim smile. 'At least I won't have to lie to Pam anymore.'

Thirty-five

London, Sunday, 12 January, 1941

Harry watches the police swarming over Sullivan's hostel like bluebottles over rotting meat. They came at dawn.

Damn you, he curses. *I really put your nose out of joint that first day, didn't I? You must have decided to search my room to get back at me. The motivation wasn't patriotism, was it? I didn't give you any reason for suspicion. It was revenge, pure and simple. What were you after, black market goods, hookey gear, some excuse to blow me up to the coppers? Just because I didn't want to 'have a chinwag.' You found more than you bargained for, didn't you?*

Harry only just managed to scramble out of the window and swing himself up onto the roof before the *police barged their way in. Now they'll be going over the room with a fine-tooth comb, Harry thinks. He has one regret. They'll find the diary of Churchill's movements, the photos of the Prime Minister watching the Blitz from the roof of the Downing Street Annexe, the plan of the War Rooms pinpointing the room where the Old Man slept. Harry slithers across the roof tiles and scrambles down the drainpipe at the back of the house, clubbing an unsuspecting PC unconscious. As he slithers down the nearby railway embankment, he swears. I was going to strike tomorrow. Now they've discovered my plans, I've got to start all over again.*

His eyes narrow. When this is all over, he decides, I'll come back for you Sullivan. You'll wish you'd never gone near my room.

Slipping away through the early morning drizzle, Harry sets about solving a problem. Where's he going to sleep tonight? He can't go near the hostels or boarding houses. There are bound to be more raids. So where? He settles on a solution and smiles. Why didn't I think of it earlier?

Harry glances at his reflection in the decorative mirror that runs the length of the restaurant. Not bad, Harry boy. You scrub up very nicely. He sees what he's been looking for. He watches the elegant, well-dressed woman dining alone in the hotel restaurant. There's something slightly sad about her, in spite of her obvious wealth. Are you a widow, Harry wonders, or are you just lonely while your husband is away at the front? He finishes his starter and leans across.

'Excuse me,' he says, 'I know I'm being rather forward but would you care to dine with me? You look like you'd be glad of some company. I know I would.'

The woman hesitates though Harry senses that she's attracted by the idea.

'I'm sorry,' he says disarmingly, 'I've embarrassed you.'

'No,' the woman tells him, 'it's not that. You took me rather by surprise, that's all.'

Her eyelids flicker invitingly and Harry permits himself a smile. She's taking the bait.

'I was just wondering,' he says, 'why such a charming lady is dining alone. I'm Hamilton, by the way.' He's adopted an urbane east of Scotland accent. 'Gordon Hamilton.'

'Margaret Coleman,' the woman tells him. 'Maggie.'

Harry gestures to the waiter and joins her. He breathes in her perfume. It's definitely preferable to the stale air of the hostel.

'I was meeting an old school friend,' Maggie explains, 'but she phoned to cancel. She lives out of town and the line is blocked. Bomb damage apparently.'

'It's a terrible thing, this war,' Harry says with exaggerated sincerity.

Maggie nods. 'Frightful.'

The waiter has arrived. 'I have Madam's order,' he says. 'Would Sir like to choose his main course?'

Harry runs his eyes down the menu. 'I'll have the special.'

Once the waiter's gone, Harry sets about charming Maggie Coleman. He knows it won't be hard. She's obviously lonely and flattered by his attentions.

'Are you a widow, Maggie?' he enquires.

'No,' Maggie says, 'Richard's serving overseas.'

Perfect, Harry thinks. When she said her husband's name, there was no glow of warmth. There's something missing in her life and he's the one to provide it. She's hooked. Now all he has to do is reel her in.

'I lost my wife a couple of years ago,' he says. 'She passed away after a long illness.' A faraway look enters his eyes. Oh, I'm playing this to perfection, he thinks. Laurence Olivier's got nothing on me. 'I've been through a difficult time myself.'

Sympathy blooms in Maggie's eyes. Harry wants to give himself a clap on the back. This is just too easy.

'Let's have a drink,' Harry says. 'Just for one night, let's try to forget about this awful war.'

A smile lights Maggie's face. Why, oh why, Harry wonders, do women always fall for the bad boys? After all, I'm such a little devil.

Thirty-six

London, Monday, 13 January, 1941

Paul and Temple found Cotton in his favourite haunt – in the far corner of the Lyons Corner House with his back to the blacked-out windows. A gas fire spluttered, fighting a losing battle against the January cold. They ordered an afternoon tea costing a shilling and sixpence. While they waited for it to arrive, Paul turned to Cotton. 'So you're homeless on top of everything else?'

He sympathised with Cotton. They were both exiles.

'Mrs Law was waiting for me when I got back on Saturday night,' Cotton said. 'She ordered me out there and then. If I wasn't gone in an hour, she would tear up Pam's lease.'

'Where did you sleep?'

'Aldwych Tube Station,' Cotton said. 'It was crowded with people sheltering from the raids but I managed to get a few hours shut-eye. I suppose I'll have to go to the authorities and ask for temporary accommodation.'

'There's no need for that,' Temple said. 'I'll put you up.' He smiled, then rubbed at his forehead. 'We've already got one stray, haven't we, Paul? Another won't make much difference.'

'Is Connie going to be all right with this?' Paul asked, 'after what's happened?'

Cotton frowned. 'Am I missing something?'

The tea and scones arrived. Temple bit into one before answering. 'Ketsch has suspended me from active duty,' he said. 'There's going to be an investigation into Saturday night. It's hardly surprising. A man's dead.'

'And your wife's upset about it?' Cotton asked.

'Connie doesn't understand why I had to risk everything on Paul's say-so,' Temple said. 'I can't blame her. We haven't told her what's really happening. She's best not knowing.'

'Then I can't impose on you,' Cotton said. 'They'll find me somewhere to doss. You never know, there might be someone at work who can help.'

'It's not that simple,' Paul said. 'It's in your interests to stay with Temple.'

Cotton waited for an explanation.

'Paul's right,' Temple said. 'I was going to ask you to stay with me anyway. It's for your own protection.'

Paul filled in the rest. 'Lud will want his revenge. You don't want to be alone.'

Cotton lowered his eyes. 'I see.'

'Look on the bright side,' Temple said. 'You would have had to move out of Pam's anyway.'

Cotton pulled a face. 'That's the bright side?'

Temple didn't answer. He pinched the bridge of his nose and closed his eyes.

'Tired?' Paul asked.

'Discouraged,' Temple answered. 'Ketsch almost had Harry but he slipped the noose. Since then, there's been nothing. The trail's getting colder with each hour that passes and I'm suspended. We're in trouble. You haven't had any more of your visions?'

Paul shook his head. 'And they're not visions,' he said, 'they're dreams. I just wish I could control them. They come and go. There doesn't seem to be any pattern.'

The three of them sat in silence then Temple saw a familiar face. 'Hello,' he said, 'here's Wallace now.'

The man was wearing a gabardine mackintosh belted at the waist. He had his coat collar up against the rain. Stepping through the door, Wallace removed his trilby and shook the raindrops from the brim. The rain-dampened shoulders of his coat started to steam in the warmer air of the café.

'You shouldn't be seen with me,' Temple said. 'You're lucky not to be serving a suspension too.'

'The fools ought to have given you a medal,' Wallace

232

said. 'I saw those three . . . things. We did nothing wrong that night.'

'I'm not sure Eric's widow would agree,' Temple sighed.

'The evil we're fighting is *real*,' Wallace said. 'I know that now. That's why I wanted to give you some information.'

'What about?' Temple asked, shaking off his weariness.

'I don't know what you can do with this,' Wallace said, 'but I'm telling you anyway. One of the MI5 boys has turned up a lead. He remembered a chap by the name of Lawrence Burton. He was a street-corner orator in the East End back in 1936, a great enthusiast for Mosley and old Adolf by all accounts. He seemed to vanish after that and he wasn't on our list of active Nazi sympathisers. So we cast our net a bit wider and found out that Burton was living out Mile End way. It's quite a big house apparently. We put him under surveillance and guess what?'

Temple waited.

'He's had contact with that pair of villains you encountered yesterday, Brooks and Savage.'

Morrison had the wrapt attention of the men around the table.

'Rumour has it from the neighbours,' Wallace continued, 'that they were seen carrying a number of office-style files. It's not the kind of thing those two usually deal in. Stolen goods is more their style.' He let the information sink in before continuing. 'That's not

233

all. They found letters from somebody called Heinrich Voss. Ring a bell?'

Temple looked thoughtful. 'Is Ketsch planning to raid the house?'

Wallace nodded. 'He's going in fifty minutes from now.'

'But you're not invited to the party?'

'I'm on office duties for a month. That's my punishment for what happened Saturday night.'

'Thanks for the information,' Temple said, 'but there's nothing I can do with it.'

'That doesn't go for me though, does it?' Paul turned to Cotton. 'Are you with me?'

Cotton struggled to his feet, sending his chair scraping back across the floor. Temple watched them go then finished his tea and scones. Wallace sat down to keep him company.

'I wish I was going with you,' Temple said.

He didn't try to stop Paul. He knew the boy could more than take care of himself.

In just over half an hour, Paul and Cotton were walking down a back alley.

'We should be able to see what's going on from here,' Paul said, shoving open a rickety gate.

Hearing voices coming from around the corner, they stopped dead. Paul inched forward and saw Ketsch. He had a pair of binoculars and was training it on the street.

'What am I looking at, Morrison?' Ketsch asked the man next to him.

'That's Lawrence Burton,' Morrison answered.

Paul didn't need binoculars to pick out Burton. Just like the hearing, he thought. Something's happening to me. He saw a short, grey-haired man with a clipped moustache. He was dressed in a flannel shirt and corduroy trousers.

'He can't have been far,' Ketsch said. 'He isn't wearing a coat.'

'He's been in the pub at the top of the street,' Morrison told him. 'I had a man keep an eye on him. He seemed to be waiting for someone.'

'It looks like this someone didn't show,' Ketsch observed.

Morrison nodded. 'I think you're right. We'll get a report in a moment.'

Burton came closer. He looked unremarkable.

'Let's go,' Ketsch said. 'I've got a couple of men down there. The moment he opens the door, they're going to follow him inside.'

Ketsch's men forced their way in. Soon half a dozen Special Branch personnel and a pair of spooks from MI5 were entering the house. Paul gestured to Cotton to stay where he was then he crept along the wall and peered through the window. They'd got Burton to sit down but he was still kicking up a fuss.

'I want to see your warrant!' he cried.

'Sit down,' Ketsch ordered. 'Under the Emergency Powers Act, I don't need one.'

Burton opened his mouth but the words never came out. Morrison seized his shoulder and jammed him firmly back in his armchair.

'Now,' Mr Burton, 'we've got a few questions. You had a visit recently from two gentlemen by the name of Savage and Brooks. We have reason to believe that they delivered some material to this address.'

'Savage, Brooks,' Burton said, 'I've never heard of them. Your information's wrong.'

'The material in question,' Ketsch continued, 'consisted of several box files. Does this ring any bells?'

'I'm saying nothing,' Burton said. 'You can't make me.'

The interview carried on in the same vein. Ketsch put his questions; Burton refused to answer them. Then Ketsch asked, 'Have you ever heard of somebody called Arminius?'

Burton's mask slipped for the first time.

'I see from your reaction that you do know the name,' Ketsch said.

Burton recovered. 'You're mistaken,' Burton said, but in the twenty minutes that followed, he gave nothing away.

'I want a word with you,' Ketsch told his officers. 'Morgan, keep an eye on our prisoner.'

Paul saw his chance. Morgan was standing in the doorway, half-listening to the conversation in the next room. Paul tapped lightly on the window. Morgan took no notice, but Burton turned. The moment Paul had his attention, he fixed him with a stare.

Paul willed Burton to keep looking. When he saw dark shapes flutter in Burton's pupils Paul knew he had him. He couldn't speak for fear of alerting Morgan to his presence but he didn't need to. He was able to plant his thoughts in Burton's mind.

What are you afraid of?

His thoughts were travelling forward, penetrating Burton's mind, descending through a mist of images painted red, purple, black or grey. Then he found what he was looking for, a tiny, flesh-coloured sliver of pure fear.

Heights, is it?

Burton's eyes widened but he didn't break eye contact. He no longer knew how. Paul had complete control over him.

Let's go on a little journey.

In Burton's mind he was floating, rising high above the rooftops.

Where shall I take you? Of course, the dome.

'No!' Burton's voice was suddenly hoarse with fright.

Morgan glanced down at Burton, not noticing Paul. He held Burton's terrified stare and continued to transport him mentally across the city until he came to rest at the very pinnacle of St Paul's.

Some view, isn't it?

'Let me down,' Burton gasped, almost inaudibly.

'Sir,' Morgan said, looking round at his colleagues in

the room next door, 'you should take a look at our suspect. Something's happening.'

Burton was now staring at the floor, his pupils wide with terror, as he imagined the city below. Paul ducked down as Ketsch and his men hurried into the room. Burton had slipped deep into his nightmare realm. Paul didn't need to maintain eye contact. He had got Burton where he wanted him. In his imagination, Burton was teetering at the edge of a precipitous drop. The streets below seemed to beckon.

'What do you want to know?' he cried. 'Ask me anything. Just let me down.'

Ketsch and Morrison exchanged mystified glances but they didn't speak, not wanting to distract Burton.

'Please,' Burton babbled, 'tell me what you want? Please!'

It was Ketsch who finally asked the question. 'Where are the files?'

The words came tumbling from Burton's lips. He guided his interrogators to a space under the upstairs floorboards.

'Is that everything?' Ketsch asked, gesturing to the pile of files and notebooks.

Burton nodded, too scared to speak. He glanced at the window where Paul was watching.

OK, you're down.

The spell was broken. Burton examined his surroundings with a single stare. In his mind, he had been walking round the roof of St Paul's. Now he was back in the shabby kitchen.

'Get him away from me,' he said, pointing at the window. 'He's a devil.'

Paul scrambled away from the window.

'Who the hell are you talking about?' Ketsch asked, turning to look.

'The boy,' Burton screamed, 'the boy at the window.'

'But there's nobody there.'

Ketsch had Burton taken to the car. The engine roared and the traitor was borne away to a local police station for further questioning, though not of the kind Paul had subjected him to. Paul gestured to Cotton. Together they listened to the police as they went through the files.

'Good God!' Ketsch exclaimed, poring over the documents. 'Burton was up to his eyes in both plots, Arminius and Rector. Look at this.'

He spread everything out on the table. 'There you go, proof that he knew Arminius. He provided him with the rifle. It seems the assassin left his notebooks with Burton in case he got caught. They were to be passed on to the next Nazi agent to try his luck.'

There was a diary of Churchill's public engagements, maps of the War Rooms and the Churchill family home at Chartwell. There were photographs of Churchill going in and out of both the War Rooms. There were also snaps of Walter Thompson.

'Look at this,' one of Ketsch's men said of a photo of the roof of the Downing Street Annexe marked with a white cross. 'It's like the material we took from the hostel.'

'The PM sometimes goes up on the roof to watch the bombing,' Ketsch said. 'That's where he stands. These Nazis know more about Mr Churchill than I do.'

He froze. He was holding a map of Chequers, the PM's weekend residence. He thought for a moment, then came to a decision. 'Gentlemen, we have five days to find Harry Rector.'

'Why five days?' Morrison said.

Ketsch pointed at the material they had recovered from Burton's house. 'Chartwell has been mothballed for the duration of the war. Whitehall we can protect. After the Arminius attack and the find in the hostel, we've erected a ring of steel around the War Rooms. No, Rector's best bet is to ambush the PM at Chequers or on the way there.' He continued his explanation. 'Chequers is the PM's country residence. It's out in Buckinghamshire. Given the location, the place won't be easy to defend. It has enormous wooded grounds, a mile long drive and plenty of thick bushes where an assassin can hide.'

Morrison stared at the map. 'I think you're right, Sir. The PM's a sitting duck. That's where Rector's going to strike.'

Thirty-seven

arry reaches the pub over forty minutes late. Debris from a recent bombing raid held up the train he was on, leaving him trapped in a tunnel. By the time he arrives at his destination, he's breathless and angry. Why did Burton have to arrange the meeting at a pub? What's wrong with his house? But Burton has insisted. For some reason, he feels safer in a public place until he has verified Harry's identity. Harry scans the bar. There are half a dozen people drinking at the round tables. None of them fits the description of Burton. Harry curses. He knows the street where Burton lives but not the number. These stupid, little men and their suspicions! He tries to summon Lud but his thoughts fall into black space. His Master is otherwise occupied. Harry is still wondering what to do when the barman speaks.

'Are you the chap Lol Burton's been waiting for?' he asks.

Harry's cautious. 'He told you he was waiting for somebody, did he?'

It seems an odd combination. Can Burton really be both wary and a blabbermouth?

'He didn't need to tell me anything,' the barman says. 'It was the way he was acting, jittery like. Every time that door opened, he looked up to see who was coming in. I've been in this game long enough to put two and two together.'

Harry decides there's nothing to lose. 'Yes, I'm the one he was waiting for. Do you know where he's gone?'

'By the look of him, he decided you weren't coming.'

'My train was delayed. Could you help me? I've forgotten which number he lives at.'

'Clickety-click, sixty-six,' the barman says, wiping a glass. 'I think he was on his way home just a few minutes back. He didn't look as if he was going anywhere further afield. He wasn't wearing a coat.' The barman obviously fancies himself as something of an amateur sleuth.

'Thanks.' Harry's relieved that he's going to find Burton after all. It will save him a lot of work to have Arminius' files in his possession. He slaps some money on the bar. 'Buy everyone a drink. I'm feeling generous.'

Harry walks out of the bar with a broad smile. It doesn't survive his first five paces along the street. Instinctively he knows something's wrong. He stops and rakes the street with a searching gaze. Years spent in Lud's service have made his senses as acute and finely-

242

tuned as those of a wild predator. They've saved him from the attentions of the police and secret service more than once. In moments he has registered danger. There's the scrape of a boot on cobbles. Police boots, Harry's instincts tell him.

Harry quickly retraces his steps to the street corner then jogs down the back alley. He listens for voices, the sound of cooking, a wireless, a heartbeat. Then he sees a man in a gabardine mac walk to a car and start loading it with cardboard files. Harry scowls.

'Special Branch,' he murmurs. 'It looks like you beat me to Burton.'

Soon the rest of the officers assemble on the street. Harry watches them clapping their hands against the bitter cold and discussing Burton's sudden change of heart. They drive away. Harry is about to leave too when a man and a youth appeared from the yard of number sixty-six.

'You!' he breathes. He recognizes the Rector family resemblance. So this is the renegade. This is Paul Rector. 'Did you bring them here?' he wonders out loud. 'You alerted the authorities to my arrival from Ireland.'

The Master is right about the boy. He might be young and untutored in his powers but he has the ability to put obstacles in the path of Harry's mission.

'Something tells me,' Harry murmurs, 'that, if I am to succeed, you must perish.'

Thirty-eight

Paul was dead on his feet, exhausted by the mind games he'd played on Burton. He closed his eyes and leaned back against a wall. How he longed to be home amid modern London's chaotic bustle. He ached for his old life, before the demons, before Lud. Then a face exploded into his mind. It was as if he was experiencing a waking dream. The face was Harry's.

You're nearby.

He hadn't meant to send the thought as a message but it travelled anyway. To his amazement, Harry's mind spoke back.

Closer than you can possibly imagine.

Paul's eyes snapped open and he yelled a warning.

'Cotton,' he cried, 'it's Harry. He's close.'

'What do you mean, close?'

Paul's eyes darted along the street. 'I mean he's here. He must have been coming to meet Burton.'

Cotton too scanned the street. 'I don't see anything.'

Paul ran in the direction of the pub, staring at the windows of each house in turn. Then he felt Harry's presence, as powerfully as if the demon assassin had broken cover and come running towards him.

'There,' Paul cried, 'it's that alleyway. I know it.'

Cotton hung back. 'We can't take him on,' he said, 'not just the two of us.'

Paul snorted his disgust. 'It's Harry. We can't walk away.'

'No,' Cotton said. 'It's too soon. You're not ready.'

Paul ignored him. 'I don't care.'

With that he entered the alley. But Harry had gone. He'd left a message cut into the wall.

Missed me.

'I should have known,' Paul said. 'I should have felt his presence earlier.'

He stood there cursing his powers. He felt like a toddler learning to walk. Some days he was strong and confident, taking great strides. Others, he just kept falling flat on his face.

'Harry's been one step ahead all the time,' Cotton said. 'At least he wasn't able to get hold of Burton's files.'

'I don't think it'll slow him down long,' Paul said.

'You're probably right,' Cotton said, 'but we got closer to him today than we have since he entered the country. Let's go.'

They found a bus stop and caught the first one that came. Paul had started to doze off when he glimpsed a familiar street sign. He sat bolt upright and stared out of the window.

'Something wrong?' Cotton asked.

They were on Bow Road. 'That's Burdett Road up ahead, isn't it?' Paul asked.

'Yes, why?'

They got off at the next stop and walked back. Paul was getting excited. He knew these streets. Many things would have changed by the time the twenty-first century dawned, but the area was recognizable. This is where he'd grown up.

'Here,' Paul shouted. 'It's the next right.'

Paul half expected the Lychgate estate to loom before him. For a moment he allowed himself to believe that it was possible to rip open the partition between past and present and return to his old life. He was in for disappointment.

'Of course,' he said, 'the engineering factory.'

It would be demolished forty-five years from now, leaving only a concrete rectangle overgrown with wild flowers and weeds, where Mum would burn all the documents relating to Harry and Samuel Rector. Paul walked over to where the estate would one day begin.

'This is it,' Paul said.

'This is what?' Cotton said, bewildered by his behaviour.

'This is where I used to live . . . will live . . .' Paul

struggled to put his thoughts into words, 'however you want to think about it. This is my home.'

Then he sank to his knees and buried his face in his hands. Never, in the two weeks he had been here, had he felt so lonely.

Thirty-nine

London, Tuesday, 14 January, 1941

'Why do *I* always have to entertain *you*?' Evelyn hissed. 'Aunty Connie makes me sound like a dancing bear sometimes.' Her cheeks and nose were red because of the forsty air as she followed Paul into the parlour, pulling off her hat, gloves and scarf and dumping them with her coat on the arm of the chair. 'Has she forgiven Uncle George?'

'Not yet,' Paul said. 'But things might change soon. Temple's up before his disciplinary board today.'

'Oh really! What's wrong with those pen-pushers at Whitehall? There's an assassin on the loose and they waste their time trying to make Uncle George a scapegoat. They've got to be complete idiots to do this to him.'

Paul knew that Temple was secretly hoping Ketsch was going to reinstate him. There were only four days to apprehend Harry so Special Branch needed every man they could get.

'Surely they'll see sense,' Evelyn said.

'I wouldn't bet on it,' Paul told her. 'Temple ignored orders. He acted on his own initiative.'

'Well, somebody had to!' Evelyn declared.

Paul smiled. 'Temple should have taken you with him to argue his case.'

'I quite agree,' Evelyn said. 'How can a few officials order somebody like Uncle George around? Don't they understand he's a hero? I would have given them a piece of my mind.'

'I'm sure you would,' Paul said. 'But remember, Sharples died because he went along with us. You've got to admit, Temple's got a lot of explaining to do.'

'He helped destroy five demons,' Evelyn protested. 'That's got to count for something.'

'Maybe,' Paul said, 'but they'd returned to human form by the time the uniformed police got there. There was no evidence of anything supernatural.'

Evelyn pouted. 'Then they were gangsters and fifth columnists. There is a war on, after all. It's so unfair.'

Temple arrived home just after one and sat down with the family for lunch. A cloud of disappointment seemed to follow him into the house.

'What did they say?' Connie asked.

'I've got another interview in three weeks,' Temple answered. 'It's going to be a long process.'

'So you stay suspended?'

Temple nodded. 'They won't let me anywhere near a live operation.'

'Wasn't there any good news?'

'Not really,' Temple replied. 'Oh, I'm on full pay. At least we won't starve.'

'Well, I think it's a disgrace,' Evelyn cried, full of righteous indignation. 'How do they expect to stop Harry without you . . .' Her voice trailed off as she realised her mistake. Paul stared at her.

'What did you just say?' Temple demanded.

Evelyn blushed to her ears and lowered her eyes. Temple turned on Paul. 'You told her?' He exhaled sharply in frustration. 'How long's she known?'

'A while.'

'For God's sake, Paul, that's classified information. What the hell where you thinking of?'

'Evelyn was with me when I met Cotton. It just came out.'

'What else? I assume there's more.'

Paul took a deep breath. 'We followed you to Euston.'

'What!'

'George,' Connie said, interrupting, 'what are they talking about? Does this have something to do with your suspension?'

'You two wait here,' Temple snapped. 'Connie, can we discuss this somewhere else?'

Paul and Evelyn listened to the raised voices in the next room. After a while George and Connie were talking, rather than yelling at each other.

'I'm sorry, Paul,' Evelyn said.

'Forget it,' Paul told her, 'it was bound to come out sometime. It was a slip of the tongue, that's all. You've done nothing wrong.'

Paul hadn't even finished the sentence when Temple appeared at the door.

'Evelyn,' he said, 'you're going to have to go home.'

'But Uncle George—'

'No buts, young lady,' Temple said. 'Whether I like it or not, Paul's involved in this whole affair. You're not. I can't have my niece exposed to danger.'

Evelyn's eyes were welling with tears. 'But Uncle George, I won't blurt it out to anyone else. You can trust me.'

'I do trust you,' Temple said, softening his voice. 'That's not the problem. In a situation as serious as this, knowledge is a dangerous commodity. I'm going to ask you to leave. It's for your own protection, as much as anything else. I didn't even want Connie to know. This has put me in a very difficult position.'

'It's my fault, Temple,' Paul said.

'That's right,' Temple said, still angry with him for involving Evelyn, 'it is, and you've been completely irresponsible. You're part of this and she isn't. You have to be here. Evelyn doesn't.' He glanced at Evelyn. 'Go home, dear.'

Evelyn snatched her coat from the peg and fled from the house. Paul heard her footsteps on the pavement outside.

'You were very hard on her,' he said.

Temple shrugged. 'It's for her own good.' He gave Paul a level stare. 'I'm not very happy with you, but if we're going to stop Harry we've got to work together.'

'I thought you were suspended.'

'The Prime Minister's life matters more than procedure,' Temple said, 'or my future. They can throw the book at me if they like but the course of the War is at stake. You say I'm going to play a major part in catching Harry. I believe you. There are only four days left to thwart the plot. Let's get to work.'

He opened a road map and set it down on the kitchen table.

'I talked to Morrison while I was down there,' he said. 'He thinks pretty much like young Wallace. He knows I've been badly treated. He explained the state of play to me. It isn't good.'

'Churchill's going to go to Chequers this weekend, isn't he?' Paul asked.

Temple nodded. 'He refuses to change his routine, no matter what Special Branch and MI5 say.' He traced the PM's likely route to Buckinghamshire.

'Just look at it. There are forty miles of country lanes between London and Chequers. Imagine the cover all those ditches, woods and hills are going to offer. Harry could take his pick of hundreds of spots to carry out his ambush.'

'And there's no progress in tracking him down?' Paul asked.

Temple shook his head. 'Harry's gone to ground

somewhere. There are no leads. There are four days left and nobody has a clue where he is. Four days!'

'Can't somebody convince Churchill to stay in London?' Paul asked. 'What about Thompson?'

Temple shook his head. 'According to Morrison, even the good Lord himself would have His work cut out persuading the Old Man. No, the PM's mind is made up. Nothing's going to get in the way of his weekend in the country.'

'We need transport,' Paul said. 'What's the news on your car?'

'I'm going to have to garage it, maybe until the end of the war,' Temple said. 'There's no chance of getting it repaired. Everything is subordinated to the war effort.'

'So what do we do?'

'Don't worry,' Temple said. 'I've got a few ideas.'

The phone rang. Temple snatched the receiver from its cradle. 'George Temple.' He listened for a moment then handed the phone to Paul. 'It's for you. It's your friend Cotton.'

'Paul?' Cotton said. 'I've discovered something. You've got to meet me.'

Half an hour later they arrived at 13, West Cromwell Place, a mid-Victorian terrace. Cotton was waiting on the step.

'Paul!' Cotton cried, rushing forward. 'Thank God you're here.' His eyes were wide and his face was flushed.

'Hello, Hugh,' Paul said. 'Why all the excitement?'

'I told you about Arthur Strachan, remember?'

Paul tried to recall. 'I'm not sure . . .'

'Arthur Strachan was a civil engineer. He was working on a project close to the Aldgate area of East London.'

'The Minories station?' Paul asked.

'That's right. Everything leads back to the area around Aldgate and Whitechapel. When you asked me about that railway line, I started going through my research. Strachan died in suspicious circumstances. He left behind a set of diaries. They're held here by his descendants. I telephoned the present owner, and she's happy for us to read them.' He lowered his voice conspiratorially. 'Paul, Strachan was murdered by the Rat Boys. There's a link with Samuel Rector.'

Paul glanced at the door. 'Is this where he lived?'

Cotton nodded. 'The very place. He was a widower. He lived here with his daughter Victoria and a few servants.' He looked into Paul's eyes. 'Your suspicions were correct. Aldgate is a portal to evil. If we can discover the link between Samuel Rector and Arthur Strachan we will be close to understanding the monster's designs.'

Temple looked on bemused. Oblivious, Cotton climbed the steps and knocked on the door. A few moments later, an elderly woman answered.

'Mrs Strachan?' Cotton asked.

'*Miss* Strachan,' she said, correcting him.

'Good morning, Miss Strachan,' Cotton said, duly

254

admonished. 'I telephoned earlier. You said we could examine Arthur Strachan's diaries.'

'That's right,' Miss Strachan said. 'Unfortunately, I can't allow them to leave the premises. They are very old, you see, and possibly precious.'

Cotton nodded. 'I quite understand. We will examine them here, with your permission.'

Miss Strachan nodded and led the way indoors. 'The diaries have a rather interesting history. Do you believe in curses?'

Cotton swapped glances with Paul. 'I've got an open mind.'

'You will need one if you're going to read my ancestor's journals.' She showed them into an oppressively dark room. 'This is the drawing room. The diaries are in that escritoire.'

'Escritoire?' Paul asked.

'It's a writing desk,' Miss Strachan said, 'in the French design. I'll get you some tea,' She left the room.

'A formidable woman,' Cotton observed.

Mad old bat, was Paul's interpretation, but he didn't say so. Cotton opened the first diary and froze.

'What is it?' Paul asked.

Cotton handed him the diary. Embossed on the inside cover of the volume was a Latin phrase: *Vince malum bono*.

'It's the inscription from *The Demon Seed*,' Paul said. 'So what?'

'You don't understand,' Cotton said. 'When I wrote

my book I didn't know the inscription had anything to
do with Arthur Strachan.'

'So where did you get it from?' Paul asked.

'They were the words spoken by the prison chaplain
the day they hanged Samuel Rector,' Cotton said. ' I
thought they were appropriate.'

'I wonder what Samuel thought,' Paul said.

They were still discussing the coincidence when
Miss Strachan returned with a tray. There was a pot
of tea, four cups, a sugar bowl, a milk jug, and a plate
of Bourbon biscuits. Paul grimaced. Just his luck. They
were the only kind he didn't like.

'There's only a spot of milk,' Miss Strachan said.
'It's this dreadful rationing. You will have to be very
sparing.'

Temple took the tray. 'Very generous of you.'

'Miss Strachan,' Cotton said, 'what do you know
about these words?'

He showed her the inscription.

'*Vince malum bono*,' she said. 'It means "good conquers evil."'

'Yes,' Cotton said, 'I know. But what's its signific-
ance?'

'It's the Strachan family motto,' Miss Strachan said.
'Mind you, it is rather ironic, given our rather che-
quered history.'

'Whatever do you mean?' Cotton asked.

Miss Strachan gave him a searching look. 'You do
know what happened to my ancestor?'

'Yes, of course.'

'Are you aware of the full story?' she asked.

'I'm not sure,' Cotton answered. 'I know he died in suspicious circumstances.'

'Mr Cotton,' Miss Strachan said, 'let's not beat about the bush. He was murdered by a gang of feral monsters, Satan's children. Circumstances don't get any more suspicious than that, young man. Follow me.'

She led her visitors to the far end of a panelled passage. She had to unlock the door to admit them. It was a long, low-ceilinged room, furnished only with a bench along one wall. They saw the inscription immediately. There it was, a six-foot long painted scroll containing letters some eight or nine inches in height: *Vince malum bono*.

'Now,' Miss Strachan said, 'turn around one hundred and eighty degrees and raise your eyes to the top of the wall.'

Paul, Cotton and the two policemen did as they were told. Cotton gasped. Gouged into the plasterwork, as if by some clawed hand, there was a second inscription: *Ut malus sim, vince bonum malo*.

'What's the matter?' Paul asked.

Cotton was trembling. His eyes were glassy and he seemed to be short of breath.

'What's wrong?' Paul repeated.

Cotton pointed at the words.

'They're the exact opposite of the first inscription,' he said. 'Do you understand my meaning?'

'So it says . . .'

'Evil conquers good,' Cotton said, finishing Paul's sentence.

Temple reached up on tiptoe and touched the deep indentations. 'How on Earth was this done? It's too rough for a chisel.'

'This was once Arthur Strachan's study,' Miss Strachan said. 'One night he was sitting here working. A child's hand clawed those words directly into the plasterwork.'

'Dear lady,' Temple said, 'surely you don't expect us to believe . . .'

'The hand belonged to his daughter Victoria.'

'Really!' Temple protested. 'This is beyond belief.'

'Read Arthur's diaries,' Miss Strachan said. 'Make up your own minds.' She walked to the door. 'One thing I can tell you, I've had workmen in three times to repair the damage. I had plans to put this room back into use. Three times the plaster fell out again within days. You explain it . . .' Suddenly her words trailed off.

'Do you smell burning?' she asked.

'Yes.' Temple ran down the corridor. 'It's coming from in here,' he said, opening the drawing room door.

'The diaries!' Miss Strachan cried.

The entire writing desk was in flames and with it Arthur Strachan's diaries. A powerful draught from the street had fanned the fire. Temple managed to put it out in minutes but there was no saving the diaries. They had been reduced to ash.

Miss Strachan slumped into a chair. 'This was no accident.'

'What do you mean?'

'Some power is determined to prevent you reading the diaries.' She sighed.

That's when Paul noticed somebody was missing. 'Where's Cotton?'

'I thought he was behind you,' Temple said.

They retraced their steps to Strachan's former study, leaving Miss Strachan to mourn the burned diaries. Cotton was standing in the middle of the floor, staring up at the inscription above the door. The words seemed to have a hypnotic effect on him.

'What's the matter now?' Temple asked.

Then Paul and the two policeman saw. The letters had filled with thick, scarlet fluid. It was blood. They were still standing there, glued to the spot, when Miss Strachan entered. She saw the letters but didn't even seem surprised.

'You were expecting something like this, weren't you?' Paul asked.

Miss Strachan passed a hand over her face. 'Expect is the wrong word,' she said. 'I was dreading it.'

'It's happened before?'

'That's why this room is kept under lock and key,' she said, averting her gaze. 'Something monstrous dwells within these walls. Things happen here; inexplicable, unnatural events. This room consumes those who enter it. It takes their minds and souls. Sometimes I believe this room is a portal to Hell. I am the last in the Strachan line. After I have gone to meet my Maker, there will be no others. God willing, the curse ends with me.' She prepared to lock the door.

'Aren't you even going to get it cleaned up?' Temple asked.

'The blood will be gone by morning.'

'That's incredible.'

'The blood vanishes. The moral stain remains. Scrub all you like, the room in which you stand will not be cleansed. The evil within is too deep-rooted for that.' She looked at her visitors over her spectacles. 'If you don't mind, I would like to be alone.'

'Of course,' Temple said. 'Thank you for your time.' He led the way outside.

Cotton was unhappy. 'Why are you in such a hurry to go?' he cried. 'There was so much I could have learned from that house.'

'You still can,' Temple said.

'I don't understand.'

'Paul's got something to show you.'

Cotton's eyes widened. Paul had a leather-bound book in each hand.

'The diaries! So what burned?'

'There were three diaries,' Paul said. 'I took the ones that mattered and left the other. I was just in time, by the look of it.'

'But isn't that stealing?'

'You heard what Miss Strachan said,' Paul replied. 'Maybe it's for the best.'

Cotton followed Paul and Temple towards the tube.

Historical research had just taken a dramatic new twist.

'But how did Lud burn the other diary?' Cotton asked.

'I wish I knew,' Paul said. 'He always seems a step ahead of us.'

But it wasn't Lud who had burned the diary. It was one of his disciples. The perpetrator had gained access through the shoved-up sash window of 13, West Cromwell Place. He was watching them from an antiquarian bookseller's shop across the road. It was Harry.

Forty

London, Wednesday, 15 January, 1941

arry is wearing a grey suit, white shirt, dark blue tie and soft, broad-brimmed hat. He borrowed the outfit, in his absence, from Maggie's husband. She asked him where he was going. Quite the possessive one, aren't you? Harry thought. He answered with a single word. Business.

Business is the trio waiting for the next tube. Harry is careful to keep them under surveillance from the far end of the platform. Paul's senses aren't yet so finely honed that they can pick him up at this distance, especially when Harry's taking care to mask his presence. The train arrives. Harry waits until Paul, Temple and Cotton are all on before boarding himself. How convenient, here they are, three of the people he wants in his sights. The fourth is Churchill. Harry sits opposite a smartly-dressed office-worker. He catches her eye and she smiles. Her name is Louise. Maggie would scratch his eyes out if she knew he was two-timing her already. Still, Harry thinks, ignorance is bliss. He chats to Louise for a few minutes without once losing track of his targets. He makes a date for tomorrow night. Here's another attractive lady with a husband at the Front. Maggie won't mind. Harry grins. There's a simple reason why. She won't know.

Harry sees Temple and Cotton get up, followed by Paul, and he excuses himself. 'This is my stop. I'll see you tomorrow.'

Paul reaches the doors and pauses. What's this? You can't know I'm here.

But Paul turns and Harry has to shrink back. Paul twists round. His gaze travels through the partition windows of five carriages but he looks straight past Harry who has dropped out of sight behind a burly ARP warden. Even at this distance, Harry can feel Paul's senses tingling. It's true, this descendant of his is special. Without any tuition in the demon's arts, he responds like a demon master. Eventually, Paul shrugs off the sensation of being watched and follows his companions out of the station. Harry follows. He's impressed. As a result of Paul's curiosity, Harry proceeds cautiously. But follow he does. He's plotting their destruction.

Forty-one

London, Wednesday, 15 January, 1941

'Evelyn!' She bobbed her head out of the living room the moment Paul arrived back with Temple and Cotton in tow. Paul frowned, remembering Temple's anger the night before. 'But I thought . . .'

'I decided I'd acted in anger,' Temple said, by way of an explanation. 'Maybe I was rather hasty. I had a chat with Brenda last night. I didn't tell her everything, of course. I just said Evelyn had got a little bit too nosy about my work. I've set out the rules and she's going to stick by them. That's right, isn't it, Evie?'

Evelyn gave him a broad smile then threw her arms round his neck. 'I'm your obedient niece. Did you know you're my favourite uncle?'

'I'm your only uncle,' Temple reminded her, 'and you're my favourite niece too, on one condition.'

'What's that?'

'There will be no prying into the present . . . emergency.'

Evelyn released him and crossed herself. 'Cross my heart and hope to die.'

'Now I don't think you need to go that far,' Temple said. 'I'm sure you're going to live a long and happy life.'

'Of course I am,' Evelyn said. 'I'm eternal, like She Who Must Be Obeyed.'

Temple explained his rules to Paul. 'You can see Evelyn. I understand how lonely you are. But I forbid you to involve her in anything to do with Harry Rector. You're young, Paul. You acted on a whim. That has to end. This business is too serious to treat it as some kind of game.'

Paul listened. 'I understand.'

'We both do,' Evelyn said.

Temple smiled indulgently and joined Connie in the living room. Cotton scurried off to the room he shared with Paul to read Strachan's diaries. Paul and Evelyn went in the parlour. Evelyn closed the door behind them and sat on the arm of Paul's chair.

'We're on our own now,' she said. 'What happened last night? Do tell.'

Paul stared in disbelief. 'Evelyn, you're incorrigible. You just promised your Uncle George that you wouldn't pry.'

Evelyn gave a mischievous grin. 'I crossed my fingers when I said it.'

'No you didn't,' Paul retorted.

'Then I did it metaphorically.'

'Your uncle would have a fit.'

'But you're going to tell me anyway, aren't you?' Evelyn asked.

Paul glanced at the door then reduced his voice to a whisper. There was an excitement about their private conspiracy. 'Yes.'

But, as Paul told Evelyn about the visit to West Cromwell Place, he was oblivious to movement outside. Harry was standing at the top of the road, using his acute hearing to eavesdrop. This time, distracted by Evelyn, Paul failed to register his presence. Every word he said was being overheard.

By late afternoon, Evelyn was growing restless.

'Uncle George,' she asked, 'would you mind awfully if Paul and I went to the cinema this evening? They're showing *Gone with the Wind*. You'd like to go, wouldn't you, Paul?'

'If that's all right with you, Temple,' Paul said. 'I'm climbing the walls and there's nothing I can do.'

'I don't know,' Temple said doubtfully. After the events at Cotton's flat, he was reluctant to let Paul out of his sight. He saw Connie gesturing to him from the hall. 'I'll be back in a minute,' he said.

'Why don't you let them go?' she asked. 'It's only a quarter of a mile to the Odeon.'

'Connie,' Temple answered, 'Paul's safety could be vital. He knows things. I can't risk it.'

'You could walk them there and back if you're so concerned.'

Temple shook his head. 'They'd still be on their own in the cinema. Connie, you don't understand how dangerous our enemy is.'

'You can't risk Paul doing a bunk, either,' Connie said. 'He went to Euston without permission. Putting him under curfew might be rather counter-productive, don't you think?'

Temple gave her a questioning look.

'Honestly George,' Connie said, 'you don't have much idea of how to manage youngsters, do you?'

'What are you getting at?' Temple asked.

'Paul's already struck out on his own once,' Connie pointed out. 'What's to stop him doing it again? If you try to keep him cooped up here, he could still slip out on the sly. From what I've seen of him so far, he's a young man with independent ideas.'

'No,' Temple said, after a few moments' thought, 'it would be reckless to expose them to danger.'

'There must be somebody you trust who can keep an eye on them,' Connie suggested.

Temple glanced at Paul and Evelyn chatting animatedly in the parlour.

'Do you really think they might go off without telling us?' he asked.

'Didn't you ever defy your parents when you were his age?' Connie asked.

That seemed to convince Temple. He might be a policeman but he was quite a tearaway in his youth. He made a phone call.

'Who are you calling?' Connie asked.

'Wallace, he said he'd help any way he could.' Having secured Wallace's services, Temple told Paul and Evelyn the good news. What he didn't know was that Paul had been listening all the time. His new, acute hearing was coming in quite useful.

Soon Paul and Evelyn were in the queue for the film. They pretended not to notice Wallace watching across the road. There was a newsreel before the main feature. When Hitler's face appeared on the screen the entire cinema started catcalling and booing. Evelyn hooted along with everyone else so Paul joined in too. Then there was footage of the raid on 29 December. The newsreader informed the audience that there had been nothing like it since 1666.

'The Great Fire of London,' Evelyn said.

Next up was a short clip in which a group of young men and women exercised to the tune of 'Keep Young and Beautiful.' Finally, a young woman was shown giving a rendition of 'A Nightingale sang in Berkeley Square.' The audience joined in, just as they had joined in the booing of Hitler.

'Sing along,' Evelyn urged.

Paul made a brave effort to mumble in time with the song. He was glad when it was over and the lights dimmed. He was surprised when Evelyn slipped her arm through his. When the male lead, Clark Gable, appeared for the first time, she snuggled close. Without thinking, he slipped an arm round her shoulder; she made no attempt to remove it. He wondered what Netty would say if she saw him now. But Netty was almost seventy years in the future. He might never see her again. He was lonely and Evelyn was sitting right next to him, reaching out. He decided to live for the moment and he gave her shoulder a squeeze. She squeezed back.

'Ow!' Paul exclaimed in mock agony.

'What's the matter with you?'

'You hurt,' Paul chuckled. 'It's all that tennis. You've got arms like King Kong.'

Evelyn realised she was being teased and nudged him. He nudged back. It felt good.

In the flickering light of the projector she caught his eye. 'Isn't this nicer than being cooped up at Uncle George's?' she whispered.

He nodded. Much nicer. When the lights finally went up at the end of the epic movie, they made their way outside. The city was perfectly dark in the black-out. Noticing the night sky, Paul stopped.

'What's the matter?' Evelyn asked, seeing him quite transfixed by the star-studded heavens.

'That sky,' Paul answered. 'I've never seen anything like it.'

It was true. In his London, the lights of hundreds of thousands of homes masked the blackness of the sky, the diamond brilliance of the stars. Evelyn linked arms with him.

'You are funny,' she said. 'It's the same old sky.'

'That's just it,' Paul said. 'It isn't.'

Evelyn rolled her eyes. 'I'm sure they have stars in, where was it, Mile End.'

'Not like this,' Paul insisted.

'Oh no,' Evelyn chuckled, 'Enfield is so much more romantic.' She started to jig along the pavement.

'*Keep young and beautiful*,' she sang, '*if you want to be loved*. Don't you just adore Eddie Cantor?'

Paul smiled. 'Definitely.' He watched her dancing down the street. She really was beautiful. More beautiful than Netty? At the thought of his old life, his smile faded. That's when he glimpsed a movement in the shadows. Wallace. Strangely, the detective's appearance was accompanied by a curious sense of foreboding. Or maybe he was just sad the evening was over.

'We'd better get back,' he said. 'They'll be worried.'

They set off down the road, just in time to hear the air raid siren.

'Isn't that just typical?' Evelyn said. 'At least Jerry didn't interrupt the performance.'

'We'd better hurry,' Paul said.

The *ack ack* had started up in the distance, then there was the now-familiar drone of German aircraft. Within moments, the thump and crump of guns could be heard. In the distance, the sky was slashed by searchlights.

'They're coming closer,' Evelyn said.

Paul saw movement down the road. Wallace again.

There was still the strange sense of foreboding, but no time to dwell on it. Moments later the raid moved closer and imminent danger made him forget all about the vague tingling he'd been feeling. Incendiaries were fizzing down, not two hundred yards to their left.

'They're hitting the marshalling yards,' Evelyn said.

There were a couple of fires like huge torches on the far side of the railway tracks. Flames were threshing back and forth. Paul heard somebody shout but he wasn't about to stop.

'Come on!'

They were sprinting now. Over the rooftops they could see the barrage balloons used to stop the raiders coming in low. The underside of the silver blimps reflected the scarlet flames.

'Look,' Evelyn cried, 'the bombers are directly overhead.'

Their shapes were etched against the sky. The roar of exploding bombs numbed the eardrums. There was one bang, more throaty, more ear-piercing than all the others. Shrapnel pattered on the road and in the gardens then there was a tremendous rush of hot air. The smell of cordite was overpowering. Hot metal was falling like rain.

A few streets from Temple's house, the sky suddenly turned a dazzling blue. A livid hail of incendiaries was coming down all around them. Evelyn screamed. Instinctively, Paul threw a protective arm around her. Then the strangest thing happened. Though fires were springing up around them like torches, not one touched them. There was a loud *pss-pss-pss* but the cascade of sparks and burning material left them alone as if they were sheltering beneath an invisible umbrella. After a few moments, Evelyn raised her head and stared in wonder. Evelyn watched the strange, fiery monsoon, then she laughed out loud. Fire and fear, Paul thought, my powers.

'Are you doing this?' she cried.

'Yes,' Paul said, watching the display of pyrotechnics with wonder, 'I think I am.' That's when he saw Wallace racing towards them, dodging the molten lead that was plummeting from the sky. Was it his voice Paul had heard earlier?

'Thank God you're safe,' he said. 'I thought I'd lost you.'

'What do you mean?' Paul asked. 'You've been following us all the way.'

Wallace frowned. 'No, I lost you in the cinema foyer. I've only just caught up.'

'So who was following us?' Paul wondered out loud.

He felt an unpleasant sensation slide down his spine. There was only one person it could be. That explained the sense of foreboding. He wouldn't treat it so lightly again.

'Are you armed?' Paul asked.

'No,' Wallace answered. 'They won't issue me with a firearm when I'm on office duties.'

There was a lull in the bombing. Bones clicked as they stretched and strained, morphing into new shapes. Joints adjusted themselves. Gristle crackled. A nose became an animal muscle. Teeth mutated into fangs.

'Do you hear that?' said Paul.

'No,' Evelyn replied, anxiety in her voice. 'What is it?'

There was a low throaty growl then a form appeared over by the rail yards. Paul saw the blood wolf but he sensed the man behind the beast.

'Harry.'

Wallace too saw the loping figure. 'But he doesn't look human.' He remembered the creatures he had fought outside Cotton's flat. 'He's transformed into a demon, hasn't he?'

Paul took a step forward. His racing heartbeat was banging in his chest. 'You've got to take care of Evelyn.'

'What are you doing, Paul?' Evelyn cried. 'We've got to run.'

'You run,' Paul told her. 'I'm staying.'

The blood wolf was advancing towards him. Paul crouched, hands starting to blaze.

'I'm going to destroy you, boy,' Harry snarled, 'then there will be no obstacle to my triumph.'

He leapt forward, claws slashing in steely arcs. Paul retreated back against a wall and ducked. Harry's claws stuttered down the crumbling brickwork, throwing up a shower of sparks. In reply, Paul threw out both hands and a sheet of flame formed to block Harry's advance. Harry simply walked through it.

'A good try for a beginner,' he growled, 'but not

good enough to stop Harry boy.' He tore again as Paul slithered away. The attack opened a rent in Paul's jacket. 'How's the family, Paul? The Master says you had an exciting couple of weeks with your darling brother.'

Paul gripped both hands together. A fireball exploded in the road at Harry's feet, making him spring backwards.

'Oh, very good,' Harry said. 'You're learning fast. That could actually have hurt me. The Master told me to be careful.'

The raid resumed. There was the crash of tumbling masonry as a nearby building took a direct hit. It was already a seething mass of fire. Paul saw the confidence in the blood wolf's yellow eyes. He had to try something. He focused on the building with all his might. The familiar dark shapes gathered and swirled in a violent circle at the heart of the inferno. Instantly, a gust of wind stirred the flames and they engulfed Harry. He howled in pain and fled backwards, cursing and staring at Paul through the firelight.

'Now that's new,' Harry said, his voice more serious, even respectful. 'It seems I've underestimated you.' Smoke was rising from his back and shoulders where the flames had scorched him. 'I won't make the same mistake again.'

He loped forward once more. This time Paul felt a surge of energy roar from Harry. It blasted him off his feet and he landed in a tangled heap fifty yards away.

Through a pall of smoke he saw Wallace dragging a reluctant Evelyn towards Temple's house.

'You like this one, don't you?' Harry said, striding forward. 'I can see why. She's a pretty little thing. That's a mistake. It gives you an Achilles heel. Our kind don't do relationships, Paul. Family ties you down. Emotion makes you weak. The demon brothers just take from people and move on.'

'I'm not like you!' Paul yelled.

Harry looked down at him as he struggled to rise. 'Oh yes, you are, more than you can imagine. There was another girl before this one, wasn't there, maybe one before that? You're no different to me. When you feel a hunger, you feed it. That's as it should be. You should come over to Lud. Together, we would be unstoppable.'

Paul redirected a jet of flame from the inferno in the rail yard. Harry skipped away easily then fell upon Paul. Paul crashed a fist into Harry's jaw. In the moment of surprise that followed, he managed to roll away from his more powerful opponent, but not before Harry had cut three painful slashes in his upper arm. They rose at the same time, blundering into another shower of incendiaries. Paul retreated into their magnesium flare for protection. The blood wolf blinked.

'Clever,' he said. 'I'll have to watch you.' Then he paused. 'Oh no I won't. Tonight you die.'

Paul crouched back, awaiting the next onslaught.

'You're getting short of ideas, aren't you?' Harry said. 'That's your inexperience. A demon brother needs a range of skills.' He glanced at the roadway. 'Watch.'

In the same instant that the words left Harry's lips, the tarmac erupted beneath Paul's feet. He hurtled through the air, cocooned in a tornado of dust and debris, before tumbling painfully to the ground. He groaned. His lungs were aching and he was struggling for breath. The blood wolf was marching towards him.

'Say hello to your brother,' Harry roared. 'You'll be reunited with John in Hell.'

But before Harry reached Paul, a gunshot cracked. Harry spun round. Temple was running towards him. He fired again and with remarkable accuracy given the difficulty of the shot. The bullet spat against the road not six inches from where Harry was standing. Paul gazed up at the monstrous face that loomed above him.

'It's just a postponement,' Harry told him. 'I'll be seeing you again soon.'

With that, he fled into the night. Temple followed for a few paces but Harry was long gone. He held out a hand and Paul rose groggily to his feet.

'You just saved Evelyn's life,' he said.

'Don't make too much of it,' Paul said. 'I'm also the one who put her in danger in the first place.'

Temple patted his arm. 'I think we both did that, old son. Connie meant well, but I should have insisted you stay inside the house. Harry was bound to come after you. Let's get back.' Temple remembered something. 'Cotton seems very excited. He says he's got something to show you.'

Forty-two

Cotton met Paul in the hallway. 'Did Temple tell you?' He held up Strachan's diaries. 'I know what Harry's after.'

'For goodness' sake, Hugh,' Temple said, 'let him get through the door before you start bending his ear.'

Hearing voices, Evelyn ran into the hall. 'Paul!' Her face drained of blood. 'You're hurt.'

'He broke the skin,' Paul said. 'I don't think there's any muscle damage. I was lucky.'

'It didn't seem like luck to me,' Temple said. 'I'd say you gave a pretty good account of yourself out there.'

Paul shook his head. 'I was out of my depth. Harry's too strong. There won't always be a bombing raid I can use against him, and if you hadn't come along, I'd be dead. I don't understand how I'm supposed to stop him.'

'I think *we* is the operative word in this case,' Temple said. 'According to this prophecy of yours, we're both essential to stopping Harry.'

Soon, everyone was gathered in the kitchen. Evelyn was using cotton wool and hot water to clean Paul's wound. Connie was cutting some gauze the right size to make a dressing.

'Now I'm ready to hear what you've found, Hugh,' Paul said.

Hugh started to read from Strachan's diary: '*I know what he wants from me.*' He paused. '*He* is Samuel Rector. The account makes it clear in another section.'

Paul smiled. He could hear the academic speaking. 'I guessed.'

Hugh looked embarrassed. 'Of course.' He continued with the reading. '*The devil is holding my child. I must serve him or lose Victoria. Dear God, it feels as if she is lost to me already. What crime have I committed to be tormented so? There is hatred in my daughter's eyes. She belongs to him now. Even if I do as he says, is it really possible for her to be as she was?*'

'So what does Samuel want?' Paul demanded.

Hugh read a second entry. '*If I do as the blackguard says, the very gates of Hell will open. The devil I have encountered, this Samuel Rector, is but a shadow of the creature that stirs beneath London. He wishes to take advantage of the construction work I have begun.*'

'Explain,' Paul said.

'I already did,' Hugh told him. 'A hundred years ago the London and Blackwall Railway Company were building a station in the Minories, not far from Aldgate. Strachan was one of the engineers on the project. He pinpoints the whole area not just as the site of one of the original gates to Roman London, but as the entry point to Lud's tomb. May I go on?'

Paul nodded. 'Do.'

'The creature possesses such satanic power it was interred many centuries ago, encased in stone so strong, and bound by magic so powerful, that his captors believed he would never rise again to terrorize the world. They were wrong. Rector has hatched a plan. He will launch an assault on the first of the four seals that bind the great temple in which Lud is held.'

'Four seals,' Paul said.

'Yes,' Cotton said excitedly, 'not just gates but seals, locks, secured through sorcery. You can't just walk into this resting place and open the coffin. Assault the seals and the magic contained within them will drive you insane or turn your flesh to flame. Strachan found the story told in chronicles from other times.' He flicked through the first diary until he found the page. 'Just listen to this: *I uncovered a mediaeval account this day. It tells of four seals. Each one must be broken before Lud can rise. The priests of old did their job well, encasing the Beast in a crypt whose defences were quite ingenious.'*

Cotton paused in his telling. 'These priests are mentioned more than once. In one account they are referred to as druids, in another as fire-priests.'

'Yes, yes,' Evelyn said, 'that's all very interesting but what about Aldgate?'

Cotton looked a bit put out but he continued anyway: '*Aldgate is the old gate, the Aeldergate. Its proportions are huge. The seal that imprisons Lud is rumoured to stretch from Houndsditch almost to the Tower of London, a construction of such prodigious dimensions it must have taken years, even decades, to build. And I am to be the architect of the monster's freedom. Dear God, can I really do this, even if the reason is the return of my only child? I will be selling my soul to the Devil himself.*'

'You said the diaries explained what Harry was up to,' Evelyn said. 'How? Isn't his plan to kill Mr Churchill.'

'That's only the first step,' Paul said, 'isn't it Hugh?'

Cotton placed the diaries one on top of the other in front of him. 'Quite. The assassination of the Prime Minister will herald a Nazi invasion. The East End's new rulers will hand Aldgate over to Harry. If I read his intentions correctly, he will excavate the entire area to expose the first seal. That's his plan.'

Temple stared. 'I thought this was just an assassination attempt.'

Soon, the gathering broke up. Temple was on the phone to Morrison, asking if anyone had been able to change the PM's mind. Connie was reading the diaries. Her face told a tale. She wasn't sure whether to dismiss them as an insane fantasy or to shrink from them as true documents of evil. Evelyn was bathing baby Denis. Paul and Cotton were sitting in the parlour.

'Do you think the others understand the implications of what's in the diaries?' Cotton asked.

'I doubt it,' Paul said, 'they're still thinking in terms of Churchill and the prospect of a Nazi invasion.'

'But you're looking beyond that, aren't you?' Hugh said.

'Yes,' Paul said, 'I'm just starting to understand what I've taken on. I don't know if I can do it, Hugh.' He rested his head on the back of the armchair. 'Even if we thwart Harry here, there will be more enemies to fight. I thought I would stop Harry and destroy Lud in one fell swoop. I thought I'd be able to go home. I was deluding myself. If I'm to defeat Lud, this is only the first of many battles. Hugh, I'm not that strong.'

Hugh stared out at the night. 'Is anyone?'

Forty-three

London, Thursday, 16 January, 1941

In just over twenty-four hours the Prime Minister would set out on the forty-mile drive through London and Buckinghamshire. Paul imagined the long country lanes that led to Chequers. They were open stretches of killing ground. For several moments Paul and Temple sat together without speaking. Soon the wintry sunlight was struggling to illuminate the parlour. There was a knock at the door.

'That'll be Brenda,' Temple said. He called upstairs. 'Are you ready to go, Evelyn?'

'Do I have to?' Evelyn asked as she came downstairs. 'It's much more exciting here.'

Connie was already opening the door to Brenda.

'Sorry, old thing,' Temple said. 'Last night you were

exposed to things you should never have witnessed. I can't change that now.' He heard Brenda's voice. 'But we came to an agreement. You've got to go home. You'll be safe there.' He leaned forward and whispered the next sentence. 'Not a word to your mother.'

Evelyn pulled a face and picked up her overnight bag. 'So that's it? No more adventures for me?' She glanced at Paul. 'You're going with Uncle George tomorrow, aren't you? You're going to try to stop Harry?'

'That's why I came,' Paul said.

'And I have to carry on with life as if nothing happened.'

'You'll be safe,' Paul said. 'That's what matters.'

Brenda popped her head round the door. 'Are you ready, Evie?'

Evelyn sighed and followed her mother.

'Bye, Evelyn,' Paul called after her.

Evelyn didn't answer.

'Don't worry about Evie,' Temple said. 'She'll soon get over it. Come with me. I've got something to show you. It'll keep you occupied and take your mind off Evelyn.'

Temple led the way out to the back garden. 'What do you think?'

'It's a motorbike.'

Temple patted the petrol tank. 'It's a BSA 350.'

'Where did you get it?'

'It belongs to Wallace,' Temple said. 'He knew we needed transport. Do you know how to ride one?'

'I do actually,' Paul said. 'My uncle took me off-roading once.' He saw Temple's look of confusion. 'We went out into the country and he showed me how to ride one.' He didn't say it was a Suzuki. That would only complicate things. He realized that this was one of the few times he had been close to making a mistake. He marvelled that he felt so at home in the past. 'Why do you ask anyway?'

Temple rested a hand on the bike. 'If something happens to me, you'll have to ride it. I was going to show you how. Now there's no need.'

They were still tinkering with the bike when Connie opened the kitchen window. 'George, Morrison's on the phone.'

'Maybe Ketsch has had a change of heart,' Temple said hopefully. He listened for a few moments then put the phone down.

'What is it?' Paul asked.

'I've got some bad news, Paul,' Temple said. 'It's Hugh Cotton. He's been snatched off the street.'

'What!'

'It happened outside the BBC. A Morris saloon pulled up. Cotton was pistol-whipped and dragged into the car. It took off at high speed.'

'You're sure it's Hugh?' Paul asked.

'They found his wallet. It must have fallen out of his pocket.'

Paul knew there was only one explanation. Lud was about to exact his revenge.

*

Hugh Cotton recovered consciousness slowly. Gradually, the shadows fell away and the room around him took on solid form. He recognized it immediately: the oak panelling, the thick, flock wallpaper, the heavy, velvet curtains that gave it its oppressive quality, its dark timelessness. Until that moment, he hadn't realised quite how frozen in time the place was. There was electric lighting but little else could have changed since Arthur Strachan lived there a century earlier. Cotton was sitting in an armchair in Miss Strachan's drawing room at 13, West Cromwell Place.

'What am I doing here?' he murmured.

Then he remembered. A man had asked him directions. He knew the tall, muscular, square-jawed individual immediately, but he was too slow to react. There was a blinding pain then he blacked out. He winced at the memory and the dull ache on the left side of his head.

'Hurts, doesn't it?' a voice asked behind him.

'You're Harry Rector, aren't you?' Cotton said, trying to turn round.

'You made a grave mistake when you warned the boy,' Harry said, still from behind him. 'Nobody crosses King Lud and gets away with it.'

Cotton tried to get to his feet but found his arms bound to the chair.

'You're not going anywhere,' Harry told him. 'My Master will be with us presently.'

'Your Master?'

'Oh, don't play the fool,' Harry snapped. 'You know exactly who I mean.'

Lud. Cotton felt the slow creep of fear over his skin. His captor stepped into view. Behind Harry the winter dusk was gathering. The moment Cotton set eyes on Harry a sliver of ice entered his blood. He remembered all the things Paul had said about him.

'You're afraid of me,' Harry said, satisfaction in his voice. 'You've got good reason, my friend. What a pity you won't live to witness the act that will make my name reverberate through the vaults of time.'

Cotton was trying to be brave but he couldn't stop a bead of perspiration working its way down his forehead.

'What are you going to do to me?' he asked, a tremor in his voice.

'Whatever my Master instructs me to do,' Harry said simply. 'Be sure of this, you will suffer all the torments of Hell before you die.' He grinned. 'Then we will send you there.'

'Please,' Cotton said, struggling against his bonds, 'you don't have to do this. You can let me go. You're a man, just like me.'

Harry laughed out loud at that.

'Why are you laughing?' Cotton demanded, appalled by Harry's reaction.

'You think I'm a man just like you, do you?' Harry asked. 'I think you might want to reconsider.' Instantly, a grotesque mutation began. Blood was oozing from every pore on Harry's body. Thick, animal bristles followed. Cotton watched in stark, flesh-numbing horror as Harry transformed himself into the blood wolf. 'Do you still think there's a human bond between us, Mr Cotton?'

Cotton moved his head slowly from side to side. 'What are you?'

'Don't you know?' Harry asked. 'I thought you'd studied my ancestor, Samuel.'

He returned to human form. A thought occurred to the terrified Hugh Cotton.

'What have you done to Miss Strachan?' he asked.

'That old hag,' Harry said. 'I showed her what her ancestor, Arthur, witnessed a hundred years ago.'

With that, he swung the armchair round. Cotton screamed. Not a yard away, Miss Strachan's corpse was propped up in an armchair identical to the one in which he was sitting. She was less a human being than a twisted mannequin, drained of colour and life. Her desiccated face was contorted into an unnatural sneer of terror. Rigor mortis had fixed the rictus grin into a macabre mask.

'It suits the shrivelled old spinster, don't you think?' Harry gloated.

'You enjoyed it,' Cotton exclaimed, 'you actually enjoyed killing the poor woman.'

He heard the cruel sweep of the wind outside.

'Of course I enjoyed it,' Harry chortled. 'Isn't that the purpose of life, to have a bit of fun? It's probably the most exciting thing that ever happened to the old shrew.'

Cotton watched the cruelty and glee in Harry's expression. That was the moment he gave up all hope of survival. It felt as if there was barbed wire coiled around his heart. Within seconds the garrotte of fear was twisted tighter round his throat. From nowhere, a hot draught blew through the house, tossing the curtains about and sending loose papers swirling round Miss Strachan's precious escritoire. A fierce whirlpool of darkness started to rage. Knowing what was coming, Cotton felt dread swirling through his bloodstream. King Lud had risen before him.

'So you thought you could defy me and live, did you?' Lud sneered. 'Well, know this, I will take the renegade in my own time. I will crush Paul Rector just as I have crushed all my enemies.'

Strangely, the very fact that all hope had gone gave Cotton courage.

'You know that's an idle boast,' Cotton retorted. 'Paul will stop you. It's his destiny.'

Lud's eyes narrowed but Cotton forced the words out, determined to manage one last moment of defiance before he died.

'I completed my studies just last night,' he said. 'I found the rest of Samuel Rector's testament, the fragment the prison chaplain hid from public knowledge. I also read Voss's notes. I know why you want Aldgate.'

'Do you now?' Lud mused. 'Well, they do say every man eventually finds his way to the Devil's door.'

'Your tomb's down there,' Cotton cried. 'You didn't conquer your enemies. They overcame you. For two millennia you've lain interred far beneath the earth, incarcerated in darkness, contained by four magical bonds.' He glanced at Harry. 'This creature wishes to set you free but he'll fail, just as all your other lackeys have failed.'

'Well, well,' Lud chuckled, 'so the little mouse now has the roar of a lion. I salute your new-found bravery, but I am unimpressed by your prophecy. It's an unequal battle, and one I will win some day soon. You see, my captors have to succeed every time if they are to contain me. But I have only to triumph once.' His eyes burned in the shadowy haze that concealed his face. 'That's the great fear of the jailer, that he can prevent his prisoner escaping nine hundred and ninety nine times in a thousand. But the poor, wretched fool will be remembered for the one time the prisoner broke free. The bolts that hold down the cover on chaos, that contain the raging power of the lord of demons, they are shaking free as we speak. It is but a matter of a time before I tear down the walls of my prison. Tomorrow, Harry here will take the first step. He will destroy Churchill . . . and Paul Rector.'

'I believe in Paul,' Cotton said.

'Take him away,' Lud told Harry. 'You know what to do.'

Harry released Cotton from his bonds and dragged him struggling to Arthur Strachan's study. Determined to resist the demon menace to the last, Cotton mustered a final act of defiance.

'*Vince malum bono*,' he yelled. 'Good conquers evil.'

'On the contrary,' Harry snorted, '*Ut malus sim, vince bonum malo.*' He shoved Cotton to the floor and knelt beside him, hissing into his ear. 'There will be no happy ending to this tale, Hugh Cotton, no redemption, not for you. Soon, the laws of your pathetic race will cease to hold sway. Chaos will be unleashed, the realm of demon kind, those who live by appetite and instinct alone. Now, look into my eyes.'

Hugh Cotton looked. He saw the black flame of madness in Harry's stare and his soul turned to stone.

'I'm going to leave you now,' Harry said. 'You're going to see what cut those words into the wall.'

Cotton heard the key rasp in the lock. Soon a shadow grew in the room. It took on human form. He could only see her from behind. It was a girl in a Victorian crinoline. Her long blond hair spilled over her shoulders. Cotton was confused.

'Hello,' he said.

The girl began to cry. In spite of the warning that screamed in his mind, Cotton took a step forward.

'Don't cry,' he said.

He'd almost reached her when her head started to turn. The girl's neck made a creaking sound like an old wooden gate. There was a final sudden twist and he saw her face. It was nightmare made flesh. Her skin was old and withered. Her eye sockets were empty. When she opened her mouth, her tongue took the form of a living cockroach. Cotton gazed at the face of Evil and started to scramble backwards. To the university teacher, all the world's horrors were now embodied in the hideous form that was rising before him.

'You're scared, aren't you, Hugh Cotton?' Harry laughed from outside the door. 'Scared to death.'

The girl came forward. Her hands weren't human. They were the talons of some predatory bird. Cotton closed his eyes and waited for the end. From the hallway Harry enjoyed the sound of Cotton's death throes for a few moments longer. He delighted in the feverish drumming of Cotton's shoes on the wooden floor as Victoria Strachan went to work on him. Then, when it was over, Harry strode toward the front door, leaving Hugh Cotton's lifeless body to the vermin. It was time to go. He had less than an hour to get over to Enfield.

Forty-four

'I think you're rather smitten with young Paul,' Brenda said, hanging up her coat.

Evelyn followed her mother into the hall of their modest semi, just over a mile away from the Temples.

'Oh, Mum, don't tease,' Evelyn protested as she too hung up her coat and dropped her hat on the hall table. She cast a wary glance at her mother. 'Did Connie say something to you?'

'I don't need Connie to tell me when my daughter's giving a boy the eye,' Brenda said. 'I've seen the way you are around him. I was young once, you know.' She reached over and rested her hand on her Evelyn's forearm. 'I wouldn't get too attached, dear. Something tells me he won't be around for long.'

'I bet Uncle George told you to say that,' Evelyn said.

'George!' Brenda snorted. 'Don't be silly. He's far too secretive to discuss his miracle boy with me.'

'What then?'

'There's something about the expression in that boy's eyes,' Brenda said. 'He's got that faraway look. Believe me, he's got wanderlust.'

For a moment she thought about mentioning the other thing she'd seen, a small flame of darkness that worried her. Evelyn didn't say another word about Paul. Instead, she walked through to the kitchen. There was a kettle and a tea caddy on a flower-patterned metal tray.

'Shall I make you a nice cup of tea?' she asked.

'Yes,' Brenda said, 'I'd like that.'

She turned on the wireless. A Glenn Miller tune was playing, *Little Brown Jug.* 'Oh, I like this one,' she said.

She leaned across to draw the curtains then jumped with fright. An image had burst upon her mind: a soulless look, a wide, smirking mouth, unnatural skin that gleamed in spite of the blackout. She recoiled, catching her hip on the corner of the sink. The jarring impact made her wince.

'What is it?' Evelyn asked, startled.

Brenda was staring outside, wide-eyed and shaken by what she'd seen. 'I could have sworn I saw someone.'

'Where?'

Brenda pointed at the bushes at the bottom of the small garden. 'Right there,' she said. 'There was a tall man. He was just standing there like a statue, watching.' She cast anxious glances left and right, sweeping the garden with a stare, then finished drawing the curtains. Already, she was beginning to wonder if she was mistaken, that she'd made too much of the floating shadows of black-out London. She shuddered, remembering the coldness of the stranger's look. 'Watching.'

Evelyn reached for the curtains.

'No, darling,' Brenda said. 'Don't.'

'I've got to see,' Evelyn said, tugging at the curtains and peering out. 'What if there *is* somebody out there?' Already, there was a name buzzing in her head. She scanned the darkened garden. 'Why don't I get the torch?'

'No,' Brenda said, 'you'll only have the ARP warden round telling us to put out the light.'

'What if there's an intruder?' Evelyn asked.

Brenda forced herself to peek out. The garden seemed to be empty. She was willing it to have been a play of the shadows. She offered up a silent prayer. *Please don't let him be real.* Then she answered Evelyn. 'I'll phone George.'

Temple was there within minutes. He prowled round the garden poking into every corner. He searched the house, the Anderson shelter, even the garden shed.

'I can't find anything,' he said.

'Thanks for coming anyway,' Brenda said. 'I didn't mean to drag you out on a wild goose chase. Sorry.'

'Forget it. I'd be annoyed with you if you hadn't. These are dangerous times.'

'I've got an over-wrought imagination,' Brenda said, seeing George out. 'I must have been seeing things.'

But Brenda wasn't seeing things. As Temple walked off down the road, Harry vaulted over the garden fence from the neighbouring garden, landing with all the velvety assurance of a cat, and resumed his surveillance. He leaned against the wall by the kitchen window. He was listening to every word they said, trying to decide when to take the girl. Such a pretty little thing, he thought, the ideal bargaining counter to use against his troublesome relative. Hearing mother and daughter enter the living room, he moved noiselessly round the corner of the house and continued to eavesdrop.

'I am silly,' Brenda said. 'Fancy dragging George out like that.'

'He didn't mind,' Evelyn said. 'What if it was a German spy?' She didn't mention Harry. Mum was upset enough already. 'You never know.'

'Honestly, Evelyn, I'm sure a German spy would have better things to do than watch you and I making a cup of tea.'

At that, Evelyn laughed out loud. 'Maybe he thinks there's a message in the tea leaves.'

'Let's just forget it,' Brenda said. 'The dark has a strange effect on the mind. Do you know, when I was a little girl my curtains had Paisley patterns. I used to scream the house down, thinking the swirls were eyes.'

She sighed. 'How I hate this war. It's turned London into a place of darkness. Sometimes it feels quite alien.'

Something was happening, something she couldn't explain. Mum obviously felt it too. That was why she'd been so disturbed by the play of the shadows outside the window.

'I'm working tomorrow,' Brenda reminded Evelyn. 'Do you want me to walk you round before I go?'

'At eight o'clock in the morning?' Evelyn said. 'There's no need. I'm almost sixteen.'

'Yes,' Brenda said, 'of course you are. There are times I wonder where the years have gone. We'll walk up to the main road together then you can make your own way.'

Outside, Harry smiled. He knew exactly when he would take the girl.

Forty-five

London, Friday, 17 January, 1941

Harry was back at half past seven. It was Friday, the day he was going to remove both Winston Churchill and the renegade Paul Rector from Hitler's path. The conquest of Britain would inevitably follow then the Master's freedom would be close. Half an hour earlier, Harry had left Maggie Coleman in bed and took her car. There would be no chance of MI5 or Special Branch tracking him down to the Kensington flat where he'd been holed up.

Harry smiled as he drove up the road. Her petrol allocation was only three gallons a month and he'd used most of it up in just a few days. What a trusting soul she was. Just think how furious she would be when she discovered that her new 'gentleman friend' had stolen her beloved car. He knew that her neighbours were already scandalized by the fact that Major Coleman's wife had got a fancy man while her husband was away fighting in foreign parts. Now they could be scandalized anew by the fact that he'd turned out to be a brazen thief as well as a blackguard.

Harry parked across the road from Evelyn's house and settled in to wait for her to emerge. Inside, Evelyn was finishing a round of toast. There was no butter left so she'd spread it with a smear of marmalade. There was only one more jar in the cupboard, meaning she had to be sparing. She wondered if she would even be seeing Paul. Today was the day they were going to shadow Mr Churchill's convoy.

'Are you ready?' Brenda called. 'I could do with leaving early.'

'Almost,' Evelyn answered. She raced upstairs and snatched her magazines and book from the bed. 'Right, let's go.'

They set off at a brisk pace. They didn't notice the Humber saloon parked on the other side of the road, or the man who had sunk low in the driver's seat to avoid being seen. At the corner mother and daughter parted, Brenda going to the left and Evelyn to the right. Harry selected first gear and drove past Evelyn, pulling up about a hundred yards further on up the main road in the entrance to the cemetery. It was the quietest spot on the route to Temple's house. That's where he would take her. Oblivious to the danger ahead, Evelyn hurried along the street singing *Keep Young and*

Beautiful. She hadn't been able to get it out of her head since that night at the cinema. She'd decided it was their tune, hers and Paul's.

Harry watched her approach in the rear-view mirror. He had the steady, hollow eyes of a predator. He liked her bobbing, carefree walk. It signalled that she didn't have the faintest idea he was watching her. He raked the main road, right and left, with a searching gaze. It was busy enough but most of the people on the street were waiting at bus stops or popping into shops. What's more, there was a convenient curtain of morning mist that reduced people to hazy shadows. He'd chosen well. He let Evelyn walk past then he called her back.

'Evelyn.'

Evelyn spun round and saw the stranger. 'How do you know my name?'

Harry didn't answer but there was enough in his gaze to set alarm bells ringing in her head. She retreated a couple of steps. That was all she had, a couple of steps. Her back was already pressed against the railings.

'What do you want?'

The answer was as simple as it was chilling. 'You.'

Evelyn's scream was shrill. It slashed through the morning air. But, before any of the passers-by could react, Harry had stabbed his finger and thumb into her throat, rendering her senseless. He bundled her into the car and clambered into the driver's seat. He put the pedal to the metal and left the handful of perturbed onlookers far behind. Heading north, he glanced at the unconscious girl beside him.

'So you think you can stop me, do you Paul?' he said to nobody in particular. 'We'll see. And if you do, I'll be able to use her as a bargaining counter.'

Forty-six

*I*n his underground crypt, Lud is restless. He should be happy. He has been waiting centuries for just this moment. His eyes roam through London, past, present and future. The borders of time don't hold him. His body is encased in stone and bound by iron and by magic. But his spirit has broken free. His fiery gaze peers through windows, gazes down dark alleys, looks over the shoulders of his disciples. He sees everything: the neon glare of the twenty-first century, the rubble of wartime, the yellowish glare of gaslight in Victorian alleyways. Lud stares down at Evelyn, her head rocking back and forth as Harry leaves the capital's northern suburbs behind.

Is this it, he wonders? Will Harry succeed? All the signs point to victory. Soon, the East End will be mine, Lud tells himself. Then Aldgate will fall. The first seal will be broken and I will begin my inexorable march to freedom. Then what fun I'll have, what mischief. Just moments later, the scarlet eyes dim slightly. There is a problem. The renegade lives. He barely understands his power. But he is dangerous. What if Harry underestimates him in spite of all my warnings? Lud is consumed with a searing rage. You will not fail, Harry. I will not permit it. My power is growing. Together we must shatter all obstacles to my rise. Heed me, Harry, Lud snarls. Mark my words. Callow youth this boy may be, but he could thwart us yet. There will be no sentimentality, my disciple. You must crush him. Yes, roast him in the fires of Hell.

Forty-seven

Temple killed the BSA's engine and pulled it up onto its stand. The engine ticked as it cooled. They were waiting to pick up Churchill's entourage.

'You're sure they're coming this way?' Paul asked.

'Absolutely positive,' Temple said. 'Morrison sat in on the meeting where they decided the route. Are you ready for this?'

Paul shrugged. If he was quite honest, he was terrified. Harry was a brutal opponent. 'We don't have much of a plan, do we?'

Temple pulled a face. 'How do you plan for a hellfiend?'

Paul caught his eye. 'I'm sorry I've given you so much trouble.'

'There's no need to apologize,' Temple said. 'Harry's the one who's giving us trouble.' He looked along the road. 'I wish I knew what had happened to Hugh though.'

'He's dead,' Paul said grimly. 'His fate was sealed the moment Harry took him.' He chewed at his bottom lip. 'He was a good man.'

Temple nodded. 'So was Sharples. We're going to stop Harry. He's going to pay for his crimes.'

'I hope so,' Paul said. He was about to say something else when he picked up the sound of three cars travelling fast. 'Here they come.'

Temple kick-started the bike and Paul climbed on the pillion seat. There were three cars in the convoy. Wallace was in the first car with two other men. Churchill and Walter Thompson were in the second, immediately behind. Morrison brought up the rear.

'Here we go,' Temple said.

They followed the convoy at a distance. Churchill's party was travelling fast through north-west London, jumping red lights and taking traffic islands on the right. Paul watched the miles of bomb damage. There were blasted trees, empty windows and scarred buildings. There were piles of broken bricks, criss-crossed with blackened roof timbers. Soon, they left the cratered city behind them. Their destination was Chequers, a red-brick manor house forty miles to the north. On the way they weaved through miles of beech woods in the Chiltern hills. Paul's eyes darted left and right. It was a perfect terrain for Harry Rector to mount his ambush.

They reached the outskirts of the capital without

incident. There was less bomb damage here. Soon, as the suburbs thinned, they entered the most dangerous phase of the journey, the long miles of open country-side. The wintry sunlight flickered through the bare trees. On a couple of occasions Paul spotted somebody standing in a field or walking along a grass verge and he would tense. Both times his heart turned over but they were false alarms. It was only ordinary citizens going about their normal business. He listened to the rumble of the engine. He couldn't believe that Harry wouldn't strike somewhere along this exposed route. No, they wouldn't reach Chequers without an assas-sination attempt. Harry would never have a better opportunity. It was getting dark. The last rays of the sun were stabbing through the trees.

Paul watched the tail lights of Churchill's car ahead. Three cars, maybe a dozen armed men. Even for Harry, taking Churchill out wouldn't be an easy task, but it would be infinitely easier than having to attack Chequers, where there would be over one hundred guards. Paul tapped Temple on the shoulder and shouted against the noise of the wind and the BSA's engine. 'How far to Chequers?'

'Twenty minutes,' Temple answered, 'half an hour at the most.'

'Then he has to attack soon,' Paul said.

Temple nodded. 'I know.'

They rounded another bend. Churchill's car took it quicker than Morrison's and a gap opened between the two vehicles. As Temple tried to close it, there was a loud creaking noise followed by a thunderous roar.

'Look out!' Paul yelled.

A huge beech was falling right in the path of Morrison's vehicle. The driver slammed on the brakes and screeched to a halt. Twigs from the uppermost branches squealed against the windscreen but there was no major damage; more than could be said for the lead car protecting Churchill. There was a tremendous explosion and a ball of flame lit the night. The black saloon was lifting off the road and the bonnet was crumpling. The windscreen blew out next and a roar filled the air. The blast from the fuel tanks swept the woods. Finally, horrifically, like a puppet, the driver erupted through the hole in the windscreen. Wallace and another man rolled out of the car, still alive but badly injured.

'Good God almighty!' Temple gasped.

Churchill's car rocked on its suspension as it squeezed past the destroyed vehicle. Temple swung the bike round the fallen tree and skidded to a halt by the two injured men. 'Are you all right?'

'The driver's dead,' Wallace said. 'We'll be all right. Get after the PM.'

Temple opened the throttle. Soon, they'd picked up Churchill's car in the beam of their headlight. A split-second later there was a loud bang and the vehicle careered wildly over the camber of the road. There was a second loud report and it skidded off the road. Paul tensed. He was about to face Harry again. Two burst

306

tyres within moments of each other. It was no coincidence. Temple brought the bike to a halt a few
metres from the stricken car. Thompson had thrown
open the rear door and was crouching behind it, gun
trained on the woods. Churchill was behind him, still
in the back seat.

'Stay where you are, Thompson,' Temple barked.
'We'll take care of Harry.'

'I thought you were suspended,' Thompson said.

'I decided not to accept the suspension,' Temple
said. His head snapped round. He'd noticed movement
in the woods. A dark figure was racing towards them.
'Paul,' he hissed. 'Over there!'

Paul didn't move. It was as if every ounce of energy
had drained from his body. Temple took the initiative,
raising his gun in a two-handed grip. He squinted and
squeezed off two shots. He couldn't believe how
quickly his target was moving. One bullet tore a
chunk out of a tree. The other spat up a plume of leaf
mould. Harry was no more than a hazy smudge in the
forest gloom but Paul felt his presence in the marrow
of his bones. He felt his ancestor's power. A malevolent energy throbbed around him.

Haunted by the memory of their last, unequal battle,
Paul froze. Temple was racing forward to meet Harry's
challenge. He was preparing to shoot for the third
time. He'd surprised Harry the night of the incendiary
attack. This time Harry was prepared. The bullet jammed in the barrel. Harry crashed into Temple sending
him sprawling. Harry continued with his forward

momentum. Within moments, he would be upon the Prime Minister and his bodyguard. At last Paul shrugged off the paralysis that had overtaken him. Imitating Harry's trick with the tree, Paul brought a venerable oak crashing down. Harry had to fling himself to his right to avoid being crushed. To Paul's relief, the beams of several torches were bobbing through the trees. It was Morrison and the other occupants of his car.

'Shoot!' Paul yelled at the Special Branch men. 'He can't focus on all of you at the same time. He's vulnerable. Fire!'

Instantly, the night was ripped by gunfire. Shots punched into the ground. They reminded Paul of the snap and spit of eggs in a frying pan. Impossibly agile, Harry spun this way and that, twisting out of the way of the hail of bullets. Temple got to his feet.

'Shoot to kill!' he yelled unnecessarily, as if the detectives were trying to do anything else.

But Harry was too fast, his powers too great. Within moments, he had fled into the murk. Even then, there was no respite. Paul picked up the sound of a lorry.

'Who the hell is that?' he wondered out loud.

Morrison had just arrived. He'd heard the engine too and turned, training his flashlight on the lorry. It pulled up on the high road, overlooking the woods. A dozen figures spilled out of the back of the vehicle.

'Who are they?'

Paul could hear their animal tread. Harry had reinforcements. 'I don't think we should wait to find out.' Morrison's car had just made its way round the obstacles in its path. 'Everybody into the car.'

'There isn't enough room,' Thompson said.

'Then we hang on any way we can,' Paul said, jumping onto the running board. 'I don't think we want to be in the open when they attack.'

Harry was already leading the dark figures in a second assault. He had taken Lud's commands seriously. Thompson got off a shot.

'The boy's right,' he said. 'Head for Chequers. Let's just hope he doesn't blow these tyres too.'

Forty-eight

Chequers, Friday, 17 January, 1941

By the time the sole remaining car limped up the mile long drive to Chequers, the place was on full alert. An ambulance had taken Wallace and the other officer travelling in the lead car to hospital. Wallace had a broken wrist. His colleague had minor burns. The driver wouldn't require treatment. He was on the way to the morgue. After the events of the last two hours, Temple was despondent. He knew the driver personally. First Sharples, now Payne.

'Don't take it too hard,' Thompson advised, gazing at the enormous wooded grounds. 'Casualties of war, I'm afraid.'

Paul overheard. Casualties of war. It sounded so heartless.

'Look on the bright side,' Thompson said. 'We've got the Old Man here safe and sound.'

Thompson remembered a snatch of conversation on the Clive Steps.

'Temple,' he said, 'is this what you were trying to tell me about that time? You were hinting at the supernatural.'

Temple nodded. 'I'm not hinting any more, Thompson.'

Paul was now standing some distance away, staring up at Chequers' mullioned windows. He let his gaze run along the walls. All those windows. All those doors. There were so many places Harry and his fellow demons could enter the house. That night they would be under siege.

'Are you thinking about tonight?' Temple asked.

Paul nodded.

'Come with me,' Thompson said to them. 'I'll give you the guided tour.'

Thompson inspected everything, down to the nearby *ack-ack* battery and the air-raid shelter under the manor house itself. He declared himself satisfied with what he'd seen. Paul was less so.

'This is no ordinary assassin,' he said. 'No matter how you organise the men at your disposal, there will never be enough to cover every possible approach.'

'You're right,' Temple said, 'and he's not alone. I dread to think what they were, those figures in the woods. We're sitting ducks.'

Thompson remembered. 'We do what we can. The rest is up to providence.'

He indicated the thick bushes over to their left. Though stripped of their colour by winter's attrition, they offered plenty of cover for an intruder, especially one as skilled and determined as Harry Rector.

'None of us will be getting much sleep until we've returned the PM safely back to London on Monday morning,' Thompson said.

'Harry's going to carry this through to the bitter end,' Temple said. 'We're in for a testing time.'

Thompson nodded.

'Our preparations are as good as they could be,' he said, 'under the circumstances.' He met Temple's eye. 'I'm going back. The PM will be getting ready for his evening meal.'

Paul and Temple walked the perimeter of the house, rarely taking their eyes off the woods. The buildings' defenders had set up a field of lamps. They were switched off for now, as the rules of the black-out demanded. But, at the first sign of attack, a switch would be thrown flooding the grounds with light. They trudged across the gravel to the manor house. There Temple was met by Morrison.

'You need to phone home, George,' he said. 'It sounds serious.'

Temple looked grim-faced when he put down the phone.

'What's wrong?' Paul asked.

'Evelyn's missing,' Temple said. 'Connie sounds

quite hysterical and I can't imagine what it's doing to Brenda. It seems Evie didn't show up at the house this morning.'

'Did Connie call the police?' Paul asked, his flesh creeping.

Temple nodded. 'The local bobbies called about half an hour ago. A young girl answering Evelyn's description was seen struggling with a man on the High Road. That was around the right time.'

Paul closed his eyes. 'Oh God, no!'

Temple looked broken. 'It's him, isn't it? He's got her.'

'There's no other explanation,' Paul said. 'First Hugh, then Evelyn. It's Harry.'

Temple scanned the woods. 'He's going to use her as a hostage. He wants you out of the way.'

Paul's legs sagged under him and he sat heavily on the stone steps. 'What do I do?'

'Our mission is to save Churchill,' Temple said. 'Sometime soon, Harry will call. He'll want you to go after Evelyn. When he does, you're going to tell him no. Do you understand?'

Paul stared at him in disbelief. 'How can you be so cold? Evelyn's your niece.'

'Don't give me lectures on how I should feel!' Temple snapped. 'I love that girl as if she were my own daughter. Don't you think this is tearing my heart in two?' He struggled to control his emotions. 'She's my twin sister's only child. Paul. She's part of me.' There was a moment's silence. 'I'd do anything to save her, but we can't give in to Harry. The fate of the country's at stake.'

Paul slipped into a subdued silence. A few minutes later, they were called to dinner. The places were set. They ate on a long table with the senior officers. Paul felt their eyes on him, wondering what he was doing in their company. Paul pushed his chops and potatoes around the plate and wondered where Evelyn was. He couldn't eat a thing. The very thought that Harry was holding her had opened a deep crack in his soul.

'Can't you eat either?' Temple asked.

Paul shook his head. Behind them, there was a lot of banging and shifting of furniture. 'What's going on?' Paul asked.

Thompson was sitting at the next table. 'It's film night,' he explained. 'The staff turn the Long Gallery into a makeshift cinema behind the black out curtains. They've lit the fire. We're all invited as soon as the place is warmed through.'

When the film started, Paul stood in the doorway. He wasn't watching the screen. He was thinking about Evelyn. When was Harry going to call? Around him, the walls were alive with the flickering of the film and the glow of the fire. Nightmare images of Harry and Evelyn darted through his mind. He'd just discovered what Hell was like.

Forty-nine

Evelyn was sitting in a windowless cellar fewer than ten miles from the PM's retreat. She had her arms tied behind her back and fastened to a steel bracket embedded into the brick wall behind her. She was sitting on the stone floor in her plaid skirt. No matter how she tried, she couldn't make herself comfortable. The cold bit through the material into her flesh. On waking, she'd spent the first hour shouting for someone to come. Nobody did. She then spent the next hour twisting and straining to loosen her bonds. But whoever had trussed her up while she was unconscious knew his job well. No matter how much she struggled, she couldn't squirm free.

'Damn,' she cried, 'damn, damn, damn!'

Mum would have been shocked to hear her swear

but Evelyn didn't care. She was cold, she was hungry and she was scared. Why shouldn't she curse?

'Hello,' she called, knowing it was hopeless, 'is anybody there?'

Her voice echoed off the walls. She vaguely remembered her abductor carrying her into this place. For a while, when he lifted her out of the car, she was swimming in and out of consciousness. She remembered the cawing of crows and their dark shapes wheeling overhead. Doors slammed. Then the light died. When she came to a second time, she found herself here, in this underground prison. She was in darkness, but it wasn't total. Her eyes were becoming accustomed to the gloom.

'I want to go home,' she yelled.

That's when she heard leather-soled shoes on the stairs. Somebody was making their way down to her. Next came the squeal of rusty hinges and the turn of the key in the lock. The sounds confirmed what she'd already suspected. The building was deserted. Most probably it was in an isolated location too. There would be little point in continuing to shout for help; nobody would hear. For a second, as the door opened, a blade of light carved through the gloom. Then it was dark again. She heard her captor walking towards her. After a moment, he snapped on an electric light. Evelyn blinked hard against the brightness of the unshaded bulb then she looked up into the eyes of Harry Rector.

'Why have you brought me here?' she demanded. 'I hope you understand that you're in big trouble. My uncle's a policeman.'

'I know who your uncle is,' Harry drawled. 'I know all about DI George Temple and his helper.'

Evelyn's heart stuttered. Her jailer was very self-assured. Her mention of the police hadn't flustered him one bit.

'Who are you?' she asked. The question was instinctive. She already knew the answer.

'I'm Harry Rector,' he drawled. 'Paul and I are family.'

'There's a bad apple in every barrel,' Evelyn retorted. 'Paul's decent and good. You're nothing like him.'

'Oh, you couldn't be further from the truth,' Harry told her. 'We're very much alike. Decent and good, you say? Did he tell you he killed his own brother? Did he tell you he'd already got a sweetheart?' He watched the doubt creep into Evelyn's eyes. 'He'll come over to us. It's just a matter of time.' He sniffed. 'If he doesn't, he dies.'

Evelyn didn't like the direction the conversation was taking. She changed the subject.

'I want to move. I'm cold. It's this stone floor.'

Harry smirked.

'Don't grin at me!' Evelyn shouted. 'You try sitting here hour after hour.'

Without a word, Harry untied her, then swung her over his shoulder and dumped her on some old hessian sacks on the far side of the cellar.

'Happy now?' he asked.

'These sacks smell,' Evelyn protested. What *was* that smell? It was sickly sweet.

'I can always put you back over there, you spoiled brat,' Harry said.

'I'm not spoiled!'

Harry leaned forward. 'Do you want me to put you back?'

'No,' Evelyn said hastily, grateful to be off the cold, stone floor, 'here's just fine.'

Harry started to retie her hands. As he tugged at her wrists, Evelyn remembered something she'd seen when she was little, at one of those Saturday matinees. It was worth a try. If it was going to work she had to keep him talking, distract him as he bound her.

'Are you going to hurt me?' Evelyn asked.

Harry looked at her as if he was considering it. 'Only if you force me to.'

Oblivious to her efforts, Harry tied the rope and secured it to another rusting bracket behind her. Had the trick worked, she wondered.

'So why am I here?'

'Surely you've worked that out by now,' Harry said. 'You do know what a hostage is, don't you?'

'Of course I do. I'm not an idiot!'

'Then you know what I've got in mind,' Harry said, 'I'm going to distract Paul. He's stopped me getting at Churchill once already. I'm going to use you to lure him away.'

'It won't work,' Evelyn said. 'He'll do his duty.'

'I don't think so,' Harry said. 'Paul's human side is strong. He'll come racing over here like a knight in shining armour.' He looked Evelyn up and down.

318

'What's the attraction, I wonder?' He gripped her chin and turned her head back and forth, his eyes lighting up in a way Evelyn didn't like. 'You're still a bit too young for my tastes but I could see the attraction for a boy like Paul.' He stroked her hair. 'Oh, he'll come running, all right.'

'You're wrong!'

'I don't think so.' Harry turned to go.

'I'm hungry,' Evelyn said, seeing his intentions.

'That's interesting,' Harry said, making for the door.

'I mean,' Evelyn shouted after him, 'I want something to eat now.'

Her words fell on deaf ears. Harry was already climbing the stairs.

'You're an animal!' Evelyn yelled after him.

Her eyes were stinging and her mind was full of questions about Paul but she refused to give in to despair. Already, she was wondering if the Saturday matinee trick had worked. She'd seen it in one of those serials, where the goodies are forever getting themselves tied to railway lines in front of oncoming trains. The hero (it was a man of course, women used to just lie there screaming) had tensed the muscles in his arms. When he relaxed them, there was just enough room to work his hands free. Evelyn tugged at the ropes. To her surprise, there was some give. It would be hard but, if she worked at it, she might just be able to set herself free. Privately, she had a feeling Harry was right. Paul would come for her.

Fifty

Finally, Harry called. Paul snatched the phone from Morrison. 'Hello?'

There was no answer. He shot a questioning glance at Temple.

'He's there,' Temple said. 'He's just toying with you.'

So Paul waited. Soon, he was able to make out low, regular breathing. Then Harry spoke. 'You thwarted me last night,' he said. 'That's quite impressive if I may say so. After all, you've served no apprenticeship in the demon arts. Who would have believed that a raw beginner would give me so much trouble?'

'Where's Evelyn?' Paul demanded.

'What, aren't you going to shout at me?' Harry asked. 'Where's the rage, the adolescent tantrum? Where's the impotent masculine posturing? Aren't you going to tell me what you'll do if I hurt a hair on her head?'

'Tell me!'

'That's better,' Harry chuckled. 'Oh, I do like a good roar.' There was a brief pause. 'Now where do you think she is?'

'Let me talk to her,' Paul demanded.

Evelyn came on the line. She sounded breathless and scared. 'Paul!'

'Evelyn, are you all right?'

Temple leaned closer to catch her voice.

'You've got to save Mr Churchill,' she cried. 'Paul, don't . . .'

Then Harry was back on the line. 'For somebody in such a weak position, you sound very confident, I'd be a bit more cautious if I were in your shoes. I rather think I'm holding all the aces.'

'What do you want?' Paul cried.

'Not yet,' Harry said. 'I'm going to let you stew a while before I announce my intentions. It all adds to the excitement.' There was a click on the line.

'Come back,' Paul yelled. 'Speak to me. Harry!' But he was gone. Paul relayed what Harry had said.

'Then we wait,' Temple said. 'Did Evelyn sound scared?'

'Very,' Paul told him.

Temple grimaced. 'What does he want?'

'I don't know.'

'I beg your pardon,' Temple exclaimed. 'You need to explain yourself. What did he say?'

'Only that he was going to let us stew a while,' Paul said. 'Evelyn's all right, thank God. I spoke to her briefly.'

He saw the dismay in Temple's eyes. 'So what do we do?' the detective asked.

Paul buried his face in his hands. 'There's nothing we *can* do. We have to wait.'

It was an hour before the phone rang again. On the third ring, Paul picked up the handset. 'Paul here.'

'You were very quick,' Harry said. 'You must have been hanging on.'

'Are you ready to tell me what you want?' Paul asked.

'All in good time,' Harry said. 'Can't we chat for a while? We are family, after all.'

'Tell me!' Paul bawled, losing control.

'Oh, don't get tetchy,' Harry said. 'Don't you want to know what your great, great uncle's been up to?'

'I already know,' Paul hissed. 'You're a killer and a traitor.'

As he spoke he became aware of a noise in the background. It was running water. Gooseflesh slithered over his skin. 'What's that sound?'

Harry chuckled. 'I'm running a hot bath. I must have left the tap on.'

'What are you doing to Evelyn?' Paul demanded, a quiver in his voice.

'It seems the poor lamb has never tasted a good glass of ale,' Harry said. 'I thought I might initiate her in the art of brewing.'

Paul's mind was racing as he tried to make sense of Harry's words. He snapped his fingers in Temple's direction and mouthed the word pencil. Temple handed him a note. Paul scribbled a message.

Ale. Brewing. Any ideas?

Temple shook his head. 'I'll ask,' he mouthed.

'Of course, she will insist on jumping in at the deep end,' Harry said, 'quite literally, I'm afraid.'

Paul was starting to understand. 'You're going to drown her, aren't you?' he asked.

'Not at all,' Harry answered. 'It's up to you whether she goes under.' He chuckled. 'Glug, glug, glug.'

'She's just a pawn, isn't she?'

'Absolutely,' Harry replied. 'Do you want to know where she is?'

'Tell me,' Paul said. 'Please.'

'It hurts, doesn't it?' Harry asked. 'You're caught on the horns of a dilemma. Are you going to leave Churchill to my tender mercies to save the delectable Evelyn? Oh, the agony of divided loyalties.'

'Tell me!'

Temple had entered the room. He handed Paul a note. *Philbrick's Brewery.* There was an address. Paul snatched the note and dropped the phone. 'Philbrick's Brewery?' he cried.

'Oh, well done,' Harry said. 'How resourceful of you to discover where we are.'

'Where's Winsham Lane?' Paul demanded.

'You can't leave,' Temple said, restraining Paul. 'I'll send Morrison instead.'

'Only the boy,' Harry's voice crackled over the phone. 'Only the boy or I kill her now.'

Paul met Temple's stare. 'Don't try to stop me,' he yelled. 'What kind of man are you, Temple? Evelyn's your niece.'

'You don't think I'm comfortable with this, do you?' Temple shouted back. 'This is killing me. But if we make the wrong decision, the country dies.'

Harry's voice eddied across the room. 'Don't squabble, chaps. It's make-your-mind-up time. Well, which will it be, the doe-eyed girl or the Prime Minister? I'd go with the girl myself. She's much prettier.'

Paul ran his eyes over the address.

'Somebody give me directions,' he said. 'Now!'

An officer entered the room and handed Temple a map.

'The route's marked,' he said.

Paul tore the map from Temple's grasp and raced from the room. He sprinted outside. Spotting the BSA on its stand, he yanked it forward and started the engine. He accelerated out along the drive in a spray of gravel. By the time Temple reached the front steps, Paul had already skidded onto the main road.

Fifty-one

Evelyn was nursing bruises from when Harry had dragged her upstairs to the brewery office to make the call. For some reason he'd wanted Paul to hear the sound of running water. She'd wondered what it was but Harry had taken her back to the cellar without showing her what was beyond the second door. That was one puzzle. The other was how she'd been able to speak to Paul without a phone or radio being used. She shifted her weight and looked expectantly towards the door. It squealed as it tested rusty hinges. Evelyn was pretty sure that the building couldn't be in regular use. Harry was able to come and go with complete confidence. After half an hour she'd come to the conclusion that there was no point shouting for help. After another hour she'd stopped tugging at her bonds. Try as she might, she'd been unable to extricate either hand. All she'd succeeded in doing was chafing the skin on her wrists. She waited for her captor to appear. She tensed as the doorknob turned. When Harry entered, his footsteps were surprisingly quiet on the stone floor.

'It's time to put you to use,' he said. He noticed the reddened skin where she had been trying to ease out her hands. 'Good try,' he said, 'but not good enough.'

His superior smile made her angry. If she got a chance, she would do a lot better next time.

'Now, no struggling,' Harry ordered.

'I heard running water,' Evelyn said.

'Did you?' Harry asked. 'Well, you're about to see what it is.'

He slung her over his shoulder and climbed the staircase. This time he took a different route. He carried her along a darkened passageway and stepped into a brightly-lit room. After so long in the murky cellar, the industrial bulbs hurt her eyes. As he deposited her on the ground, Evelyn was at last able to make sense of the building in which she was being held. It was a brewery. Of course, that sickly, sweet smell, it was hops. They'd visited relatives in Kent last summer. The smell had been everywhere. She also saw why it wasn't in use. There was a huge hole in the roof where a bomb had smashed its way through without exploding. Moonlight flooded in. The Luftwaffe had probably been offloading any they had left after blitzing the East End. The brewery had taken a hit.

'What are you going to do to me?' Evelyn asked.

Harry scowled. 'Don't you ever shut up?'

'Not for somebody as rude as you, I don't,' Evelyn retorted.

Harry didn't like that. He knelt beside her and grabbed her jaw between finger and thumb. A hard knot of fright formed in her throat.

'One more comment like that,' he snarled, 'and I'll ruin that pretty face.'

Evelyn saw into his eyes. She didn't doubt his ability to hurt her very badly. Satisfied that she wouldn't give him any trouble, Harry set about opening a valve. There it was: the sound of running water. Evelyn tried to see what he was doing, then her heart turned cold. Oh no. The bomb had missed the key parts of the brewery and it was still in good working order. She could hear freshly-brewed beer sloshing into a huge vat. At last, she understood his intentions. The thought of the ordeal to come tore open a gash in her mind. Her scream was a shrill alarm in the stillness of the abandoned building.

'No,' she murmured, 'you can't.'

'Don't tell me what I can or can't do, little girl,' Harry snapped. 'My kind don't obey rules. We break them. Where's the fun in doing what you're told?'

He seized the struggling girl and dragged her to the edge of the vat. She looked down and saw the frothing brown tide starting to climb the walls.

'Please, no!'

'Oh, it's *please* now,' Harry said. 'Funny how you

find your manners when you think your life's in danger.'

He suspended her over the side. He'd driven a hook into the wall of the vat and was looping the ropes that bound her over it. The moment they took her weight, a terrible pain lanced through her shoulders. She screamed. It was as if her arms were being torn from their sockets. She tried to find some way to support herself. She kicked for a moment or two then discovered another hook driven into the wall some way below. She rested her feet on it and took the weight off her shoulders. Though her upper back and chest still burned with agony, she managed to achieve a kind of respite.

'Well done,' Harry said, 'you found the support I hammered in for you.'

'You're a monster,' Evelyn gasped.

'Oh, don't be so melodramatic,' Harry scolded. 'I'm not trying to torture you. I'm a gentleman.'

'You're evil!' Evelyn cried.

If only she were stronger, she would wipe that sneering grin from his face.

Harry smirked. 'Sticks and stones may break my bones but words will never hurt me.' He glanced at the foaming gallons of beer working their way towards her feet. 'I'll be getting in touch with lover boy quite soon.' He winked. 'With Paul out of the way, there will be nobody strong enough to prevent me completing my mission.'

Harry straightened up.

'Don't leave me,' Evelyn pleaded. 'I'm begging you.'

Harry gave her a pitiless stare. There were footsteps behind him. For a moment, Evelyn dared to hope then she saw Harry smile. What she saw next made her veins run cold.

Fifty-two

*L*ud watches events unfold with growing satisfaction. Well done, Harry. You hold all the aces. Lud has always worried about Harry's arrogant streak. He has had one overriding concern. What if Harry insisted on doing it all alone? But here he is enlisting the support of his demon brothers. It's only a matter of time, Lud thinks. His spirit is racing back and forth through time. He relives his triumphs and his defeats. He sees himself young and free, riding into battle with a sword in his hand. He sees himself summoning the powers of the night and avenging himself on his enemies. Then he relives the cruel day when the priests of Beltane laid their trap for him and condemned him to twenty long centuries of imprisonment and despair. But your victory will only prove temporary, Lud declares in his underground mausoleum. Within days my bonds will be loosened.

His eyes are incandescent with a brutal joy. Then they narrow. No, Lud tells himself, you must not surrender to triumph. You must be composed, clear-headed, ruthless. The renegade may yet have some say in this matter. I have made this mistake before. I must be prepared for the possiblility of failure. He ponders the matter and smiles. This is an unequal battle, boy, he snarled. You fight on one front. I fight on many. It barely matters what happens here. His spirit roars back through time. Regardless of the outcome at Chequers, the demon master will be free, and soon.

Fifty-three

Harry's new companions were creatures of the night.

'Wolfmen,' Evelyn murmured.

'Observant little minx, aren't you?' Harry said. 'What gave it away? The fur, the fangs, the claws.'

Evelyn felt six pairs of night-dark eyes on her and looked away. 'You won't succeed.'

Harry suppressed a yawn. 'Oh, I think I will, you know.'

He watched for a while as the tide of ale reached Evelyn's knees. He enjoyed the way it frothed around her. Like brown blood, he thought. Evelyn fascinated him. Young and strong, she was struggling gamely. What fun. She was impaled on the point of her own terror.

'You've got pluck, little lady,' he teased. 'I wish I'd

invented a more interesting ordeal for you. Don't you just hate it when your imagination fails?' He put on a toff's accent and mimicked a suburban office worker leaving home. 'Still, I'm off to work. Bye bye, dear. Do have a smashing time.'

Evelyn hated his taunting. She tried to look straight ahead.

'What, no kiss on the cheek, darling?'

Evelyn twisted her neck to look at him. This time she didn't speak at all. Instead she stared him out, putting all her hatred into those heart-stopping eyes of hers. Harry simply laughed and sauntered away towards his comrades. He led the shadowy figures of the other demons out of sight.

The brewery was a small family concern. It was situated at the end of Winsham Lane, as long and lonely a country track as you could find anywhere in Buckinghamshire. Rebuilding wasn't scheduled until war's end. The night birds were the only witness to her plight. Would Evelyn live or die? Harry wondered. Would Paul arrive in time? He had a kind of detached, academic interest but he didn't really care, so long as the renegade was out of the way when he launched his final assault on the house.

He slid into the driver's seat and fired up the ignition. His fellow demons scrambled into the car or clung on. Already, Evelyn was forgotten, a mere detail of his broader plan. He was going to park a mile or so from Chequers. He didn't need the headlights, even the narrow slit permitted by the black out regulations. He could drive perfectly well by relying on his own Hell-given night sight. With a low murmur of satisfaction, he pulled away.

Inside the ruined brewery, Evelyn could feel the cold tide rising up her thighs. She was trembling violently from the cold. But there was one cause for hope. Fired by a burning hatred for her captor, she had redoubled her efforts to squirm free. Though the skin on her wrists was being peeled back and blood was trickling down her arm, she had almost released her right hand. With a final tortured scream, she tore it loose, ripping the exposed flesh. Just for a moment, she sobbed with the pain then set about untying the rest of her bonds. The hurt might be wracking her wrists and shoulders, but she wasn't going to give in. Gripping the hook from which she had been suspended, she started scrambling up the slippery sides of the vat. Time and again she managed a metre's progress before the worn soles of her shoes failed to grip. Time and again she slid back, sobbing with frustration. But, at long last, kicking off the shoes and letting them drop into the climbing tide of ale, she succeeded in scaling her way upwards and gripping the edge of the vat.

'Come on!' she shrieked at herself. 'All that tennis must have given you some strength, girl. For God's sake, pull.'

And pull she did, heaving herself up until she had her elbows on the concrete floor around the vat. Writhing and twisting for purchase, she finally hauled herself out. She rolled onto her back and lay on the floor for long moments, panting, her chest rising and falling as she sucked in lungfuls of air. She stared up at the winter sky and started to laugh out loud.

'I did it! I beat you.'

Then, barely recovered, she raced out of the brewery and ran down Winsham Lane in search of help. The winter cold bit through her damp clothes. At the same time, Paul was roaring towards her. Twice he took wrong turns. It didn't help that the road signs had been removed or painted over in case of Nazi invasion. But each time he realized his mistake and returned to the crossroads to take the correct turning. As he swung into a long, tree-lined road, he was overjoyed to see Evelyn running towards him. He stopped the bike and went to greet her. He threw out his arms and awaited her embrace but Evelyn simply stared at him.

'What have you *done*?' she murmured. 'You abandoned Mr Churchill for me?'

She took a moment to gather her thoughts then she came to a decision. 'Turn that bike around. If you matter as much as that creature seems to think, you've got to get back. He seems to think you're the only one who stands in his way.'

'I only wanted . . .'

'What?' Evelyn demanded. 'What did you want, Paul, to rescue your damsel in distress? That's a bit rich, don't you think? Who's this other sweetheart?'

'Evelyn, don't . . .'

'Just don't talk to me for a while, Paul. It's time you turned your mind to helping the Prime Minister.'

335

'Evelyn.'

'Paul, just go.'

She jumped on the pillion and wrapped her arms round his waist. Paul squeezed the throttle open and set off in the direction of Chequers.

Fifty-four

arry races through the bracken and flattens himself
against the perimeter wall. Any moment now, it's
going to start. His brother demons don't let him down.
Floodlights snap on and small arms fire rattles through
the night. Urgent shouts tell him the assault on the north
side of the grounds has thrown the defenders into confusion. He hears a couple of engines splutter to life as the
officers in charge rush reinforcements across the grounds
in military vehicles. He smiles at the crackling bursts of
machine gun fire. Listen to that, the music of the night.
Harry closes his eyes so he can enjoy the symphony of
war. Bullets spit against trees. A grenade sends sparks
dancing like fireflies. But where are the sounds of his
comrades? Soon he hears the first scream. His eyes
sparkle with pleasure. It's time to move.

Harry scrambles up the wall and drops lightly to the

ground on the far side. He listens for sentries then creeps forward through the tangle of undergrowth. As he jogs forward through the webwork of roots, he starts to transform. The blood wolf feels bare branches whipping against his face. He gives a low growl and moves on. He sucks the chill air deep into his lungs. It's a good night for a kill.

Through a gap in the trees, Harry sees the manor house. Contrary to the rules of the black out, every light is burning. Harry smiles. That makes me a greater danger than the Luftwaffe. How wonderful. In the haunted moonlight he discovers the first unsuspecting guard. The private can't be more than nineteen years old. He has his back to Harry, watching the fire flashes that are lighting the woods to his left. The blood wolf leers. This is all too easy. He falls upon his victim and tears a ragged hole in his throat. The soldier's eyes lose their hold on life and his life slips away. Now for the house.

Fifty-five

Paul had the throttle full open. The bike was eating up the distance between the brewery and Chequers. Evelyn watched the flashing trees with a mixture of terror and exhilaration. She was leaning forward, her face pressed against Paul's cheek. At first she was reluctant to lean over with him on the bends. She was so angry. Was it true, what Harry had told her? Gradually she started to shadow Paul's movements and the journey became smoother. Paul was intent, intense, focused on the road ahead. In that moment, she regretted her anger. What made her think somebody like Harry would tell the truth anyway?

What is the truth about you, Paul? she wondered. It hardly seemed to matter. She knew, when she looked at his taut, mask-like face that he'd already put the incident aside. If he felt shame that he'd chosen her ahead of his duty, he didn't show it. Then, as she held on to him in the last few hundred yards leading to the main gate, she felt his breath catch.

'What is it?'

He couldn't hear her against the howl of the wind.

'What is it?' she screamed, repeating the question.

Then she saw. A plume of flame leaped among the trees. There was a simultaneous explosion that tore a hole in the buffeting of the wind. Paul stopped the bike. Without another word, he ran towards the battle, leaving Evelyn alone at the gate. It was a scene of carnage in the grounds. The dead and wounded lay in grotesque, twisted shapes on the ground. Fire was sheeting down on the dead and the living alike. Among the dead, Paul saw three werewolves. Their fur was silvery grey. None of them was Harry.

'You there!' a voice barked suddenly. 'What the hell are you doing in the line of fire?'

Paul turned to see a burly sergeant striding towards him.

'I'm looking for—'

The sergeant cut him off in a harsh Welsh-accent. 'You're in the middle of a full-scale battle. Are you trying to get yourself killed?'

Paul was about to have a second stab at an explanation when Morrison appeared. 'That's all right, Sergeant Bevan. I know who he is.'

Bevan grimaced. 'Is that right? Well, he's your responsibility. I'm not here to nurse-maid lost boys.'

The words were no sooner out of his mouth when a silver blur burst from the nearest clump of trees. Paul saw the gaping jaws, the bared, serrated fangs. Bevan reeled backwards, eyes wide in terror, as the demon snapped just inches from his throat. 'Get down!' he yelled.

There was no conscious thought behind what Paul did next. Instead, he let instinct guide him. He placed his palms together as if he was praying and pointed his fingers at the creature's heart. It broke off its attack and howled in pain. Paul's hands glowed. Concentrating every atom of his being on his fingertips, he started to unglue his clasped palms. Threads of flame were transferred to the werewolf's chest, stitching themselves inside. It started to twist its head back and forth, then its rib cage split asunder, burning entrails spilling over its knees. The beast's insides boiled then the two halves of the demon lay on the ground, identical pools of fire. Bevan stared in a kind of shocked respect.

'How did you do that?' he gasped.

'I don't know,' Paul said.

It was true. It was as if he was rediscovering some primal knowledge, following the choreography of an ancient dance of death.

'I don't think the lad needs nurse-maiding,' Morrison said, 'do you, Bevan?'

Paul's eyes roved round the battlefield. 'How's the battle going?'

Bevan got to his feet and brushed himself down.

'This is the one we were looking for, the last of the beasts to be roaming free. We've got the surviving pair pinned down over there.'

'Is one of them the blood wolf?' Paul demanded urgently.

'The *what*?'

'The blood wolf,' Paul said, 'a werewolf whose fur glistens with uncongealed blood. Have you seen him?'

Bevan shook his head slowly, as if he thought Paul was quite mad. A blast of cold fear struck Paul. He started running towards the blazing lights of Chequers. Morrison followed.

Evelyn was standing barefoot in the woods, rubbing her arms against the cold. The battle raged barely a hundred yards ahead, the impact of bullet and grenade making the air tremble around her. She wanted to run after Paul but, for once, she did as she was told, staying put in the chill of the woods. After a few minutes she heard the rumble of vehicles and the shrill ringing of a fleet of ambulances. The first vehicle pulled up and the driver peered out of his window.

'What are you doing out here, young lady?' he asked. 'You'll catch your death of cold.'

'I've been told not to move.'

The driver examined her with a brief glance. What was she doing out here in the woods? She couldn't have been more than sixteen. Her hair was plastered to her scalp, her clothes were wet through and her bare legs were smeared with mud up to her knees.

'Who told you that?' he demanded. 'You've got no shoes or coat and it isn't like your even safe from the bullets. No, you'd better get in.'

Evelyn hesitated. 'But Paul said . . .'

'I don't know who this Paul is you're talking about,' the driver said, 'but he can't have your best interests at heart. I'm telling you this isn't the place to be. You're better off with us.'

Reluctantly, Evelyn climbed into the ambulance and it sped off.

Harry had heard the motorbike approaching but he too had to shut out every distraction. Two men stood in the way of his prize – the policeman Temple and Thompson. Once they were out of the way, he would destroy the Old Man. He would penetrate the mind of the man who had remained steadfast against Hitler through all those bleak months. He would seek out his deepest fears. Churchill would die, his mind obliterated in the Hell blast of endless terror. Then Harry could turn his attention to the renegade boy.

He advanced towards the Hawtrey Room. Inhuman eyes picked out the door behind which his prey was waiting. Harry reached for the handle and twisted. It was locked and barricaded. He smiled. It wouldn't hold him long. That's when he heard running footsteps. Spinning on his heel, he saw Temple racing towards him, pistol in hand. He remembered another such confrontation but this time, with no Paul to distract him, he had the measure of his opponent. Harry's eyes glowed and Temple dropped the gun, howling in agony. His palm was covered in crimson welts where the hot metal had burned. Harry strode forward and laid him low with a vicious, clubbing blow. For a moment the blood wolf stared down at the senseless detective before returning to the doors that were barring his way.

He gripped the door handle and watched in satisfaction as the metal dripped to the floor like wax. Then he entered. In response, Thompson got off several shots. Harry was moving fast, weaving from side to side. One bullet shattered a lamp, leaving the carpet strewn with shards of glass. Another embedded itself in the wall between two huge tapestries. A third succeeded in hitting Harry but, to Thompson's horror, the sheen of blood enveloped it and prevented a serious wound. He carried on across the room with astonishing agility and struck Thompson a back-handed blow. Thompson fell, striking his head on the fender of the fireplace that dominated that end of the room. Harry's eyes swept back and forth across the room. Where was the Old Man hiding?

'Show yourself,' he snarled. Then his voice relaxed. 'Is this a game?' He adopted a sing song voice. 'Come out, come out, wherever you are.'

He listened. There. A heartbeat.

'You may as well show yourself,' Harry said. 'I can hear your heart beating. Come on, Prime Minister, you must know the game is up. Speak to Harry.'

But the next voice he heard belonged to Paul, not Churchill. 'Turn round,' Paul said.

Harry faced his young descendant. 'I suppose it was always going to come down to this,' he said. 'Are you insane, boy? Do you really think an untrained youth can stand against one such as I, a disciple steeled in battle? Why don't you just walk away and leave me to my task?'

'You're not going to kill anyone else,' Paul answered. 'I won't let you.'

Harry heard both fear and doubt in the boy's voice. He grinned.

'You know you can't win, don't you?' he demanded. 'You're sick with fright at the thought of what I'm going to do to you.'

It was obvious what Harry was doing. Already he was searching Paul's soul for his deepest fears. Paul responded the only way he knew how. His powers were fear and fire. He ignited the air before him and Harry recoiled. The spell was broken. But Harry was in no mood to break off the attack. He exhaled and the ball of flame rolled back towards Paul. Struck by the force of the sudden whipcrack of air, he landed heavily, winding himself. Harry strode forward and seized him by his shirt collar, lifting him off his feet. His lips peeled back and the deadly fangs glistened.

'Too easy,' Harry hissed, 'all too easy.'

Along the corridor, Temple stirred. For a moment he was unable to focus, then he remembered where he

345

was. Behind him, a pair of cautious, fear-stricken soldiers were working their way up the stairs.

'Give me your rifle,' Temple ordered.

The nearest soldier gave up his weapon without any protest. He was glad to leave the fighting to the detective. Temple winced as he gripped the stock with his burnt hand, then he ran towards the Hawtrey Room. Harry was about to sink his fangs in Paul's throat. Temple waved Paul out of the line of fire and squeezed the trigger. The detective stared in disbelief as Harry flung himself backwards with superhuman agility. There was a trickle of blood where the bullet had broke the skin on his scalp, but the damage was slight. Paul seized the moment and buried his fingers into the flesh of Harry's face. Harry shrieked in pain. His flesh had caught fire. He writhed and twisted, desperate to tear free of Paul's grip.

'Do it,' Paul yelled at Temple and the one soldier who was still armed, 'shoot him before he can recover.'

But Harry was already fighting back. He crashed his skull into Paul's face. Paul's entire head crackled with pain. Then Harry turned his attention to Temple.

The ambulance had stopped outside the front door. Evelyn was trying to convince herself that she hadn't ignored Paul's instructions. If she stayed put in the cab, that would amount to the same thing as waiting in the woods. Then, through the open window, she heard Temple's cry.

'Uncle George!'

Without a moment's hesitation, she threw open the door and entered Chequers. She started climbing the stairs to the first floor. She forgot Paul's order. She forgot the pleading expression in his eyes. At that moment, there was only one thing on her mind. Some-body was hurting her beloved uncle. She reached the top of the stairs and raced towards the Hawtrey Room, from which the sounds of a terrible struggle were echoing.

'Uncle George!'

Harry moved with incredible speed, shoulder-charging Temple against the wall and snatching the weapon from him. Armed with Temple's rifle, Harry fired. The young soldier to his left felt the cordite flash against his face but he wasn't hit. The bullet flew past him and found a different target. Paul returned to the fray. Grabbing Harry's upper jaw with one hand and the lower one with another, Paul forced his mouth open. Blistering flames were licking along Harry's lips. Harry dropped the rifle.

'Shoot him,' Paul yelled. 'Somebody, for God's sake, shoot him.'

Temple recovered his rifle and tried to take aim.

'It's no good, Paul,' he cried. 'I might hit you.'

Paul smashed Harry's head against the floor, trying with all his might to focus on the pulse of energy in his hands and arms. He was aware of reinforcements arriving up the stairs, Morrison, Bevan and twenty soldiers.

'Finish it!' Paul yelled, terrified that Harry might yet turn the tables. Harry was screaming as the heat scorched his face. Then Paul saw something that tore his soul apart. He slackened his grip. The blood wolf hurled himself through the window and made his escape.

'Evelyn!'

She was lying on her side, a pool of blood already forming. He ran over to her and cradled her in his arms. He willed her to be alive but her chest was stained scarlet. Harry's bullet had passed straight through her heart.

'Oh God, no! Somebody get a doctor.'

But there was nothing any doctor could do. Temple knelt by his side and put his fingers to Evelyn's throat. In a voice heavy with despair, he told Paul something that, in his heart of hearts, Paul already knew.

'She's dead.'

Fifty-six

Harry stumbles from the field of battle defeated. He's confused. How could a mere boy overcome him? He makes his way through the threshing bracken and discovers a pool of rainwater. He tries to cool his burned flesh by splashing it over him. It gives him little relief. His mind is racing. What next? How can he turn the tables on the renegade?

'Master,' he roars. 'I need you now. Where are you?'

But the Master doesn't come. Harry's alone. At that moment Harry realizes that he has been fooling himself. He isn't Lud's right-hand man, merely another foot soldier. Harry's mind is racing. He must think. Think! All is not yet lost. Maybe he can yet recover the advantage. But his brother demons are all dead. The enemy forces have regrouped. Their guns would cut him to shreds. He wants guidance.

'Master!'

Harry looks around and there they are. At the top of a rise, in a clearing, four hooded men stand watching him. The priests of Beltane! The blood wolf snarls his hatred. They can't touch me, Harry thinks. They're ghosts. He has no cause to be afraid of them. But Harry avoids their unwavering stare and plunges deeper into the woods.

'Master!'

At last Lud appears.

'He's coming,' Lud says. 'You know what you have to do, Harry.'

Harry hangs his head. 'Is there no other way?'

'No, Harry,' Lud says. 'You have failed but you can yet snatch victory from the jaws of defeat. Do it, Harry, sacrifice yourself and deliver the boy to me.'

Then he's gone. A moment later, Harry hears a twig snap behind him. He turns. It's Paul.

Fifty-seven

Paul strode through the forest gloom and unleashed a stream of fire that raked the ground in front of Harry.

'What kind of monster are you?' he yelled. 'All you do is bring suffering. Evelyn's dead.'

'Really?' Harry said, no emotion in his voice. 'I didn't know.'

'You're to blame,' Paul said. 'You're to blame for everything. You fired the bullet that killed her.'

Harry met Paul's gaze. His eyes were dark and alert. 'For once, it wasn't my fault. It was an accident.'

'Don't try to evade responsibility for her death,' Paul cried. 'You're the one who kidnapped her. You're the one who left her to drown.'

'Yes,' Harry said, 'I did all that.' He remembered Lud's instructions and played his part. 'What's the matter, Paul? Aren't things going the way you expected? You thought you were going to be the hero, didn't you? You were going to journey back in time and kill my Master. It isn't that easy, is it? There's no victory without sacrifice. Wherever you go, whatever you do, there will be death and suffering. That's the way of the demon. Are you ready? Can you go through all that pain?'

Paul didn't say a word. He gazed down at Harry with hollow, steady eyes.

'Say something, Paul,' Harry taunted. 'But for me, Evelyn would still be alive. Go on. Don't you want revenge?'

Tears pricked Paul's eyes but he didn't give in to them. Instead, he held Harry in his stare, still not saying a word.

'I killed Cotton too, you know,' Harry said. 'He died alone and afraid. How does that feel, Paul? He was your friend.'

'Where you're going, no friend or ally can follow. Can you handle the loneliness? Can you endure the sacrifices? Evelyn's only the first.'

He thought of something and laughed at his own joke. Then he started singing:

Keep young and beautiful,
If you want to be loved.'

'Remember?' Harry asked. 'She sang that the night you went to the cinema together. Didn't you have a lovely time? She was so young and alive.'

That was the taunt that pushed Paul over the edge.

A fireball roared towards Harry. Harry ducked and the tree behind him exploded.

'There will be more Evelyns,' Harry sneered. 'I wonder, what was it like seeing her lying there? Did you see the fresh blood drenching her blouse? Did your heart break as you witnessed the white mask of death? You loved that face. Are you really telling me you can go on looking down at such sights? Can you take the responsibility? I don't believe you, Paul. You're not that strong.'

Paul responded with a shriek of rage. He rushed forward. Raw energy exploded from him. Harry felt the blast of a furnace in his face. The rush of super-heated air pinned him to a tree. Harry winced as he eased himself away from the bark. He started singing again: '*Keep young and beautiful . . .*'

Paul roared his despair and hatred. All around, the trees started to bend and thresh in the hot wind that emanated from him. Harry felt his flesh starting to roast. He tried to respond with his own powers. The earth opened beneath Paul's feet. Paul simply stepped forward. Harry slashed with his razor-sharp claws. Paul seized his wrists and flames rushed over Harry's flesh. He screamed.

'It hurts, doesn't it, Harry?' Paul said.

'I'll tell you what hurts,' Harry retorted defiantly, 'the talons of a hell-fiend. That's what killed your friend Hugh.'

He gave a demonic grimace. Paul responded by seizing his jaw. He squeezed tight. For the second time, Harry felt the boy's power. Flames danced over his skin. Foam spilled from his lips. His body twisted and convulsed. This was the sacrifice Lud had demanded, the agony he would have to endure to draw Paul into the demon master's service.

'That's it,' Harry hissed, 'kill me. Take it all out on me, all the rage, all the darkness, all the despair. Then you know what, Paul, you will finally embrace your true destiny.' He forced his words out through blistered lips. 'I was like you. I struggled against Lud to begin with, you know. When I was thirteen, I hated the Master. I denied my identity. Oh, you've resisted it longer, that's true, but you'll come round in the end.'

Paul didn't answer. Flames licked around Harry's face and he screamed. Still, he spat his defiance.

'Rage is joy,' Harry said. 'It opens your heart to the Master. Do you feel your power, Paul? Do you enjoy making me scream in agony? That's how it starts. Go on. Show no mercy. Let the darkness flood into your soul. Soon you'll be able to do anything you want. The power, Paul, the power.' He begged for his own death. 'What are you waiting for? Finish it. You hate me. So destroy me. Let the rage blaze out from you. In the moment of conquest, you will go to Lud and serve him in my place.'

At that moment Paul's rage was all-consuming. He saw with Lud's eyes. He felt Lud's malice.

That's when another voice erupted in his head, breaking the spell. 'Let him go, Paul.'

Paul half-turned. It was Temple.

'He killed them,' Paul groaned. 'He killed Hugh. He killed Evelyn. He's got to pay.'

'You're right,' Temple said. 'If I had your powers, maybe I'd be behaving just the way you are now.'

Paul could feel Harry twisting and writhing as the flesh round his jaw blackened and blistered.

'As I followed you here, I even thought about shooting him myself. But revenge is wrong. Can't you see what Harry's doing? He wants you to give in to rage and despair. Then your heart will be so poisoned, Lud will have you. Vengeance isn't the way. Let him face the justice of the courts, Paul. There has to be law.'

'Law!' Harry snorted in disgust. 'There's only one law. The strong rule. You want to be strong, don't you, Paul? Just imagine. You'll be able to do anything you want. You can have anything you want. You can have a thousand Evelyns.'

But Harry had just overplayed his hand. Those six little words turned Paul from Lud. 'What did you say?'

'You can have any woman you want. There are thousands out there like Evelyn, millions.'

Paul cast Harry aside in disgust. 'That's where you're wrong,' he said. 'There never was anyone like her and there never will be again. She was unique and now she's gone.'

'Rubbish!' Harry snorted. 'What's so special about one wretched girl?'

'That's the reason we're different,' Paul answered. 'I know and you don't.' He glanced at Temple. 'Give me your gun.'

'But I thought . . .'

'I'm not going to kill him.'

Temple handed over the Weobley. Paul shot Harry twice, first in the right hand then the left. The once mighty Harry knelt on the ground, whimpering wretchedly.

'I'm going to tell you how to control him,' Paul said. He knelt next to Harry. 'You're going to face justice, Harry. You're going to be tried in open court. In eighteen months you will hang like a common criminal. That's *your* destiny.' He rested a hand on Temple's shoulder. 'This is why I had to protect you, Temple. Your destiny wasn't to save Churchill, it was to save me.' He heard the heavy tread of infantrymen's boots. 'Now you've succeeded.'

Fifty-eight

London, Friday, 24 January, 1941

Paul and Temple were standing in the driving rain, watching as Evelyn's coffin was lowered into the ground. They were set apart from the other mourners. Brenda blamed them both for her daughter's death. She hadn't said a word to them since they arrived. Paul knew it must hurt Temple terribly. He stood there, a broken man, the rain trickling off the brim of his trilby, reliving the moment when he saw Evelyn lying lifeless on the floor of the Hawtrey Room. The shroud of rain continued to move across the churchyard, drenching the mourners. Nobody seemed to care. As they started to file away, Temple tried to approach his twin sister.

'Brenda,' he said, 'I'm so sorry. If I could turn back the hands of time I would.'

'But you can't, can you?' Brenda retorted bitterly. 'Nobody can bring my Evelyn back. But for you and your bloody job, she would still be here with me.' She shot a fierce stare at Paul. 'He's the reason she's dead. Why did you have to bring him into our lives, George? He's unnatural. He's a monster.'

Paul hung his head. Brenda trembled as she wept. 'There's no putting things right, George,' she said. 'God knows if I'll ever be able to talk to you again. As things stand, I don't want anything more to do with you.'

With that, she walked away. Temple stayed rooted to the spot, rigid as a statue while the rain sluiced over him. Heavy, dark stains formed on the shoulders of his overcoat. Connie walked over.

'Let's go home,' she said.

'She'll never forgive me,' Temple said.

'She will,' Connie said, 'in time. You didn't kill Evelyn. Paul didn't either. We all know that.'

Temple walked to the car like an automaton. They drove back to Enfield in silence. At the house, it was as if some force had torn the life out of the house. It seemed cold, a shell of bricks and mortar. Paul walked around the places Evelyn had been. He looked out of the window and watched the icy, driving rain hissing across the city. He turned on the wireless. After half an hour he heard the song he'd been waiting for: *Keep Young and Beautiful*. He listened to the end then he looked in on Temple and Connie. They were sitting side by side in front of the fire, quite silent, while baby Denis slept in his pram in the hall. Paul was haunted by an image of Harry's face, scornful, mocking. If this was victory, what did defeat taste like? Remembering the things Harry had said, he came to a decision.

'Where's Paul?' Temple asked about half an hour later.

'Do you know,' Connie said, 'I'm really not sure.'

Temple prowled round the house, becoming increasingly concerned.

'Paul,' he shouted, 'Paul, where are you?' He threw open the door and peered out into the rain. 'Paul!'

Connie was at his side.

'He's gone,' Temple said. 'I think I know where.'

Connie understood. 'Go after him, George.'

Temple rode the BSA through the rain-lashed streets of London at high speed. He left the bike outside Bank station and ran down the steps to the platform where Paul had first appeared. At first it seemed deserted then Temple saw a hazy figure, ghost-like and quite translucent.

'Paul!'

Paul turned and smiled sadly. Temple rushed forward.'You don't need to go,' he cried. 'You can't throw your life away. Lud will destroy you.'

But he couldn't reach Paul. The boy had passed into another place. There was nothing but his after image.

'It's something I have to do,' Paul said. 'I left my

family. This is hard, but I've got to leave you too. I've got no choice.'

Then a ghost train pulled into the station and Paul climbed aboard. Temple watched the train vanish into the darkness of the tunnel. He would never see Paul again.

Fifty-nine

*P*aul feels hollow. He sits in the lonely carriage, tears running down his cheeks. It was never meant to be like this. Harry was right about that at least. When he left his home, his mother and friends, he imagined himself a lone hero fulfilling his destiny. He never expected this pain in his chest, this terrible sense of loss. It's as if he's lost two families, two loves. This war will not end soon. It will be fought over centuries. It will cost innocent lives. Lud's power is rising. He is tearing at his chains. And who is standing in his way, Paul sighs. Am I ready? He isn't sure. Somewhere, at the end of this long, sulphurous tunnel, there will be more of Lud's followers, more struggle. Paul wonders if he will have the strength to go on.

The train rushes on, oblivious to his thoughts. It plunges into the hellish darkness. Then Paul hears what he has been waiting for. It's a man's footsteps. He turns round. Just as he has been expecting, it's the ticket inspector. But there's a surprise in store for Paul. He looks different, wrapped in a long robe with a hood.

'Your ticket, please.'

Paul hands over the London Underground ticket, dated 24 January, 1941. He is issued with one bearing the imprint of the London and Blackwall Railway. There's a date one hundred years earlier.

'This will take you where you need to go,' the hooded man tells him.

'Who are you?' Paul asks.

'My name is Cormac, first priest of Beltane. I speak for the fire priests.'

'I don't understand.'

'You will in time,' Cormac says. 'I've been watching you, Paul Rector. You did well. You destroyed the disciple and delayed Lud's escape.'

'Delayed?' Paul asks. 'Is that all?'

Cormac glances out of window. There's a point of light in the distance. 'I don't have much time.'

'Tell me what you can,' Paul urges.

'You know about the seals that contain him?'

'Yes.'

'Lud's power is great. Some day soon he will break the bonds of his prison. Events have been set in motion that will lead to his liberation. That he will rise is certain. Nothing can prevent that outcome. The question is when.'

'If he is going to escape why does it matter when?'

'During the long years of his incarceration,' Cormac

explains, 'his power has grown. Twice you have held back his advance. That's good. If he had escaped into your time or Harry's he would have been unstoppable. You must delay his return as long as possible. That way, you may prevail against him.'

'How many battles must I win?'

'That depends on their outcome.'

'If I am to destroy Lud forever and prevent his return,' Paul says, rephrasing his question, 'how many?'

'The number will be decided by the courts of destiny. But know this: great battles will be fought for the four gates of London and you will be at the heart of them. Some you will win, some you will lose.'

'Which will I win and which will I lose?' Paul demands.

'That is up to you,' Cormac answers. 'Destiny is not the same as predestination. The battles you have to fight are unavoidable. Their outcome, however, is in your hands. You are free to triumph, but you are also free to lose. Already, Lud's forces are assembling in the back alleys of London town, stronger than ever. Even the dead are being enlisted in support of Lud. Are you ready to face them, Paul Rector?'

Paul listens to the screech of the brakes. It reminds him of human screams.

'I'm ready.'

Cormac's form has become translucent. His face creases with frustration.

'I am being called back into the shadows,' he says. 'I must go. We will speak again.'

Cormac turns his back and walks away. Already he is fading from view.

The point of light grows. The third battle is about to begin.

EXCLUSIVE EXTRAS

Behind the scenes with Alan Gibbons . . .

Journey into the heart of London during
the Second World War

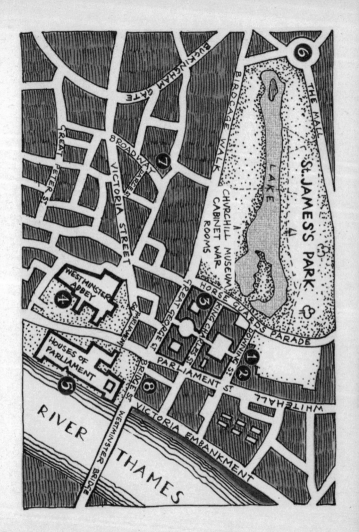

Fact Zone:

Setting the Scene for

The Demon Assassin

1. The prime minister's residence, 10 Downing Street

2. The chancellor of the exchequer's residence, 11 Downing Street

3. The Cabinet War Rooms

4. Westminster Abbey

5. The Houses of Parliament

6. Queen Victoria Memorial

7. St James's Park Underground Station

8. Westminster Underground Station

About the Author

Name: Alan Gibbons
Place of birth: Warrington, Cheshire
Lives in: Liverpool
Occupation: Author and educational consultant

What is your earliest memory of being afraid?
When I was little my bedroom window was cracked
for a while and a slight draught blew through. My dad
taped it while we were waiting for it to be repaired.
One windy night the tape peeled off. Soon the wind
was lifting the curtains. I thought it was a ghost and
howled my head off with fright.

Do you believe in family curses? Not in a supernatural way but in some families there is a medical
condition that affects each generation and it can put
the family members under great strain. That gave me
the idea of the demon seed.

**If you were King Lud for a day, what would be
your top priority?** King Lud's purpose in life is to
cause the maximum chaos and mayhem so I would
be one of those politicians who starts wars. They
really know how to mess things up! Lud would be
envious.

Which is scarier – truth or fiction? Truth. Mankind
has committed some terrible crimes throughout

history. You can control the ending of a story and make sure the good guys win. Life isn't always like that.

Know any good jokes about ghosts? I wouldn't call it good but this is it:
Q: What do you call a ghost with a machine gun?
A: Sir.

What would your code name be? Panther. That's what I would like to be like, sleek and powerful, but Cuddles is probably more like the real me.

What is your favourite London landmark? The Palace of Westminster. It is still one of those iconic buildings everyone recognizes in an instant.

Hallowe'en and Beltane – what's the difference and which is more important for the spirit world? Hallowe'en is based on the Celtic festival of Samhain, a celebration of the end of the harvest season. This was when the boundary between the dead and the living weakened. The festival has sadly been cheapened by commercial exploitation. Beltane was to do with the coming of summer. Fire meant hope and purification. I have interpreted Samhain as ushering in the bleakness of winter and Beltane as introducing the light of summer. It seemed a good metaphor for the battle between good and evil.

𝕴 chose the setting for *The Demon Assassin* because I wanted a time when my character Paul's nemesis, King Lud, could unleash his henchmen on a weakened city. When better than the darkest years of the Second World War when Britain was facing the threat of invasion by Hitler's legions? At that time Britain was being pounded night after night by a huge aerial bombardment and many thought a Nazi invasion was imminent.

Second, the strength of the first book in **Hell's Underground**, *Scared to Death*, is that readers can visit the sites of the Jack the Ripper murders and peel back the present day environment to discover the savage past that always lies beneath. Churchill's London is still there to be discovered.

Finally, I have always been fascinated by Britain during the Blitz. When I was growing up in the northern industrial town of Crewe, reminders of the war were everywhere. I used to see one of the veterans on his walking sticks. He had lost a leg and the empty trouser leg used to flap in the wind as he made his way down the street. I don't know why he didn't have an artificial limb. Crewe Works, the engineering factory that dominated the town, was still painted with wartime camouflage. My own great uncle died in the fighting. Crewe was too small a canvas, however. London is the universal city of this country. So it was time to unearth the wartime narrative of the capital.

Historical Background

According to historians, there really were numerous plots against prime minister Winston Churchill's life. There was also a significant minority of fascist sympathisers in the United Kingdom. There had been a movement called the British Union of Fascists, led by Sir Oswald Mosley, which openly sympathised with fascist Italy and Nazi Germany. Many of its supporters were interned during the war. The events in Germany are also based on real events. RHSA leader Reinhard Heydrich is an historical figure. Berchtesgarden in the Bavarian Alps was Hitler's retreat.

The British background is similarly accurate. Walter Thompson is a real person. He was Churchill's bodyguard for many years. The War Rooms were exactly as described and you can visit them today. Churchill really did go up on the roof to watch the bombing though it was a terribly dangerous thing to do. Chequers is a real place, still used by prime ministers for meetings. The film shows happened exactly as described. The menus were as described. Only the demons are fictional!

Research

Mainly, I read. I devoured several biographies of Churchill and a shelf full of books about the war years. I read about rationing and even the sleeping arrangements for the air raid shelters in the London Underground. I read accounts of life in Nazi Germany and biographies of some of the Nazi leadership. I read novels set in the time such as *The Eagle has Landed* by Jack Higgins.

One of the first things you have to do as a writer is find out as much as you can about the historical period you intend to describe. Then you put most of what you know to one side and forget about it. That might sound a bit stupid but a novel isn't a history lesson. If the author starts showing off how much they know, it can get in the way of the story. Out of every hundred historical facts you know, you might use five or six. Your aim is to tell a story and you don't want to clutter it with too much useless information, no matter how interesting it is.

The second thing I did was try to immerse myself in the period. I listened to the music and the radio broadcasts of Alvar Liddell, the BBC presenter. I looked up the movie posters. I chatted to my mum, dad and mother-in-law Maisie who gave me a feel for the period.

Then I went walking. I would go down to London and roam around the East End looking for locations then jump on the tube into central London and investigate Whitehall itself. That's the best bit of research, walking your locations. There are few more exciting square miles of ground anywhere in the world than Britain's centre of power. It is all there crowding for your attention: Trafalgar Square, Whitehall, Downing

Street, the Houses of Parliament, the Embankment, St James's Park. You can almost feel history crawling up out of the pavement. If you are bored by London, you don't have a pulse! During those walks I became a time-traveller like Doctor Who, staring at locations and imagining them in wartime as the bombers rumbled in the distance and searchlights played across the sky. Finally, to complete the mosaic, I visited the Cabinet War Rooms and the Imperial War Museum. Now I was ready.

Walk **The Demon Assassin's** *London*

If my novel does nothing else, I hope it persuades some readers to explore their nation's past. If you want to relive Arminius's attempt on Churchill's life, get off at Westminster tube and walk just two minutes to the Clive Steps, just off Whitehall. Stand at the bottom of the steps with the statue of Clive of India behind you.

Now look across the road at St James's Park. Here you will be able to imagine Churchill, Thompson and Temple taking their walk round the lake. Gaze across at the trees and decide which one Arminius used as his vantage point as he got Churchill in his crosshairs.

Turn to your left. Set into the building at the bottom of the steps are the Cabinet War Rooms. Today, they have been converted into an evocative and exciting museum that will tell you just about everything you want to know about London in the Blitz and the life of the wartime prime minister Winston Churchill (later Sir Winston Churchill).

When you come out of the War Rooms turn left and go round the corner. There before you is the Palace of Westminster. Imagine this great building during the war when explosions echoed across the Thames and great fires lit the sky. This is the city where Paul Rector embarked on his mission to save Churchill and thwart the assassin sent by King Lud.

If you have time, catch the tube to the Imperial War Museum. Not only does it have an amazing collection of tanks, aircraft, uniforms and weapons. There is also a wartime Air Raid Shelter where you can sit and experience the bombing (safely, it has to be said).

Alternatively, you could get off at Bank station and retrace Paul's pursuit of Temple through the blazing streets. Follow him to St Paul's Cathedral and gaze up at Sir Christopher Wren's famous dome. Now imagine how it must have looked that January in 1941 engulfed in smoke and fire as the bombs rained down. Most of all, never forget that it was millions of ordinary British people who fought and died, or simply endured, to defeat the horror of the Nazis and make it possible for us to live the way we do today. We stand on the shoulders of giants.

The Demon Assassin is the second book in a series that began with *Scared to Death*. Writing a saga of six three hundred-page novels is a new departure for me. I usually write stories that are completed within the structure of a single book. That is true of many of my most successful books, such as the real-life thrillers *The Edge* and *Caught in the Crossfire*. Even *The Legendeer Trilogy* happened almost by accident. I wrote the first book *Shadow of the Minotaur* as a single novel. Then it won the Blue Peter Book Award. Suddenly, readers started to e-mail me asking for more and I thought, Why not? *Vampyr Legion* and *Warriors of the Raven* followed. But I wrote them as a novel and two sequels rather than a trilogy I had planned out from beginning to end as a single narrative.

I suppose I always wondered what it would be like to plan a long series as a longer tale, divided into parts. That is **Hell's Underground**. Almost by definition, a series has something of an epic quality. Now, epics usually involve a great journey across vast distances. You think of Frodo and Sam's progress from the Shire to Mordor. I decided to structure **Hell's Underground** differently. I have been a fan of Dr Who since the early episodes back in the 1960s and I love the great time-travel stories that came before and must have inspired it. There is H.G. Wells's *The Time Machine*, Ray

Bradbury's *A Sound of Thunder* and Mark Twain's *A Connecticut Yankee in King Arthur's Court*.

My hero Paul Rector embarks on a journey back through time to confront King Lud, his monstrous nemesis. Often, when you write a story dealing with the supernatural you give yourself a huge amount of freedom. You can do anything with magic. I decided to decline the gift. Instead, I set myself some strict rules. Although the action would sometimes stray outside the square mile of East London which lies at the core of the tale, the ancient districts of Whitechapel and Spitalfields would be the dark heart of the action. What's more, each of the historical periods in which Paul confronts the demon brotherhood would be depicted in as historically accurate a way as possible.

There are other constraints in writing a series. Each book has to exist in its own right but it also belongs to a greater whole. I knew the ending of the series before I even put pen to paper. In an extended story like this I think it helps to know where you are going from the very beginning. That way, all the events point towards the final resolution. I think my ending is a humdinger but readers will have to wait until 2012 to discover how everything is resolved.

So here is what readers of the series can expect. Book III, *Renegade*, takes Paul to early Victorian London where his ancestor Samuel Rector lies in wait for him. Book IV, *Witch Breed* (July 2010), visits the witch hunts that erupted across the eastern counties of England during the Civil War. The fifth volume will take the reader through the ferocious conflicts between the Anglo Saxons and the Vikings. The sixth and final book will take us to the final conflict as Boudicca's revolt threatens to engulf Roman London.

Writing such an ambitious chronicle is a challenge but it keeps me off the streets!

Alan Gibbons